Spoilers

John Stamp

Cover Art:
Michelle Crocker

http://mlcdesigns4you.weebly.com/

Publisher's Note:

This is a work of fiction. All names, characters, places, and
events are the work of the author's imagination.

Any resemblance to real persons, places, or events is
coincidental.

Solstice Publishing - www.solsticepublishing.com

Spoilers
John Stamp

Spoilers

Chapter One

Aleister Fitzpatrick rested on the couch in front of the stage and watched through THC occluded eyes as a young eighteen-year-old blonde from the upstate contorted and squirmed clumsily out of lingerie. She tried and failed to keep in rhythm with the head thumping bass track blasting out of the club's speaker system. He suppressed a chuckle as the girl worked her way out of her clothes, trying to keep her eyes on him while she fumbled with the straps and snaps. The girl, a newly minted freshman at the Baptist College up the road, was going for seductive, but her facial features came off more confused than sexy. Largely, Fitz let that slide, the girl could be taught to shake her ass, and do it right. He focused on the pert tits and tight ass that jiggled just so as she moved. She was the right commodity for the gentleman's club, young, white and with a vacant head. Fitz watched diligently until the music ended and he waved her over. He suppressed a laugh over how out of breath the girl was.

"Have a seat, sweetheart," he said.

The girl beamed as she perched on his knee. She arched her back so that her chest stuck out. Fitz studied her for a moment.

"What did you think?" she asked.

"I like it," he told her, stroking his fingertips up and down her spine, "You put a lot of heart into it. It's not easy work, is it?"

"No."

"Yeah." He looked into her eyes and saw that need for approval that a lot of the new girls came in with. He didn't know if the old adage of daddy issues or some other pathos drove them to him. Maybe good girls just wanted to be bad? He didn't care. Fitz only knew that every August,

5

he had a steady stream of young girls who wanted to dance for a living. He made a gesture of looking at his watch,

"Wow," he said, "It's getting late, or early depending on how you look at it."

The blonde laughed playfully.

"I'm famished and you must have worked up an appetite by now. Want to get something to eat?" That was step one every time he had a new girl and it had yet to fail. Charming at dinner, flatter the naive, hungry ego, then complete the conquest in the back of his car. A perfect formula.

"Yeah." She giggled.

"Okay." He whapped her on the butt just so. "Go get changed and I'll meet you outside."

The girl hopped up and he watched her perky ass as she flitted off toward the wardrobe in the back. He noticed the heads of several customers, mostly workers from the port and military from the Air Force or Navy Bases in the area watch the same thing he did as she left.

Little girl is going to be a gold mine.

With a satisfied groan, Fitz stood and headed for the front door.

He gave a nod to the bartender and bouncer who watched him as he left. The bartender, Harris, who'd been his muscle behind the bar and otherwise since the kid was freed from Lieber State Correctional five years before was chuckling so Fitz flipped him off on his way out.

Fitz stepped into the humid low country night and immediately smelled the marsh and plough mud that surrounded his place, the 'Tasty Kitty.' He shook a finger in one ear as the sudden cessation of head splitting hip hop music threatened his equilibrium. He took over ownership of the place a decade earlier after deciding to invest his take from fifteen years of smuggling for the Columbians in something a little more stable. He'd bought the place outright from an old time Dixie Mafia boss who fell on hard times. Old man started dabbling in his own product, everything from coke to Meth, and slid down the drain with the speed of an Olympic sprinter. Gravel crumbled under his feet as Fitz made his way to the gleaming black, Chrysler 300 that sat in his specified parking spot next to the front door. The parking lot was quiet as it was a light crowd on a Sunday night. A welcome change from inside though the muted bass track could still be felt out in the humid low country air. Instead of starting the car up, he leaned against the driver's side door and reached for a cigarette as he waited for... What was her name anyway?

Fitz shrugged it off and went on lighting his cigarette until the first pop shattered the rear passenger window next to him. He started, his mind not registering what was happening until the staccato tat, tat, tat of a semi-automatic rifle preceded the impact to his chest and abdomen by a millisecond. Fitz flinched and tried to run as his primitive mind raced into survival mode but it was too late. The pain of his internals being shredded so quickly didn't even register. He fell to the gravel as a heavy round broke through his spine. Two more rounds carved out his brain case like a Halloween pumpkin. What was once Aleister Fitzpatrick lay twitching in a haze of dust and gravel.

Chapter Two
Friday

Lieutenant Peter Banks waited in the front passenger seat of the Charcoal Grey Jeep Cherokee and watched the small, crumbling row house on the corner of the street. The engine emitted a minor hum through the car as the team of four narcotics officers waited. In the driver's seat sat Sergeant Max DeGuello, the second row of the SUV held Detectives Poppy "Pops" Montague and Esteban Viejo. Each officer scanned a different area surrounding the vehicle, looking for signs of counter surveillance, or just the meandering crack addict that could spoil the pending operation with one wayward glance inside the vehicle. They all wore their standard tactical gear, a level III bulletproof vest, and webbing overlay that held numerous pockets for their radios, blow out first aid kits, and extra ammunition for their .45 caliber Glock model 21 sidearms. Poppy and Max each had a CAR-15 assault rifle. When the radio clicked, they all sat up straight in their seats.

"Wilkes is coming out," came the crisp voice of Detective Eric Thompson who was perched in an abandoned apartment overlooking the residence.

The team strained in their seats to get a look at their undercover officer leaving the target. A quick burst of static and Thompson was transmitting again.

"He gave the sign, target plus six."

"Let's go," Banks ordered. He keyed his own mike, "All units Execute, Execute, Execute."

Max stepped on the gas and the Jeep chirped as the rear wheel drive caught on the hot asphalt. A block away two more uniform patrol vehicles each carrying two officers moved in their direction.

Max pulled the Jeep to a silent halt three houses down from the target and the four dismounted quietly. Wilkes was waiting for them already shedding a ball cap and flannel shirt. Poppy handed him his vest, which he threw over his head and strapped on. He pulled the .45 from a holster mounted on the vest and press checked the weapon, ensuring a round was in the chamber before falling in behind the team. Wilkes and Poppy split off from the team as they hit the break between the houses. The two made their way quietly to positions to cover the rear of the building, using two trees for protection.

Max, Banks, and Viejo mounted rickety old wooden stairs, which cracked and popped under their weight. Thompson, after sprinting from the apartment perch, fell in behind them. In approaching the door, each member of the team covered a different field of fire. Viejo was on point carrying a battering ram. The two patrol units pulled up in front of the house and the officers dismounted to provide perimeter security.

Viejo paused at the front door. Thompson locked eyes with a perimeter unit before turning and squeezing Banks' shoulder. In sequence, Banks squeezed DeGuello's shoulder who in turn squeezed the shoulder of Viejo. Viejo grinned.

"Police! Search Warrant!" Viejo yelled.

When Viejo hit the door, the heavy iron battering ram struck just under the doorknob. The door was ancient, its brittle wood shattering under the impact. Viejo backed up a step and hugged the wall of the tight porch. Max charged the door and hooked to the right. Banks was second in the door and covered the left side of a small living room and set of stairs leading up that side of the house. Thompson smoothly cruised past Max and Banks and made his way further into the house. He and Max cleared room by room as they went. Banks held his position until he felt Viejo behind him and they made their way slowly up the stairs.

"Police!" they called at random intervals, "Show your hands!"

Banks and Viejo mounted the second floor and quickly secured the upstairs. They reached the final room of the second floor and yelled, "Clear," signaling they had found nothing. The two detectives looked at each other before filing back downstairs,

"Quiet in here..." Viejo's comment froze in his throat as a sudden crashing sound rattled the house.

"Shit," Banks breathed, "Coming down!" he yelled as the two men ran down the stairs.

Banks hit the first floor after leaping the last four stairs and landed with a boom on the warped old wood. He could hear breaking furniture and shattering glass coming from a room to the rear of the living room where they had entered.

He and Viejo were steps from the doorway when two figures burst from the room. Banks was just a step too late for the first but the second was just a step too late to get away. Banks threw his non-gun hand out and caught the fleeing suspect with a clothesline and dropped the man to the floor in a huff.

"Police!" he shouted, "Don't move!" He locked eyes with the suspect, a kid maybe in his twenties. He was white, wearing checkered shorts and a polo that could only be described as the brightest orange he'd ever seen. Banks put the muzzle of his forty-five in the center of the kid's chest and ordered, "Don't move," but he knew even before the kid flinched that it was on. The briefest of flashes behind the suspects blue eyes telegraphed what was to come.

The kid roared and swiped at the pistol. Banks yanked back to protect his gun and had to duck and block a wild punch with his non-gun hand. The kid scrambled to his feet like a cornered animal and took another swing at Banks before breaking for the rear door. Banks gritted his teeth and just before the kid was out of reach lashed out with a front kick to the small of his back. The boost in momentum carried the kid off course from the freedom he was willing to assault a police officer for and he ran smack into the peeling paint and wood of the doorframe. The impact stunned the suspect and he crumpled to the floor, holding his hands over his face. Blood bubbled through his fingers. The kid moaned as he slowly rolled into the fetal position.

"I bet that hurt," Banks said. He yanked the suspect's hands behind his back and handcuffed him as the kid howled. A quick pat down revealed a quarter of an ounce of what looked like weed and a handful of pills he figured was ecstasy. "You sit tight," he told the kid and left him to wallow as blood streamed from nose and split lip.

Banks looked out the rear door to see if the other suspect had gotten away. He chuckled when he saw the kid, another white kid dressed much the same as his compadre except wearing a pink polo shirt, lay sprawled on his back as if he were in the process of making a snow angel. He looked unconscious. Poppy and Wilkes stood over him. When Banks looked at her, she shrugged her shoulders while cradling her CAR-15 as if she'd just found an abandoned puppy

"Right," he said quietly.

The room where the sounds of a house demolition had come from had fallen silent. Banks crested the doorway and saw four bodies sprawled across the floor, each on their stomach with the hands bound in either handcuffs or zip ties. Three of the four were bleeding from the face while the fourth, a Hispanic kid wearing jeans and a t-shirt, cried into the rubble covering the floor.

"That sounded pretty intense," Banks said from the doorway as he looked over his team none of whom were scratched though Thompson was covered in what looked like flour. The large black man grimaced under the coating of white powder. It made him look like a sad faced mime. Banks tried not to laugh and failed.

"Not funny L-T," Thompson growled.

"Uh-huh."

"Hey L-T those frat boys didn't hurt your feelings did they?" It was Max speaking up, "That one looked like he had you there for a minute,"

Banks didn't respond but to say, "Let's get to it."

He waved in Poppy and Wilkes from the backyard. The two helped their prisoner up from the ground and kept him on his feet while guiding him into the house. Banks then went to the front of the house and released the two patrol units that had been holding perimeter for them during entry. As he returned, he noticed that Max and Viejo had started marshalling their prisoners in the small living room at the front of the house.

"I checked everything in here L-T," Viejo said. "We're going to keep them in here until we're ready for the wagon to come get'em."

"Works for me," Banks replied. "Once the kitchen's clear, start talking to them in there one by one, see if anyone wants to help themselves out." Banks noticed his own prisoner, who had sat up into a lotus position on the floor, glaring at him. "If they've got nothing on them cut'em loose, all except for Antwan and the two pastel wearing runners. They seem a little far afield, I'm sure one of them is going to want to talk to us."

Viejo moved off to search the kitchen. While the rest of the team spread out to search the house, Banks approached his charge,

"How you feelin?" he asked.

The kid looked at him and did not speak.

"Suit yourself," Banks said and reached down to help the kid to his feet. "Next time, I would advise you to stop when a cop tells you to stop,"

The kid scoffed, "You have no idea who I am, do you?"

He got the kid to his feet and took him by the arm. "Nope but I bet you're about to tell me," he said patting the kid down for a wallet, which he found in the back pocket of his checkered shorts.

"Ever heard of Congressman Tulley, asshole?"

"Yup, I voted for him." Banks responded, flipping through the wallet.

He sat the kid down on a ratty sofa next to one of the other five prisoners and pulled the ID from the billfold.

Aw, Hell, moaned a paranoid little voice in the back of his head.

"Let me go and maybe you get to keep your job, asshole,"

Banks held up the ID to the kid's face. "Yup, Andrew Tulley, what brings you to these parts, Andrew?"

"I'm not saying shit. My dad is going to have your ass,"

"I bet. What's your daddy going to think about you getting caught by the police with you pockets full of dope, Andrew?"

Tulley scoffed again. "Wait and see,"

"I sure will," said Banks, then he whistled holding up another card from the wallet, "Wow, the Charleston School of Law, and a senior to boot." This time, Banks was the one to scoff. "What's Dad going to think when law school dumps you out on your ass?"

"Tsss, never happen," answered Tulley.

"We'll see." Banks looked back to Viejo who waved him over to the kitchen. He glanced back at his prisoners. "You all just sit tight,"

Viejo was in the kitchen waiting for Banks. As the lieutenant walked in the door, his eyes went wide. Viejo had the freezer open. The compartment was stacked surface to surface with gallon sized zip lock bags, each bursting with little white pills. Viejo was holding one of the bags in his gloved hand. Banks got a closer look without touching the bag.

"Shit, Este, looking good."

"Wilkes did it again," Este said. "But I don't think even he saw this kind of take coming,"

"Not a chance." Banks slipped a latex glove out of his pocket and held it between his fingers and the bag as he took the evidence from Este. "Bag it carefully, I want fingerprints. This just got bigger than a couple of ghetto rats and college kids scoring for a Friday night. We just created a lot more work for ourselves."

"Yes, Sir."

Holding the bag as gently as he could, Banks returned to the living room in time to see Tulley and the actual resident of the house, Antwan Tate, whispering. Tulley was all but spitting at Banks' main subject. When he came out of the kitchen, all hissing ceased and the six prisoners seemed to melt as Banks presented the evidence to them. All that is, except Andrew Tulley.

"You have up'd your game since the last time we took you down, Antwan," Banks addressed the long time drug dealer. He had first arrested him for dealing crack-cocaine at the age of twelve. Tate was now twenty-one and only out of jail six months after serving a year for distribution of cocaine. Another charge Banks and his team had put on him.

Tate didn't respond.

Banks dropped the bag of ecstasy on an old, chipped coffee table in front of his charges and clapped his hands. "All right, most if not all of you know how this works. I'm going to take each of you into the other room where you will have your chance to come to Jesus. This will be an opportunity to help yourselves out. Like all good things this will not last. Attorney Tulley, you're up first."

Tulley huffed. "Pass."

Banks shrugged. "Good." He was beginning to look forward to locking the little prick up. "All right then, you." He pointed to Tulley's partner in fashion. The kid looked like he was about to vomit. He shook like a leaf. "You're up."

Suddenly a whistle sounded from the bathroom across from the kitchen. Banks held up his hand to the kid and looked toward the bathroom. Wilkes poked his head out of the doorway and gestured for him to join him.

"Whatcha got, kid?" he asked.

Wilkes was kneeling next to the sink. The cabinet doors were open. The young detective reached in with his gloved hands and produced a compact assault rifle from under the sink.

"Wow, I didn't think Tate was in the gun running business."

"Me either," Wilkes responded. "It never came up when we met. There's something else." He handed the weapon to Banks.

"What?"

"Look it over," said Wilkes.

Banks studied the weapon. It was an even more compact version of the CAR-15 that his unit carried. A rail system covered the barrel. The weapon had a traditional iron sight system and receiver similar to their weapons but the grip and the buttstock were almost non-existent. Banks gingerly pressed a lever near the stock and the buttstock telescoped out to a normal distance for support. However, design and the way it collapsed gave the weapon a tight aspect that made his long guns look like an old World War Two era M-1 Garand. Despite all that, the receiver still seemed to be a little bulkier than his assigned weapons. The

15

main section of the gun that contained the majority of the weapon's internals felt bigger in his hands. Like an AR on steroids.

Damn.

Then he noticed something else. Banks gently rotated the gun, looking around the receiver.

"There's no serial number," he said surprised. "No manufacturers stamp."

"I know."

"What the hell is a two bit crook like Tate doing with this?"

Wilkes shrugged his shoulders.

Something wasn't right, "You don't by any chance have a fuming kit with you do you?" It was unusual but Wilkes had a thing for forensics. Banks let him play with his toys every once in a while during a raid.

Wilkes nodded, his eyes widening.

"Do your thing then, but keep it quiet and in here. I want to know who's laid their hands on this thing."

"Yes, Sir."

Chapter Three

Adler Harrison was fidgeting. He was messing with his hands, tracing the lines on his palms with his fingers, snapping his joints. It was his tell, the signature thing he did when he was under stress. He spent forty years in boardrooms, committee halls, even in front of congress and was able to suppress his nervous response—until today. He silently reprimanded himself over the lack of self-control. He had dedicated himself decades ago, while on the debate team at Princeton, to mastering himself. He conquered his natural, stress-induced tendencies during his years in the Ivy League. Used his discipline to always keep his opponents guessing whether professionally, politically, or even in his own household. However, today, as he sat on the cold paper covered examination table, he was at a loss to control his nervous tick.

Harrison knew in his gut that things weren't going his way. That during the greatest challenge of his life, even with his vast resources, his own body was failing him. The realization hurt. He wanted to jump out of his own skin and beat on his body like a pissed off motorist kicking at his broken down car on the side of the road. His body was breaking down and the knowledge of that left him feeling undone, as if there was some grand list he had not completed.

The door to the exam room opened and the sight of Dr. Steffanson broke Harrison out of his stream of consciousness. He dropped his hands to the paper on the table; he hated how the paper always stuck to his skin. It made him feel like he was somehow unclean. He watched as Steffanson closed the door at a very deliberate and controlled pace. Harrison was a student of human behavior, that was how he had been the negotiator, the master salesman, and the corporate field general that had associated his legal firm with every major corporation on the East Coast. Harrison suppressed a sigh as he noted the man's tight lips and crow's feet at the corners of Steffanson's eyes.

"Doctor," he said. He always wanted to be the one to start and finish a conversation. It was a power position, and gave him control of the meeting.

"Adler," Steffanson responded.

"You don't look so good."

Steffanson almost laughed. "I don't like days like this, Mr. Harrison. I'm sorry but unfortunately the early intervention we attempted was unsuccessful. The mass in your pancreas has grown, and it appears there are signs of it spreading throughout your abdomen. There is a general inflammation in your lymph nodes consistent with metastasis."

Harrison nodded, the doctor confirming what he had suspected for the last month. "So?"

"So there are options we can try. However, the disease has advanced very aggressively, giving our chances of success a sharp decline."

"Is there any option with a chance of working?"

"I'm sorry, Mr. Harrison, the disease has just progressed too quickly. We will attempt any treatment you feel could benefit you. Once I explain to you in detail what treatment options I believe we have, we can decide on how we progress."

"Bottom line, Doctor, is there any option we are going to try that will cure me?"

Steffanson's shoulders sagged. "None that I am aware of. I'm sorry,"

Harrison hopped down from the table and reached for his leather jacket. It was amazing to him that he felt fine, maybe a little tired every now and then but he was after all seventy-two years old. Seventy-two, it didn't feel like nearly enough.

"How long do you think I have, Doctor?" Harrison swung his arms into his coat.

"Up to a year, maybe more, maybe less. I'm sorry, Adler, but there is no sure measurement."

Harrison paused for a moment, thinking about the fact that he was literally on the clock. Finally, he looked up at Steffanson as he opened the door.

"Thank you, Doctor, you take care of yourself," he said.

Chapter Four

As much as Peter Banks loved his job as a cop, there was no getting used to the sheer amount of bureaucracy that came with executing a simple arrest. When he was younger, a term that he could feel more and more every morning when he got out of bed, he fought against it. Argued that the tide of paper required just to do his job kept him from doing said job to the upmost of his ability. Then a little later on, when he was a detective working property crimes and later homicides, he took solace in the ideal that requiring so much data to justify depriving a person of his or her freedom was a part of the checks and balances system that kept law enforcement from putting away the wrong people. He would argue with himself that the volume of notes, reports, statements, etc. would ferret out exculpatory material if it existed, thereby clearing someone's name through documentation. Now, seasoned as he was after twenty-four years as a City of Charleston Police Officer, he simply sighed. As the Supervising Lieutenant of a Special Operations Command, all the paper fell to him.

He looked up from his pile of documents as Wilkes held another stack of reports for him to sign.

"Use of Force for me and Pops, and the statement for the buy bust."

"Thanks, Ben," Banks responded, taking the documents.

"Somethings up, Lieutenant," Wilkes said.

Banks looked up at him from his seat in the small break room adjacent to roll call where a shift of uniformed police were getting their marching orders. Wilkes waited while a young patrol officer fished a bottle of Pepsi from the vending machine and left the room. He gave the hallway outside one last look before returning to Banks.

"That kid from the raid," Wilkes said. "His lawyers are here."

Banks frowned. "Already?" Though it felt like hours since Banks shed his tactical gear and planted himself at the small table to start sifting through reports, he looked at his watch and realized he'd only been there twenty-five minutes. "That was fast. Wait... did you say lawyers, as in plural."

Wilkes nodded. "And the Chief and Assistant Chief are here. They took one of the suits back to the chief's office."

"How do you know they're here for the kid?"

"Desk Sergeant Miller told me. Seems they got him a little spooked too."

Banks reviewed the information in his head for a moment. "Is everything taken care of?"

"Yup, the dope is in the locker. Poppy and Este are processing the prisoners now. Should be finishing up in a few."

Banks nodded. "All right, give them a hand then tell Max to cut you guys loose. I'll see what's going on."

The young undercover left the room and Banks tried to go back to his paperwork. He hadn't made it ten words into Poppy's narrative about using the necessary force to affect an arrest before his department issued phone chirped. Banks had to fish it out from under a stack of evidence receipts before studying the screen. It was the Chief's office.

That was quick.

"Banks," he answered.

Assistant Chief Andrew Vaden was on the other end of the line. Banks listened for a moment.

"Yes Sir," he finally said and gathered up his paper.

He took his time collecting his file from the table and even paused to organize it slightly by category before heading to the Chief's office on the other side of the building. Banks had been through this kind of thing before. He didn't see any reason to rush.

The Assistant Chief was waiting for him when Banks arrived at the office. He and Andy Vaden had worked together since Banks was a rookie patrol officer and Vaden was his first squad Sergeant. Banks could see the grimace on Vaden's face,

"What's up, Chief?" he asked playing dumb.

"You've got a thing for kicking hornets nests, Banks, I swear," he said.

Banks didn't respond. He knew that silence was something Vaden couldn't let stand.

"That kid you brought in today. You know who that is?"

"He told me he was Congressman Tulley's kid,"

"He wasn't lying!" Vaden tried to control his voice. "The Congressman's Chief of Staff, lawyers, the Deputy Mayor, and a DA are in there with the Chief right now."

"Huh."

"Huh." Vaden took a step back. "That's all you got is huh? Are you kidding me?"

"I don't set the line-up for which shit bags are going to be at my raids. You would think some silver spoon douche would've taught his kid to say no to drugs." Banks tried not to laugh,

"That's not funny, asshole."

Banks was about to respond when the door to the Chief's Office swung open, silencing both men. Banks didn't recognize any of the expensively suited political operatives when they filed past him. He tried to lock eyes with each of them, three men and a woman who could stop traffic as they passed by. She was the only one who had it in her to meet his eyes.

"Ma'am," he said with a nod of the head.

The woman looked shocked that he had the guile to speak to her. Banks found that thoroughly entertaining.

Over the years, he had run in's with all walks of life. Everything from superstar sports figures and celebrities to political hacks like this lot, in addition to his usual cast of degenerates, dealers, and other bottom feeding criminals. In all his dealings with people, he had found something that remained consistent; elitists were elitists no matter what their socio-economic status.

The people in the middle, the nine to fivers, folks who went to work every day, put time in on the weekends, and did whatever else they had to do just to make ends meet, were usually humble, quiet, respectful. These folks just wanted to get along and do what they had to do. The rich and the so-called poor on the other hand were another matter entirely. Banks had worked in and around the projects for the majority of his career. He dealt with people who were part of the entitlement system day in and day out. Though the majority of even those people were just trying to get along, there was still that element of elitist. Those people, part of the generational welfare system who expected and demanded that the government give them shelter, food, even pay for clothes and cable television. Those people and the elitists on the other side of the financial system always gave him the same look. That look of, "How dare you? Do you know who I am?" The similarities in attitude in contrast with the vast differences in wealth between the two groups never ceased to stop him in his tracks.

That was what Banks was seeing now as this file of politicos walked passed him. Most wouldn't meet him in the eye. Not because they were intimidated, but because they thought he and the assistant chief, and even the chief were not worthy of their time. It told him all he needed to know about the congressman they served, and the prisoner they were trying to spring.

When the entourage exited the office the Chief, who had held the door for them, waved Banks in.

"Chief," Banks said as he entered the office.

"Have a seat, Lieutenant," Chief Gerald Nesmith told him.

Banks did as he was told and immediately noticed the man in the grey suit looming over him. He was younger than Banks, maybe early thirties, and his jet-black hair stood at attention above his head. Banks wasn't big on hair care products, but even he took notice of how plastic the younger man's hair was. Banks knew he was a prosecutor at the District Attorney's office. He'd seen him in the halls of the DA's Office but he didn't know his name. The young lawyer stood with his arms crossed over his chest, scowling at Banks. Banks stared back at him until he flinched. It took about five seconds.

The prosecutor was about to speak when the chief cut him off.

"Lieutenant Banks, this is Deputy District Attorney Marlon Hansfield. He's going to be handling the Tulley case."

"Yes, Sir." Banks studied the Chief who seemed to be grimacing from the inside out. "That was quick. Sir, I haven't even finished the report yet." Banks gestured with the folder in his hand.

"I'll just take what you have," Hansfield said, reaching for the report.

Banks pulled it back out of Hansfield's reach. The ADA glared at him.

"As I said, it is not finished yet. I've only completed the reports for the narcotics charges." Banks looked directly at the prosecutor. "I haven't gotten to the resisting arrest and assault of a police officer charges yet."

Hansfield turned red and seemed to choke on a flood of unspoken thoughts. He looked at the chief. "There won't be any resisting arrest or assault on police charges."

Banks was enjoying pushing the little prick but his building rage was getting hard to tamp down. Before the chief could speak, he filled the dead air.

"Mr. Tulley attempted to flee the scene and when opposed struck an officer, me. He will be charged with both resisting and assault."

It wasn't so much the fact that this suited weasel was trying to get Tulley off before the ink was dry on the reports Or the fact that no one was trying to get Antwan Tate or any other kid from the ghetto out of his jam. Sure Tate was a piece of shit that his unit had taken off the street time and time again, but this Tulley kid was just as guilty of the same racket. Both assholes sold poison for a living.

Banks wasn't naive; he'd been around long enough to hear the stories of some big wig, or their straphanger, getting off after they were caught with their pants down. This wasn't the first time it had ever happened to Banks. But this was not then. He wouldn't let this happen again. He looked at the chief and saw the man had already wilted under the pressure the herd of suits had put on him. After all, he was a political animal; he served at the pleasure of the mayor. The mayor and Tulley, and probably this apoplectic fool standing in front of him in a grey suit would someday serve the same donors who filled their campaign war chests and paid for favors they would receive when their subjects gained office. The difference was that the chief took an oath, just as Banks did. He was paid by the city to enforce laws. He never read anywhere that some laws didn't apply to certain people. He tried to calm himself as he squared off with the prosecutor and the chief.

"Banks," Nesmith finally said, it seemed more like a plea than an order. "Come on, you know what this shit is."

"I'm beginning to Chief."

"G..." Hansfield was cut off when Banks continued.

"But it's kind of hard to swallow, letting a subject carrying felony weight in pills and struck a police officer go. Doesn't seem right."

"Grow up," Hansfield blurted.

Banks' dark eyes narrowed and he started toward the prosecutor.

"Stand down, Lieutenant!"

Banks stopped and came to attention. It was an instinctual reaction, more muscle memory than anything.

"Give Hansfield the file and go home."

"You're both ordering me to drop charges on a subject based on pedigree?"

Neither man answered.

***

The chief wouldn't look at him and the prosecutor smirked. It took every ounce of restraint Lieutenant Peter Banks had to hand the unfinished case file over, knowing full well that Andrew Tulley would never suffer for his crimes the way Antwan Tate would, and all because of who his daddy was. Hansfield took the file and without leave, Banks left the room.

In the hallway outside, Vaden was waiting for him.

"That's about how I thought you would look," he commented.

Banks walked past him. There was nothing he could say in that moment that wouldn't get him suspended or fired, and he still considered Vaden a friend. After a few steps, Vaden stopped trying to follow Banks as the lieutenant headed for the back door of the station.

"Don't do anything stupid," the assistant chief yelled.

"Hmmm."

Chapter Five

The whiskey in his glass tasted like piss. The bar was loud and crowded. People filtered around Peter Banks who was hunched over a sweating tumbler crunching on ice. The team was scattered throughout the bar. Wilkes, Poppy, and Thompson were at a table playing quarters with a couple of drunk college kids while Este and Max were in a booth, conspiring about something or other. Banks had shown up simply because that's what leaders did. They show their appreciation, built unit cohesion. Normally, any given Friday night his team invaded some nightspot or another and did all they could to drain the bar of harsh liquor and cold beer. Tonight, however, Banks was only there for show.

He'd known as soon as he showed up that Max was on to him. The hulking black man with close-cropped black hair trimmed in flecks of salt and pepper had had his back since the two of them split a patrol car fifteen years ago. They'd seen riots together, buried brother policeman together, and bled together. After that much time, and that many high impact incidents, people could feel each other's instincts. Max DeGuello knew Pete Banks was on the warpath before Banks did himself. He had done a quick hello around the squad when he'd arrived and played off like he was going for a drink before he could field any questions. All of his detectives had seen the power players skulking around 7-5, the code used for police headquarters, before cutting loose for the night, and they all wanted the inside scoop. Banks wasn't sure how to put it to them so he'd retreated to the bar, hoping to get lost in the crowd. He drained the tumbler of melting ice and Jameson Whiskey, and rapped the glass on the bar looking for another. The bartender gave him a nod and Banks stiffened as he felt Max coming up behind him.

"What's going on?" he asked and not in the way of greeting.

His partner was prying like a sledgehammer on a safe.

"Congressman's son walked." Banks growled.

DeGuello sighed. "We had to know that was going to happen."

Banks nodded.

"So what now?"

"I don't know yet."

"That's what worries me."

"Huh."

DeGuello held his glass up and shook it for the bartender. "Orders are orders, man."

"I know."

"Still sucks though. Kind a like a kick to the balls."

Banks knew his friend wasn't going away so he gave in. He turned to DeGuello. "You know the worst part? The part that is eating away at me the most?"

"What?"

"Tate."

DeGuello scoffed. "Antwan, really?"

Banks nodded but didn't say a word.

"Man, screw that guy. What does he got to do with this?"

Banks turned away from his friend.

"Come on, spit it."

Banks sighed; he already knew how this was going to sound. "I get he's a piece of shit drug dealer. I just can't swallow the fact that some asshole politician's kid, who's a total dick, gets to go back to law school and the expressway to his daddy's seat someday while a kid like Antwan is going to do ten years for doing the other half of the transactions Tulley's kid was in on."

Banks cringed as DeGuello broke out laughing. "Way of the world, man. Shit. How long we been at this? Twenty something years and you get a conscience now? You better keep drinkin."

"I know. I don't get it either."

"That kid was an asshole though."

The bartender dropped a new set of tumblers full of amber liquid in front of both men. Banks took a hefty swig and started crunching ice again. "I know."

Chapter Six

Judge Henry Mercer wiped sleep out of his eyes and blinked into focus the figures of Marlow Hansfield, Andrew Tulley, and his assorted entourage of three lawyers, none of whom Mercer recognized. Hansfield and the defense, as Mercer characterized them, spoke quietly while Tulley, who looked nothing like a man who had gone to jail the night before for felony level narcotics trafficking, yawned and slouched at the defense table. The young man was oblivious to the thousands of dollars in time, and promises that were swirling around him. He wore a blazer and a pair of dark jeans. Mercer could swear that if he caught the light just right, Tulley's face sparkled with glitter.

"Jesus Christ." Mercer breathed.

He turned on the microphone on his bench and looked to his stenographer who glared at him. Nancy Paulette had been at his side, documenting proceedings for over twenty years. She knew exactly what was going on in the courtroom. Mercer found it funny that there was a stenographer present to document this slap in the face to the justice system however statute required all judicial proceedings be recorded so without Paulette banging away at the steno machine, nothing he declared would have any legs. On the flip side, the fact that there was any recording of this hearing period made Mercer's spine tingle. He was planning on retiring in the fall and the donation he had received from Congressman Tulley made his transition to pasture a path lined with gold. He could live with that.

"All right," he said into the microphone, "Let's get this over with."

Hansfield and the rest of the lawyers sprang to their separate sides of the courtroom. Mercer found that ironic and he saw Paulette roll her eyes. He wondered if the dream team before him had paid her off as well or did they not see her from so high up on their perch. As for Hansfield, that kid dripped with unencumbered ambition. He would sell out his own child to get into the state house, his oath of office was nothing more than a speedbump where his own career was concerned. Tulley for his part at least sat up straight-ish in his seat.

Hansfield straightened his tie one last time and cleared his throat as he waited for Mercer to wave him forward. Mercer creased his brow as he hastily waved him up.

Get on with it.

Hansfield took the file that he had strong armed from the chief of police the night before and approached the bench. Mercer took the file and looked up with a start when he heard the door to the back of the courtroom burst open. A sudden spark of panic rushed the room. Merceer felt as though he were back in his childhood, caught raiding the cupboards while his mother was not looking. He growled under his breath while watching the detective stroll down the aisle toward the small gate before the court.

"Judge Mercer, sorry for the interruption but I don't think you have the complete file related to my investigation."

Mercer didn't respond. He looked to Hansfield who watched Banks closing on them with unhindered disdain.

"Judge, the file is complete as I received it from the police department."

"Judge, I would recommend you look at the reports that have not been approved for dissemination, nor have all the reports been filed. You have an incomplete file, Judge, to include the lack of charging documents for all the violations related to Mr. Tulley's case."

Banks was looking at Tulley when he said it and Tulley matched his stare. There was plain and clear murder in the eyes of the defendant. Banks knew that look; he'd seen it before though coming from the congressman's son, it piqued his curiosity. Banks filed that away for later.

Mercer cleared his throat. "Detective, this file looks appropriate, if not complete in every sense of the word. I believe we have enough to move forward."

"Judge, you lack charging documents for resisting arrest and assault on a police officer," Banks stated.

Mercer looked down at his desk for a minute, considering threatening the son of a bitch in front of him with a contempt of court charge. When he looked up again, he had to swallow the fire in his belly when he noticed a new player standing next to Banks. The girl was all of maybe twenty years old, wearing thick horned rimmed glasses. Her hair had a neon shade of blue coating the ends and her clothes looked as if she couldn't decide if she was homeless or a schoolteacher.

"Who are you?" he ordered more than asked.

"Anna Flagherty, City Paper, Judge. Thank you for your time."

Banks watched the room around him meltdown silently as every person present stared at their shoes. He reveled when he saw shoulders drop and heads fall, all except for one. The stenographer, sitting off in her small corner, was grinning from ear to ear.

***

Max DeGuello leaned against the cement wall around the corner from the Chief's Office. He arrived a little late and could hear the booming report of the chief screaming at who he could only guess was Peter Banks. Banks had a way of riling people up. Though he was decorated three times over the years for bravery, every now and then he came down on the wrong side of the command staff. Usually it was his casework and his close rate that helped him walk through fire. DeGuello sighed, wondering if there was anything that was going to save his ass this time. Max was only able to pick up every third word or so through the thick concrete block walls. What he did gather though was colorful. The Chief must have threatened his job four times in the last five minutes that he'd been listening. The tirade was impressive. Max was not immune to the occasional ass chewing; less so now that he was on the far end of the scope and winding down career wise. Nowadays, it was usually he or Banks handing out the ass chewings when one of his bobble headed detectives turned their brains off momentarily. Regardless, he didn't know the chief had it in him. The guy, a retired fed who came in after the last chief stepped down a few years back, was less fiery than the average cop. Probably from years wading through the ocean of worthless paper that was federal law enforcement, he was more bureaucrat than anything else.

Not today though. Max had to suppress a grin a few times as curse words made their way through the walls into the quiet, Saturday morning hallways.

It was another ten minutes before the chief must have worn himself out. Pete emerged from the office keeping his expression as blank as possible for any possible onlookers hanging around. He nodded at Max who fell in behind him.

"You still employed?" Max asked.

"Yup."

"You still a lieutenant?"

"Yup."

"You still running narco?"

"Yup."

"Wow you really do walk on water," Max said.

"Good call with that reporter," Pete said in a low voice.

Max scoffed. "Wasn't me," he said, "Este's been banging her for the last six months. Did it on his own."

"Este is banging a reporter?"

Max nodded. "Uh-huh."

"Stupid kid."

The two detectives left police headquarters through the back door and rounded the corner of the building so that they were out of range of any of the closed circuit television cameras that covered the exits and entrances around the complex. When Banks stopped, Max waited patiently,

"This is a weird one, Max."

"I've noticed. I've also noticed you're not taking it too well."

Banks looked at his friend. DeGuello was right and Banks knew it. The rule has always been 'hit'em and forget'em.' They put people in jail. What the system did with them after that was not their problem. But this case was grinding on him. He knew why but his justification was just as perplexing as the case itself. Seeing a judge and the Chief of Police bend over for a congressman, and the fact that the gun they found was not supposed to exist, given the lack of identifiers and design, told Banks they couldn't let it go. There was more to this case and there were a lot of heavy hitters involved. He was a stray mullet swimming in a shark tank.

"You're not wrong," he said. "But I'm seeing this case through. I've got my twenty in, worst they can do is fire me. I'm not asking you or the rest of the unit to come along."

DeGuello looked across the road to the Ashley River that flowed passed the old headquarters building.

"Shit, I've got my twenty in too. And that shit bird hit a cop. No one walks for that. I don't care what the Chief says."

Banks followed his eyes across Lockwood Avenue and saw the squad waiting in the parking lot. Wilkes and Thompson were laughing while Viejo and Poppy were watching him intently. He studied them for a moment, trying to figure out a way he could keep them out of it.

DeGuello must've read his mind, "I hate to break it to you but where you go, those youngsters are going to go too. They've been around long enough to know what happens when a unit like ours goes through a shakeup. None of them want to go back inside, you know that."

"I know," Banks replied. "Bunch of morons."

"Hell of a lot smarter than we were at their age."

Banks nodded, he wasn't kidding. "All right."

Chapter Seven

The open hand slap across Andrew Tulley's face sounded like a whip cracking over a bulls head. The twenty-four year old law student reeled, retreating from his seat at brunch to get some distance from the old man.

His father, Congressman Andrew Tulley Sr., had welcomed his son home after his long journey through the gutter. He embraced him in both arms and guided him to the dining room where Milley and Ferris were preparing brunch. Senior had seated him and even prepared a Bloody Mary himself. He served it with just the right type of spice and heavy on the expensive Russian vodka he kept their 'city home' stocked with.

Tulley Jr. was apprehensive at first. He expected all hell to rain down on him after that asshole cop got his charges continued at court. Son of a bitch even had a reporter there to back him up so that no one could do anything about him. Remembering the way the pig sauntered up the aisle staring at him the way a hawk looks at a rabbit. Junior's blood rose and he noticed his breathing increasing as he thought about what had happened. Not his father though. As Junior sipped on his red drink, Ferris brought the plate in, and he saw that the staff had prepared his favorite, quail eggs over easy, resting on a bed of toast and smothered in hollandaise sauce. Junior had smiled, feeling relaxed for the first time since that horrible experience with Antwan Tate. He took a silver fork in his right hand, a silver butter knife in his left, and reached for the meal.

Junior saw it coming out the corner of his eye but was too slow. His father moved faster than any seventy year old should. In a flash, the man flipped the meal of steaming eggs onto Junior's chest and face. The slap that followed caused him to flee his chair.

"Son of a bitch!" the congressman bellowed, stalking him as Junior tried to get away. "Never in my life have I seen a simple swap so mishandled, so fucked up as this." Charging Junior, the congressman laid another ear splitting slap across the already burning cheek of his son. "Boy, if your mother was still alive, she would be downright ashamed to admit you were a product of her loins."

"I'm sorry," Junior blurted. He tasted blood and realized he had bit his tongue.

"Sorry! That's not the half of it, son. You were sloppy. You were weak!"

Junior kept backing away from his father but didn't speak.

"I give you one simple mission. I try to bring you in, get you on your way in this world, and you fucked it up like a virgin on prom night!" Senior's fists were balled and his shoulders were hunched as he followed his son around the table. "I figure you troll the gutters, you know people infesting the sewers of this godforsaken city, and you do! I tried!" his father screamed, spittle flying from his mouth in a rabid foam. "And you can't perform a simple task. You know what you've done!"

"I'm sorry," Junior whimpered.

"You are sorry! And that's not the half of it! You put it all at risk with your bullshit, trying to add to the plan for yourself, trying to get yours. And with pills of all things. Your bullshit side business with that vermin has put everything this family has built since your great-great grandfather first took the halls of the state capital, since our people first sank their boots into the mud on this fucking continent!"

His father closed on him again and Junior prepared himself for another blow. It would not be a punch that he knew. His father never hit him with a closed fist. You hit a man with a closed fist, he would tell him, you're not worthy of a closed fist. Junior had been hearing those words since he was nine years old. They hurt worse than the actual assault.

"I can fix this," he tried to say as another slap rattled his skull.

His father grabbed a fist full of his shirt and pulled him to within an inch of his hot, vodka soaked breath. The old man's eyes burned, the whites of the orbs stood in stark contrast to the puffed red skin of his face.

In a quiet voice he growled, "You will fix this son. Or you will die trying."

His father threw him away and walked toward the door. "Clean yourself up, you're coming with me."

As Junior recovered, watching his father stomp from the room, he caught a look at himself in the mirror over the bar. Snot ran down from his nose and tears streaked his face. Andrew Tulley hated what he saw.

Chapter Eight

This is a hell of an opening salvo.

DeGuello leaned against the doorway leading from the evidence drop to the front desk of the station.

"You need to hurry the hell up," he said.

"Yeah, yeah," Banks replied, working the old rusty lock on the evidence drop box with a set of lock picks.

He delicately felt around the inner workings of the lock with two probes. Trying to feel for the tumblers and gently twisting the mechanism hoping it would fall his way. Banks had been trained over a decade ago in lock picking as part of his role in breaching doors on the SWAT team. He sucked at it and would rather knock down a door with a battering ram any day than fiddle with tweezers. He felt sweat beading on his forehead as he tried to keep his composure while dealing with the damn World War Two era locking mechanism that secured the evidence drop box, which was nothing more than a retired dome shaped mail box. Luckily for him, it was a Saturday, and late morning, so the usual traffic through the area was relatively non-existent. The desk sergeant, Thomas, was still around though, lurking between the booking area, break room, and restroom. At any given second, he could pop up out of nowhere and Banks' pseudo guerrilla war against the Low Country political elite would end before it began.

"You gotta move. Thomas is on his way back." Max hissed behind him.

"Almost got it," Banks lied, he could get it in the next five seconds or take another ten minutes. He had no idea. Suddenly the bolt sprang open and it was such a shock he didn't realize it for another couple of seconds.

"Shit," he said, surprised by his success.

Banks yanked the door open and quickly found the gun. Sitting next to the weapon, surrounded by a collection of other evidence items seized by police officers over the last day and a half, were heavy paper bags holding the pills they had taken from the crime scene where Tulley and Tate were arrested. Banks grabbed both the weapon and the drugs, and shut the door as quietly as he could.

As he stood up, he froze when he looked into the eyes of Sergeant Thomas. The old man was staring at him from behind the glass partition separating the desk area and the workroom. Banks tried to recover and, grabbing a pen from his shirt, he smiled at Thomas with a nod and started filling out the chain of evidence form attached to the paper bag holding the pills.

"How's it going, Sarge?" he asked, acting as if it were just another day at the office.

Thomas looked at him with a grim scowl while Banks kept himself busy filling out the form for the weapon and then amending the clipboard over the evidence box to keep the property chain following the evidence intact. It was irregular, to say the least, to remove evidence that had already been put in the 'drop box.' Evidence in the drop box was technically only a safekeeping mechanism before being entered into the official department evidence custody system. Banks could think of a handful of policies he was breaking by doing what he was doing. As he filled out the forms documenting every action he took, he was making a paper trail for others to follow. Technically doing everything in the open. Regardless, he figured after the morning's festivities, there wasn't much more he could do to get on the Chief's bad side.

Banks finished signing the custody form and hung the clipboard back up over the evidence box. He grabbed the paper bags and box the weapon was secured in, and walked out of the room with Max in tow. All the while, Thomas watched them from the front desk.

"Can't get much closer than that," Max whispered as they made their way toward the back of the station.

"I'm still not sure we actually got away," replied Banks.

Chapter Nine

The ride to Kiawah Island was shared in silence between Congressman Tulley and his son, Andrew. The two clung to their respective sides in the back seat of the Lincoln Town car they shared, and each did their best to ensure the integrity of the gulf between them.

Andrew stared out the window as the James and John's Island slid by him and concentrated on his resolve. His face burned where his father had hit him. The lingering sensation of the assault was like embers stoking a dying campfire back to life. He felt his face flush several times and he fought to keep himself calm. There would come a time when his father would not so easily be allowed to strike him, Andrew told himself. He was a man in his own right now. He had his own income stream across several separate avenues, discounting the unfortunate setback with Antwan Tate. Andrew stood on his own. He was no longer reliant on his father or his family's support. The way his father slapped him, open handed only to add insult to the pain, made Andrew sick with himself.

Never again, he told himself. *That man will suffer if he ever tries to hit me again*, he promised.

As the drive came to a close, Andrew gave a sideward glance toward his father, who even on a Saturday wore a heavily starched suit and tie. The man sat like he was commuting to his office at the state house. He read a newspaper that was neatly folded around his reading area. The driver pulled to a stop in front of a monstrosity of a beach house on the Eastern side of the island, two men in sunglasses and polo shirts opened a door for each of the Tulleys. Before getting out of the car, his father slapped the paper down on the leather seat between them and grabbed

Andrew's arm. Keeping him from leaving the vehicle, he spoke quietly.

"Keep your mouth shut in there. This is the big leagues, son, let me handle it."

Andrew glared at him but didn't say a word. He nodded slowly after a moment then freed himself with a yank of his arm.

The steps leading up to the house were hewn stone, which matched the trim around the structure that was primarily of brick construction. At the top of the stairs were two men that Andrew had met only once before. Michael Brigston was the CEO of Old South Armorers, a rifle manufacturer out of the upstate near Greenville. The massive beach house was his. Next to him was Niles Davidson, an executive from some defense contractor. Andrew wasn't sure which one. When he asked his father after their last meeting, his father had told him it wasn't important. Both men wore suits like his father did. Andrew wore a blazer that sparkled every now and then with glitter he'd accumulated from a couple of young coeds he'd run into last night in downtown Charleston. The jeans and Van sneakers he sported did not help him blend in as he climbed the stairs. He reached the landing and shook the outstretched hands of both men.

"Tough break yesterday, Andrew," Davidson said.

Up until that point, Andrew had feared what awaited him at the meeting. A degree of relief swept over him as Davidson provided an air of sympathy. The gesture was much appreciated.

Brigston, on the other hand, said nothing. Decorum required the two shake hands. When they did, Andrew saw only mildly veiled disgust in the man's facial features and looked away.

Andrew slid past the two men as his father made his entrance. This was a practiced maneuver he had started in grade school. Whenever his father went anywhere, he had the appearance and mannerisms of the president crossing the rose garden after disembarking from Marine One—a stern countenance and a purposeful stride. Andrew slipped behind and off to the side of Davidson and Brigston, and watched the two take a couple of steps toward the congressman. For a man nearing his seventies, Tulley Senior was strong and healthy. There were no creaking or knee troubles as he took the stairs like a conquering general. His smile was broad but controlled, looking professional with just the right amount of humanity mixed in. His hand rose in perfect timing with his step to meet Davidson and the two shook vigorously. Tulley Senior followed the handshake with his weak hand to Davidson's corresponding shoulder. His father repeated the same gesture with Brigston with just a hint of less enthusiasm as if to ensure Davidson and Brigston knew their place in the hierarchy of the two men. After a brief flurry of pleasantries, the three men turned toward the massive double oak doors and entered the grand house as servants opened the portal for them. Andrew was all but swept aside by the three men and fell in step quietly behind them. This was the second half of the long-standing maneuver. As always, Andrew was here for show, to be seen, to have the right smile, the right nod, maybe even the supportive laugh when his father made a precisely calculated joke. He knew his role and would follow the script as he always had.

Once inside the massive foyer, the three were ushered to a rear sitting room, which overlooked the ocean. The beach on this side of the island was private, for meetings just like this one. The pristine beach glistened under the hot sun and a rising tide lapped lazily at the shoreline. The four men were each seated in a relative circle and provided a scotch before the meeting started. After everyone had had their first pull of the aged liquor, Davidson put his crystal tumbler down next to him and sat casually with his legs crossed and his hands resting in his lap.

"What happened, Andrew?" Davidson asked.

Junior's head popped up, thinking for a moment that the question had been directed at him. His father didn't even look at him before answering. He noticed that Davidson wasn't looking at him,

"You see, Niles, things hit a little snag there yesterday, minor snag, you see but there's nothing to worry about I don't think. We already have a couple of avenues we're looking at to fill the void left by our last pipeline."

Niles Davidson had a practiced face, almost as honed as the congressman's. "I heard we had a snag. I also heard we hit a second snag, followed very closely by a third. Tell me, Congressman, where is Mr. Brigston's sample as we speak."

Congressman Andrew Tulley didn't even blink. "The sample is secure. It remains under our control and in the hands of trusted people even if not our own."

"Good," Davidson responded flatly. "Good, so then we have nothing to worry about given Andrew's current legal situation?"

"No." The congressman waved a dismissive hand imperceptibly. "No, that too is well in control."

"I'm glad to hear that, Andrew," This time Davidson looked toward the younger Tulley. The attention surprised Andrew. Without pause, Davidson turned back toward the congressman. "And what of this man, Tate, and Wyatt Friehurst?"

Andrew was stunned as he saw, maybe for the first time ever, his father pause. He didn't stutter, or stumble, the man only paused. The silence would have been imperceptible to anyone else except Andrew. He knew every characteristic, every habit, every tell that came from the man.

"Those issues are being worked at the moment by our same trusted associates."

"I see, so a three time felon and a pantywaist aristocrat floating loose in the legal system fits your definition of controlled does it?"

There was another pause, this one longer, less controlled.

"Well..."

"Well," Davidson repeated. "Given the light of the previous weeks failures, it has been decided that we will be overseeing your role in the operation for the foreseeable future."

Andrew was shocked when his father's jaw dropped.

"Excuse me?" Senior asked.

Davidson set his drink down on the small table beside his lounging chair. His posture did not change, nor did his facial features. However, when he spoke, the air in the room turned cold.

"Within the last month, you have lost our cleansing mechanism for getting Mr. Brigston's product to market, and worse you." Andrew shriveled as Davidson's eyes found him. "Have lost a sample to law enforcement. A weapon that does not exist and is in violation of every firearms regulation in effect in this and many other nations."

The congressman stuttered but Davidson continued.

"So you must understand, Congressman, when those at corporate start to show concern when a major aspect of an operation begins to fall apart."

"I will not have it!" His father huffed. "This is my state, I call the..."

Now Davidson leaned in toward the Congressman, he kept his voice icy calm. Andrew was scared. He had never seen his father ever challenged, much less what was happening here.

46

"Do you, Mr. Tulley?" Davidson asked, elbows resting on his knees, hands forming a steeple aimed at the congressman.

Andrew could see his father fume when Davidson did not use the title of his office.

"Do you call shots?" Davidson asked. "We and our concern have funded you over numerous terms in office, as we did your father before you. You have been a loyal and well performing employee for quite some time now. Deep down, do you feel as though you have 'called the shots,' as you put it? No, you have not just as your predecessor did not, just as those that follow you will not." Davidson paused for a moment to look at Andrew again.

The young law student suddenly felt like bait on a hook. Davidson returned his focus to his father and Andrew observed his father staring at him.

His father's jaw was slack, his eyes somewhat lost. Andrew Tulley barely recognized the man. They looked at each other, the younger studying the older, trying to figure out what he saw there. Was it embarrassment? Or shame? Maybe fear?

Then he realized what the foreign look was that he was seeing in his father's eyes... defeat. His father was defeated by this man, this terrifying man wearing an expensive suit. When Davidson returned to his relaxed position in the lounger, his father's eyes dropped to the drink in his hand.

"Now," Davidson said, as if he were chairing a board meeting. "As I said, there will be a degree of supervision over the resolution of the current issue. Once things are resolved, we will re-evaluate our position." Davidson's face changed to a grin, as if he were offering a pep talk during half time. "Not to worry, Congressman," he said, "We value the relationship we've had with the Tulleys for two generations now, and we look forward to the future." Davidson again glanced at Andrew, "We simply need to get past this current unfortunate situation."

Davidson retrieved his cell phone from the breast pocket of his suitcoat and entered a code. The door to the adjacent room opened and Andrew watched as three men walked in, each wearing a suit on par with Davidson's. They did not say a word, simply stood before them. Andrew watched the three men. He knew the look. They had close-cropped hair, stern jaws, and their suits failed to hide the hard muscles moving beneath the material. They were military men or something like it. The three had a confidence that was uncommon to most of the people Andrew dealt with on a daily basis. He'd seen men like this on foreign visits, even one to Kabul, Afghanistan with his father a couple of years ago. These were men who had struggled at some point in their lives and won. They appeared to Andrew to be used to winning.

"These three gentleman will be assisting you, Andrew, in the resolution of our current situation."

Congressman Tulley huffed. "Me, I..."

Davidson leered at the old man, "Not you, Andrew. You." He pointed at Andrew Junior.

"Me?" Andrew asked, "Why me?"

"No they most certainly will not!" The congressman shot out of his chair and Davidson met him face to face.

"How hard do you think you would be to replace, Congressman?" Davidson asked, keeping that calm, customer oriented voice icy cold.

Congressman Tulley puffed out his chest, his nostrils flared, but he did not say a word.

"Where would you be without our millions burying your skeletons during every campaign? If our money was not there to silence your competition, or pay to block the other side's access to media?" The congressman slowly sat down. Davidson followed him. "Where would you be if your history was suddenly revealed to your constituents, or the FBI?"

Congressman Tulley turned his face toward the door. Davidson stood back straight and focused on Andrew.

"Andrew," Davidson said. "Your father saw fit to bring you into this world. He gave you a chance to 'be a man,' as he is wont to say. You managed to get arrested with a weapon that should not exist, and a dump truck load of ecstasy that in no way should have been part of this operation."

Andrew felt his insides trembling under the stoic, placid face of Niles Davidson. The man's smile was at once predatory and sympathetic. It was terrifying.

"Now, you will assist these men in resolving this matter to the best of your ability. Any less than your full cooperation will be met with more than just an openhanded slap to the face. Are there any questions?"

"No." It was a hoarse attempt at speaking, but Andrew was too scared to make a sound.

"Good." Davidson clapped his hands together, causing Andrew to jump. "Let's get started shall we. The sooner we can put this whole sordid affair behind us, the better."

Chapter Ten

When they pulled behind the large quiet office building, Max looked at Banks quizzically,

"This is your plan?" he asked.

"This is the best place for this gun," Banks said. "We need to get it out of CPDs hands and figure out where it came from."

"And you think the ATF is going to help us with that?"

"Not the ATF, Pak."

"Shiiiit." DeGuello shook his head sadly.

"Whoa, where did you get this?" Yao Pak asked in hushed tone as he studied the weapon.

The rifle was zip tied into a cardboard box, which now lay on a butcher paper covered examination table in the Bureau of Alcohol, Tobacco, Firearms, and Explosives laboratory. Banks and his team lined the table taking turns looking from Pak to the gun and then back to Pak.

"This happened to show up at a raid we did yesterday," Banks said.

"Some kind of raid," Pak observed as he lowered a flashlight to an oblique angle over the weapon. The low angle of the light brought out shadows along the grooves and mechanisms of the weapon. It was also a handy way of identifying hard to see trace evidence like hairs and fibers.

"Yeah, this wasn't the only VIP there. The local congressman's son also was in attendance, though not as cooperative as the gun was. That's why we're here."

Pak's head shot up from studying the gun.

Banks took a step back. "Everyone from the DA, to the chief, to the congressman's own straphangers have already braced me. This case and this gun will disappear if my people handle this. I figured this is the best place for it."

50

Pak's eyes furrowed under the clear plastic examination lenses he wore. "You said this was a rush job, not some personal fight, Banks." Pak looked to DeGuello. "He letting things get personal, yeah?"

DeGuello looked at Banks. He took a step back from the table. "He said it partner, not me."

Pak dropped his head and sighed.

Banks looked around the table at his squad, and at Pak. He was putting all their careers at risk by letting them come along with him, and he knew that. He also admitted that part of him wanted Tulley in jail. In all his years, that smug son of a bitch could be in the top ten people he'd run into that grinded on him the way the little shit had. But then there was the weapon sitting in front of him. There was more to the story of that weapon, Banks needed to know what the story was.

"Banks, sometimes the system don't work like we want. Sometimes people don't go to jail. It above your pay grade."

"Pak, look at that gun," Banks blurted. "All of you look at that gun," he said to the rest of the table. "It's an AR that you could almost fit in your pocket. Aside from how dangerous this thing would be in the hands of some jackass gangsters—look at it. There are no stamps identifying this thing. No serial numbers. The receiver is half polymer. That's some next level shit. It doesn't belong in some ghetto flophouse. Where did it come from?" He looked at Pak. "I just need to know what you can figure out. Just look at it, that's all. We're above board here; the chain of custody is clean. Who gives a shit what some congressman wants, or the DA in his pocket wants to do with this case? I just want to run this down."

Pak stared at the gun on the table again.

The rest of the crew was looking at Banks. Viejo was the one to speak up. "So what do we do?"

Banks took a breath. "I'm not ordering any of you to do anything. No matter how clean we are here, the powers that be will try to sink us. I'm going to hang here and wait for Pak to do what he can."

"And the rest of us?" Wilkes spoke for the group.

Banks sighed. "We're going to run this like any other investigation. We need to track down these pills. Where are they on the street? Who are the major distributors? Are any of the clubs involved? And we need to get back to Antwan, see if he wants to talk. We build our case just like we would any other and deliver it to the prosecutor just like any other. Thanks to Este's girl at the city paper, the DAs and the command staff feel the heat from the press. We'll use that to our advantage and maybe save our jobs in the process."

Chapter Eleven

Antwan Tate spent the night at the police lockup before being transferred to the Al Cannon Criminal Justice Facility the next morning. The in-process at county was the same as it had been the last two times he had gotten locked up. Tate spread his ass cheeks, changed his clothes, gave his belongings to the property clerk, got his scrubs, flimsy blanket, lace-less slippers, and made his way to his pod.

He was admitted to Pod-5. When he checked in with the corrections officer, or CO, he got the usual 'don't fuck up or you'll pay' speech from the bloated prison guard and answered "yes boss," when it was expected. He kept his mouth shut when that was expected too. Finally, he was shown to his bunk in a cell. The eight by ten cell was constricting and made him edgy. Tate dropped his blanket and other issued property on the bunk and sighed. He stared at the thin, plastic covered mattress trimmed in cold aluminum framing. All he wanted to do was sleep, to climb into that bunk and shut his eyes til his day in court. He knew he was going up for a while this time. This was the third time Banks and his boys got him for dealing. The first time it was weed, not much but enough to put a felony on him. The second time, he'd been selling crack rocks for Jamal Washington. That one was bad, he had just re-upped from Jamal and was loaded down with a couple cookies when they got him. Antwan had done seven months of a three-year bit and got out on parole cause of overcrowding. When they got him this last time, the pills made the crack look like crumbs from a box of Cheerios.

He knew that was too much dope to try and move quietly. He should have listened to his instincts that were screaming for him to run when Tulley came to him with the proposition. But he jumped, like he always did, right into the pit. Admittedly, the money was good for the run they had. Tulley was getting the pills from somewhere down south. He never said and Tate never asked, wasn't his side of the business, and less is more when it came to that sort of thing. All in all, he and Tulley made a good team. They had a pretty good split though Tulley got a little bit bigger pinch since he was bringing the stuff in but Tate didn't care. The pill game made the crack game look like trippin through a sewer, dealin with crackheads day in day out. Bored off his ass standing on some street corner just waiting for the damn cops to come throw him up on a wall or some shit. Dealin' pills was like handing out Jordans at a high school, everybody wanted some. He was in at every club in the city, even the high side ones that never would let him in before. Hot white chicks and college kids lit up his pockets with cash. And that ecstasy made them girls so horny, Antwan smiled as he recalled what he had done to some of those college girls in the bathrooms of some of those clubs.

"Out! Let's Go. Get down stairs," A guard yelled from out on the landing.

Antwan had forgotten that the guard was still out there. He nodded and did what he was told after taking one last look at the crappy bed that called his name. He walked the pace of a man with nowhere to go as he made his way down the stairs to the communal area. All the pods were two stories. Mostly cells on the second floor and wash rooms. There were a couple of pods on the first floor but largely the wide area was filled with chairs and a couple of bookracks. Four televisions were situated in the corners of the large area. Antwan checked out the room and saw a couple of familiar faces seated around the lounge. He didn't see anyone that he had a beef with so he figured that was a plus. With a huff, he flopped down in a plush reading chair and breathed deeply. The faint smell of Clorox and the mammalian scent of too many men living in close confines was a familiar odor and one that Antwan never got used to. He resigned himself to the fact he was going to be sitting in county for a while and tried to block out the rest of the world.

His thoughts went back to Tulley, to the last meeting they'd had, right before they got pinched. He had brought the machine gun with him, he and his dip shit friend, Wyatt. Tate was suspicious of that dude, Wyatt, from the start but what he really had been concerned with was the gun. The damned thing looked like something from the SEALS or some shit. Tate never much got into guns, even in the crack game. He'd seen people shot before and been shot at when he'd gotten caught up in somebody else's drama. Word was that his daddy got shot but he was never sure. His momma never talked much about his old man before she ran off too.

That gun. Antwan knew they were gonna put that gun on him. The piece was going to make for a long bit. He tried to push the weapon and Tulley from his mind and close his eyes. He was almost in that blissful state between sleep and the perennial boredom of jail when he snapped up.

"Tate!" the CO called. "Visitor."

"Shit." Tate growled.

Chapter Twelve

Marlow Hansfield would have been raging if anyone else had called him in to work on a Saturday. As circumstances had it, the prosecutor still had murder on his mind but it wasn't for the fact he was walking into police headquarters instead of laying on the beach in front of his family's Isle of Palms beach house. Instead, he was truly pissed at the fact a simple detective had out played him. He hated the whole affair with the Tulleys. In fact, Marlow Hansfield had only met one person he hated more than Andrew Tulley, that smug son of a bitch, in his entire life, and that was the prick's father, Congressman Andrew Tulley. But the Tulleys were plugged in and held the keys to the door of low country politics, and possible beltway politics, if he handled the situation right. So far, the situation had been handling him. The sight of that damned reporter standing next to Banks earlier that morning incensed his normally casual demeanor. If he had not been standing before a judge, and had Banks not towered over his lithe frame, he would have attacked the man.

Banks had won the round; he'd outmaneuvered not only Hansfield himself but also the entire team sent by the Tulleys, and the judge who had to have been in on the plan. The backers of the Tulleys had handled the news far better than Tulley himself who launched into a tirade. Hansfield could hear him bellowing curses and insults through the phone one of Andrews's lawyers used to break the news to him. Hansfield had considered the fact he was not the one to tell the congressman his son's prosecution would go forward was a small victory in what had to date been an ass kicker of a Saturday.

Then Hansfield had received a phone call. It was a couple of hours later after he'd had time to calm himself outside of court. The congressman's staff needed to review the evidence against Andrew. As was expected, Hansfield lodged the proper protests and pointed out all of the regulations and laws allowing such a thing would violate. Once the assurances that he would be taken care of were put forward to his satisfaction, Hansfield was more than willing to make the trip to police headquarters.

Since there was no court on weekends, police headquarters was relatively quiet. An old, tired looking desk sergeant flipped through a fishing magazine, barely looking up at him from behind the glass partition,

"Can I help you?" the old cop grumbled.

Hansfield held up his credentials, "Assistant District Attorney Hansfield. I need to review some evidence."

"On a Saturday?" the desk sergeant, his nametag read 'Wagner,' asked, arching a bushy eyebrow.

"Tell me about it," Hansfield responded.

Wagner shrugged, "The evidence custodian's not here. When was the evidence brought in?"

"Should have been yesterday."

"Oh," Wagner said putting down the phone he'd just picked up, thinking he would have to call in an equally old and soon to be pissed off evidence custodian, "Well everything that's come in since yesterday will be locked up in the evidence drop. Go in the room there and check the log. If what you're looking for was dropped, it'll be there. I'll have to call the duty commander to get the key,"

"Thanks," Hansfield said, acting as cheerfully as he could.

Truth was he hated dealing with cops. They always asked too many questions. Thought they knew how he should present his cases. Most of them barely had a college degree, and they thought they could tell a lawyer how to do his job.

Stepping into the small room, not much more than a cubicle next to the windowed sergeant's desk, Hansfield found the clipboard over the old mailbox type evidence container. A second after his eyes hit the page, his breath caught in his throat.

Wagner made the call to the duty commander and set the phone back in the cradle. When he looked up to tell the lawyer that the CO was on her way in, the prosecutor was nowhere in sight.

Chapter Thirteen

Banks sent Wilkes, Poppy, and Thompson to start running down the ecstasy they'd taken the day before. The three youngest members of his team would get a handle on places to start looking for dealers and later that night, would hit the Charleston night scene and start working their informants. That left himself, DeGuello, and Viejo sitting around the ATF lab watching Pak go to work on the rifle.

At first, they were interested in watching the analyst do his work. After a half hour of photographs and measurements, the interest in the laborious process faded and the three started milling about like seven year olds at a museum. Pak scorned Viejo three times for touching the delicate scientific equipment before the three cops finally got the message and found perches around the lab to sit and wait.

The hours wore on and soon the sun dipped over the horizon. Banks looked at his watch and noticed he'd been shuffling around the lab for going on six hours while Pak ran tests and documented every detail of the strange, unmarked weapon they had brought him. He found Pak mounting the rifle over a large tank of water and his interests piqued. He approached Pak careful not to get in the way of the short but fiery scientist and found that Viejo and DeGuello were flanking him. Pak noticed the rejuvenated audience his actions had attracted,

"You guys seem curious," Pak commented.

"Seen this part on CSI," offered Viejo.

"Mention that show again and you are thrown out of this laboratory for life," Pak said without looking up from tightening down a mounting bracket along the weapon's receiver. "Basically what we have here is a souped up AR-15," he continued. "The receiver is a slightly larger scale than the rifle you guys and the military are used to and the venting system is a design I've never come across. Whereas your run-of-the-mill AR recycles the gases from the combustion of the charge in the round through one vent in the barrel this one has two. I can't be sure as to why quite yet but I think the extra gas vent may help with the cycle rate, meaning the weapon will fire faster than the traditional version."

Pak looked up from the weapon momentarily and noticed that his onlookers may have understood half of what he was saying. Like most gun-toters, he knew they just want to hear the weapon go bang. He pulled a 7.62mm round out of his pocket, slid the cartridge into the weapon's chamber, and released the charging rod putting the weapon into battery.

"Was that a seven-six-two?" asked Banks.

"It is. This weapon also varies from the traditional platform in that it carries a larger round."

"Thing's a monster," said DeGuello.

"It does seem so," responded Pak.

He retrieved four sets of hearing protection from a rack mounted to the side of a large tub of water and distributed them to his guests. He then went to the weapon and ensured the three were following proper protocol by putting the safety gear over their ears. They did so without question and Pak reached for the trigger.

"Fire in the hole," he announced and squeezed the trigger.

BANG!

The discharge of the high-powered weapon in confined space was considerable even with the ear protection. A small burst of water plopped at the surface of the tub briefly. Pak looked up at the three cops and saw that they were waiting for more.

"Sorry," he apologized. "There's really not much drama to see." They seemed deflated. "But if anything will tell us where this weapon comes from it will be this."

He opened the lid to the large tub and used a small net, not unlike the kind used for a fish tank, to retrieve the core and jacket of the bullet he'd just fired into the water.

"Let's see what she can tell us."

Chapter Fourteen

Tate was herded by the corrections officer out of the pod where his cell was and passed through three control doors before being ushered into the visitation room. The guard escorting him motioned past the row of cubicles where inmates met with loved ones and other visitors toward a separate room. The heavy iron door swung open for him as he approached and he all but choked when he stepped inside.

"You gotta be kiddin me?" he asked as he took in the two detectives.

"How ya settling in, Antwan?" Wilkes asked from a bench on the other side of the room.

Antwan slouched against the wall as the guard removed the shackles he'd worn from the pod to this meeting. "Bout how you'd expect bein in jail and all." He glanced from Wilkes to Poppy and slowly looked her over, lingering on her hips and chest.

"Can I help you?" Poppy asked nonchalantly.

"You have no idea," responded Antwan.

"I've had better offers in here before," she said.

"Doubt that," Antwan retorted. "So." He turned back to Wilkes, "What the fuck you want?"

Wilkes held his hands out in a beseeching gesture, "Same as always, man, see if you want to help yourself out."

"And Banks sent you? Shit, your dumbass put me in here."

"You're the one who dropped those pills in my hand, Antwan, so there is that. You're also a three striker, so there's that. But you know as well as we do that you're not the top of the food chain. We're looking for the shot caller, like we always do. You want to help us out?"

Antwan was quiet for a moment, leaning against the cold, seemingly damp concrete block. This wasn't his first time in a cell, nor was it his first time being approached by the cops after an arrest. This time he was going up and he knew it. Even if he helped these fools out, he was going to get a couple of years in Lieber State Correctional. In and of itself that wasn't a huge deal to Antwan, just another jail, and he didn't much care about anyone out on the street anyhow.

"What do you want to know, man?"

"I want to know what Andrew Tulley was doing in that house with you."

Shit.

Antwan tried to play off the shock of hearing Tulley's name come up. He figured Tulley and his boy would already be out, runnin free with the rest of his daddy's friends.

"Who?"

"Right." It was Poppy coming at him this time. "It doesn't piss you off that rich pricks like him play at being a gangster then walk once the heat gets to them. While you and yours end up doing time that should be on their heads?"

Antwan took the opportunity to study the lady cop's body once again. Her hips, thinly covered in tight jeans, were cocked just so against the wall. She had a plaid shirt over a tank top, all earth colors. Antwan could see how tight her tummy was. She didn't have huge tits but he could see just enough of their bulge to guess at what they would feel like in his hands,

"So," he responded.

"So you want to help yourself out, tell us everything you know about that asshole. Maybe we can get something done for you."

"Maybe, but I need to know you gonna take care of me."

"Don't give me that shit, Tate, you know how this works. We took care of you last time, and the time before that if I recall."

"Correction, Wilkes, if that is your real name. Max and Banks took care of me last time, not you."

Wilkes sighed. "Either way, man, the game is the same."

Antwan saw Poppy cross her arms over her chest and saw a hint of cleavage roll out of the low cut of the tank top.

"All right then," he said. "He's the guy."

"Who is?"

"Tulley, he been the man with the pills for a while now. We just got tight last couple of months. He says he get his shit from somewhere in Europe or somethin. Prague or some shit. Says he met some boys over there when he was backpackin, whatever the fuck that mean."

"What about the gun?" Poppy asked.

Antwan crinkled his nose. That was what was going to get him, and it wasn't even his. That was the worst part. The gun charge would get him the most time and Tulley was the asshole that stashed it at his house. Antwan knew better. Knew better when Tulley had shown up with the damn thing, and knew better than to expect to get it off his jacket now. But what the hell.

"It was Tulley's. I never even touched the thing."

"Lie," said Poppy.

Antwan shrugged. "All right, I touched it, but I never shot it. I hate guns, man. You guys never got me with a gun before. Specially no Star Wars shit like that."

Wilkes was about to ask him something else when the door he was leaning on clanged as the bolt fell. He moved aside as the door swung open and in stepped a stunning blonde wearing a black pant suit.

"Shit," Wilkes muttered.

She shot him an icy glare that he grinned at. For some reason, Wilkes loved it when attorneys or other self-important tools tried to intimidate him.

"Mr. Tate has retained counsel. This meeting is over."

"Of course it is." said Poppy, stepping off the wall.

"Please excuse us."

Wilkes looked from the high priced lawyer to Tate who was grinning like a five year old at Christmas. Something wasn't right,

"Careful Tate," he told the convict as he left the room.

Tate didn't respond.

"So much for that," Poppy said as the two made their way out of the jail.

Chapter Fifteen

Pak had the bullet he retrieved from the tub mounted to a comparison microscope. The Asian scientist was hunched over the device and rotating the knob slowly so he could study the striations left on the bullet as it passed through the rifle barrel.

After the excitement of the test fire into the tub, the three detectives had again spread out around the small lab, trying their best not to distract the forensics expert from his task. DeGuello was leaning against the doorjamb to the lab when the sudden scratching sound from the outer offices caught his attention. He turned and looked for the source of the sound and after it continued, followed by a beep he turned to Pak.

"You expecting anybody, Pak?"

"Probably just an agent."

"On a Saturday?" DeGuello offered, "Never seen a fed work a Saturday."

The statement brought Pak up from the reticle of the microscope. The look he gave DeGuello was best described as surly.

"Present company excluded," said Banks as he and Viejo slid past where Pak was working toward DeGuello and the sounds of company.

"Jig might be up," said DeGuello.

"Pak, we just need to know where it came from."

"I know," was the bored response.

Banks looked at the two detectives that he had probably gotten fired for following him on his wild goose chase. He should have known better. One detective against the Police Command Staff, Mayor, Congressman, and District Attorney's office. What did Banks expect was going to happen? He figured Vaden or someone had gone behind him at headquarters and deduced that he took off with the evidence against Tulley. He tried to tell himself he was doing the right thing, that he was doing his job, being a thorough detective but he couldn't even sell himself on the deal much less his men. He heard the electronic lock open with a beep and a thunk. Whoever was coming had them dead to rights. His adventure was over.

"Sorry guys," he told DeGuello and Viejo. "I'm going to tell them you were here against your will."

"What the..."

DeGuello didn't get to finish his slur as a white male with the most intense, piercing stare he'd ever seen seemed to float above the cubicle maze twenty yards away from them. On instinct, the three detectives started reaching for the handguns at their belts. There was something off, but none of them could explain it. Was it the sight of the lone white male walking across the office space in front of them?

The question was suddenly forgotten as the guy turned at an intersection before them and with speed and smoothness born of long hours on the range, raised a now familiar weapon in their direction. The rounds fired through the modified AR-15 came so fast and the percussion was so severe in the enclosed space that Banks, DeGuello, and Viejo clumsily scrambled away from the assault.

Throwing themselves to the floor, they each low crawled behind a cabinet or a bench,

"You guys okay?" Banks called over the din of automatic weapons fire.

He saw each nod. DeGuello popped up from his bench and fired three rounds in quick succession at the intruder. Viejo did the same. Following Viejo, Banks likewise fired on their attacker who was advancing slowly as he wielded the rifle. Banks saw the man's long black coat jump in answer to his shots but the shooter did not go down. Banks ducked back to the floor and heard DeGuello call.

"Body armor. Aim for the head!"

In unison, the three detectives again leapt to their feet and fired. This time, Banks observed clinically as two rounds took the man in the face, one through the left eye and the other through the right cheek. The man crumpled like a marionette with his strings cut.

Moving smoothly and precisely, Banks, DeGuello, and Viejo converged on the downed gunman. DeGuello kicked the weapon away and handcuffed the subject then went to searching the man's pockets. There was not even lint on his person.

"We need to call this in." DeGuello looked the man over.

"Do it," said Banks and turned away from the body, "Pak!" he called then stopped and turned around.

DeGuello and Viejo looked up at him.

"What?" asked Viejo.

Banks wasn't quite sure himself. There was something in the background noise and his ringing ears he couldn't pick out. Viejo and DeGuello must've sensed it too. They stood next to him and all three were suddenly switching out magazines. That's when they heard it.

The chime was so benign that it didn't seem to mesh with the reality surrounding the three men. Then two more men dressed similarly to the first they had dispatched entered the ATF Office and opened fire on them.

"Fuck!" Banks heard Viejo yell as the three men fled in different directions.

They all fired as they moved, dodging from workbench to workbench. Chunks of wood, plaster and plastics swirled around them. Banks dodged a swarm of hissing and snapping rounds biting at the air as he ducked behind a hood system. Looking up to find his detectives, he spotted an emergency exit to the left rear of the lab.

"Exit, one o'clock!" he yelled.

He heard confirmation and saw the others clambering through the debris toward the exit. Banks started moving himself but not toward the exit. First, he needed to find Pak.

"Pak!" he called and moved between the items in the lab.

He got no response. The silence from the small forensic scientist was deafening when compared to the staccato bursts from the advanced assault rifles. Diving between workbenches, Banks looked up to see a lab coat covered shoulder poking out from behind the steel tub.

"Pak," Banks called, sliding toward him, trying to stay as low as he could.

He made it around the corner and came face to face with the scientist. Time stopped for Peter Banks for just a moment, as he looked the poor man over. The cracking and popping of bullets striking all around the detective seemed distant, happening somewhere else. Pak had taken a round through the thigh, must have been in the opening salvo of the attack on his lab. The man's belt was wrapped around his leg, as a tourniquet against what Banks guessed was a damaged femoral artery, judging from the massive pool of blood covering the floor and his legs. The man was slouched in a sitting position as if exhausted, like time had simply run out on him.

The world snapped back in with Peter Banks as a chip of wood, a fragment from one of the benches, stung his face. He crouched low. When he did, he saw something in Pak's hand. It was dark metal with what looked like notebook paper wrapped around it. He wrestled the object from the dead man's grip and fled toward DeGuello and Viejo, who were screaming for him to retreat.

Banks remained crouched and fired with one hand as he ran for the door. Diving under the firing of DeGuello and Viejo, he got his feet under him on the first row of steps leading down a twisting concrete staircase. Banks yelped when he came face to face with another man wielding another of those damned rifles. The darkly clothed white male must've been creeping up on DeGuello and Viejo when Banks surprised him. He was in a crouch on the landing below. Banks started shooting on reflex, watching the opposing muzzle of the man's rifle, just waiting for the devastating weapon to end him in an instant. He cranked off rounds in a panic and continued to charge the man. He fired wildly until the man crumpled over onto the rifle. Banks kicked the man off the gun and grabbed it. He could barely breathe enough to call out to his teammates.

"Let's go!" he yelled.

The three men fled, a cloud of 7.62 millimeter fire chasing them out of the lab.

Chapter Sixteen

Myra Ross tilted the rear view mirror of her Toyota Corolla down so that she could check out her makeup one last time. Her uniform was crisp and the brass insignia on her collar along with her nameplate and silver badge gleamed. She was fit to pass any inspection the patrol lieutenant might throw at the returning night shift. So why did she feel so scared?

Is it fear? Maybe not. Maybe not fear. Is it shame? Or embarrassment?

Myra brushed some lint off the crown of her cover and stepped out of her small sedan, careful not to put her shining black Bates Boots down in any soft mud or even sand. She wondered at her own actions, and the strange knot she had in her stomach as she approached the rear entrance to police headquarters. She had never been reprimanded for her appearance, and up until last week, she was in a rush to get to the roll call room. She knew she shouldn't feel ashamed for what happened the week before. In her mind, she knew that she had done everything right. That he had managed a lucky blow that landed her on her ass and with a black eye that fortunately had blended in well with her dark brown skin. Only a couple of swipes of makeup had rendered the remaining bruise invisible.

It was a fight, things happened in a fight and sometimes one side or the other got lucky. At least that's what the corporal had told her and she agreed. Fighting that drunk had not been her first go-round despite the fact this would constitute her first true shift without a field-training agent. Maybe that was it? Was she scared to go out on the street alone?

Myra reached the rear entrance and punched in her code to get in. With a click, she yanked on the heavy steel

71

door with every bit of her ninety-five pounds. At four feet
eleven, Myra Ross had set a new standard at the Charleston
City Police Department by two inches. She was the shortest
person ever to put on a CPD badge. She heaved her way
through the door and immediately her stomach twisted in
knots.

She realized where her anxiety had come from; they
were standing at the end of the hallway. Pluretti and Beach
were her squad mates—two massive, hulking, bald headed
white males who could be playing linebacker at USC. As a
matter of fact, Beach had played linebacker at the Citadel.
She wanted to hide at the sight of them—to tiptoe her way
down the hall like a mouse scurrying against the wall until
she could dive into the roll call room. She forced herself to
walk directly at them.

She approached, steeling herself against the
disapproval she would see when they noticed her. The way
they sized her up and dismissed her so quickly. When
you're four-eleven, you get that all the time. Myra thought
she had gotten over it until she started feeling that guilt,
that weakness, right after Beach had kicked that guy off
her. He'd helped her up and asked her if she was okay but
she could see it even then. The guy, some drunk getting
loud at a bar in West Ashley, had over powered her. Just
another woman that couldn't carry the load was what they
were thinking.

But it wasn't true she wanted to tell them, to make
them see. She had had the guy, was about to get him on the
ground but he spun and twisted her up. Even on the ground,
she hadn't been scared, or thought she was losing anything.
Beach showed up all of a sudden and hit the guy so hard
that when EMS transported him, he was still unconscious.
She could have handled it, she knew it.

She was standing right next to him before Pluretti
noticed her. When he looked at her, she didn't see any of
the disappointment she expected. His eyes were somewhat

blank like he didn't know how to explain what had happened.

"Can you believe this shit?" was all he said.

Myra followed his gaze to the old television mounted in the tiny break room where he, Beach, and the rest of the shift stood. On screen was the night anchor for the local news. Floating on screen next to his head was a graphic that read "Wanted." Imposed on the graphic under the word were the faces of her department's Narcotics Unit.

"No way," she whispered.

***

Antwan Tate was in his cell before lights out, studying the paperwork his lawyer had dropped off for him. He sat on the thin wafer like mattress, reading each page over and over again. It read that he was going to be released on his personal recognizance. Though the word was tough to pronounce, he knew what it meant. After his first arrest years ago, the judge had released him on personal recognizance. At the time, Antwan had only heard that he was getting out of jail. After the Sheriff's deputies had picked him up for missing his hearing, he had found out that he had been found guilty of that first charge in his absence and had to do six months any way. One of the deputies had been nice enough then to explain to him that personal recognizance didn't mean he was free and clear, it just meant that he could be out on the street until trial.

He knew better now and the fact that he was getting out blew him away. The lawyer, that fine blonde white girl, he still couldn't believe she was a lawyer much less his, was sent by Andrew Tulley. She told him that Tulley felt bad for Antwan and wanted to help him out. Antwan had been around the block long enough to know what that meant. He worked for Andrew Tulley and he had no problem with that. He knew that as soon as he got back on the street, Banks and his people would come at him again. Try to get him to flip on Andrew to save himself. The lawyer, all Antwan could remember was her tits struggling under her tight suit, and her ass as she left him with the paperwork. He couldn't remember her name but she told him she would be handling his case from start to finish and not to worry about anything. Antwan Tate felt like he had just won the lottery.

He heard the call for fifteen minutes til lights out and ignored it. He was already in anyway; he heard the officer's downstairs calling out orders for the other inmates to wrap up whatever they were doing.

The order for lights out came and two minutes after that he heard the loud schnick of his cell door locking and the lights around the jail were snuffed out. Antwan waited another thirty minutes then reached for his prize. When the lawyer had gotten done explaining things to him, she had offered him a smoke from a pack inside her briefcase. She moved smoothly to cover the camera angle and block the view while he had slipped one from the pack and hid it in the sleeve of his shirt.

Though it had only been a couple of days since his last cigarette, Antwan was almost shaking with anticipation when he put the filter to his lips. He ducked under his covers to light up then took a deep drag and held it in. Before exhaling, he bunched up a thick wad of blanket and exhaled into the material hoping to capture some of the fumes.

The rush hit him fast. The world spun for just a second and Antwan had to catch himself. He was surprised. It had been a long time since he was buzzed from a smoke. He loved it. He took his second drag and held this one just as long before exhaling again into the blanket bundled in his hand. The rush was there again but this time he could control it. Though the substance racing to his brain sent him on a biochemical joy ride, he was ready for it and further enjoyed the ride.

Then his heart started racing, really racing. Antwan swung his legs that suddenly felt like logs from a redwood tree over the side of his cot and planted himself on the floor. His chest pounded and his heart thundered in his ears.

"Shit." He wheezed.

Antwan put a hand to his temple that was likewise pounding like someone was beating on the inside of his skull trying to get out. The pain increased, spreading to behind his eyes and down the sides of his neck. He strained against the pain and tried to get up to go to the door. This wasn't right.

"Ahh."

He wheezed again He couldn't catch his breath.

His ears screamed with the pressure building throughout his body. When he tried to stand, his legs buckled under him.

Antwan Tate hit the cold concrete floor of his cell and suddenly there was silence. He couldn't move, couldn't see. The cold of the floor was both refreshing and frightening but at the same time the fright was distant and growing more distant. The pounding in his chest and head was gone. Antwan knew that should scare him, that there was something wrong.

Like everything else, the sensations were so distant, dark and distant...

Chapter Seventeen

Andrew Tulley couldn't breathe. The noise and the savagery of the concussive blasts of the rifles, even from outside the office, had been the worst experience he had ever been through. He tried to tiptoe around the coating of shattered glass and shards of plastics and wood as he surveyed the destroyed office area. Brigston's men were ahead of him doing something. He was vaguely aware of papers being thrown and things being shoved around somewhere in the distance.

Tulley made his way beyond the cutoff between the office cubicles and the lab area of the law enforcement space and had to pause to note the damage to the doorjamb and heavy-duty workbenches around him. They looked as if some monstrous rat had gnawed on the furniture and walls like they were made of candy. He stepped further in and stopped.

"Where are they?" he asked.

He was ignored for a long moment then the leader of the three men, one now dead and laying off to the side in the cubicles, that sight in itself had almost made Andrew Tulley soil himself. Finally, the man answered him,

"They retreated," he answered dispassionately.

"What do you mean they retreated?" Tulley was shocked.

So they had failed. These men to him seemed to be a mutant bastardization of Rambo and the Reservoir Dogs, and they'd failed.

The leader, who had not deemed it necessary to reveal his name or any of his employee's names, stopped and fixed him with a dead stare that brought Andrew up cold.

76

"They were not the mission. The weapon was the mission." He turned to another of the remaining mercenaries. "You got it?"

The man in question held up a plastic bin with metal parts as well as a notebook.

"Good," the leader said. Then he turned to Andrew and pointed to the floor next to him, "This may make you feel better," he said almost absently.

Andrew followed his gesture and went to the spot behind one of the workbenches. Before he could see the body, he noted a thick pool of blood coating the floor. It was more blood than he had ever seen; the sticky fluid seemed to have an orange froth on its surface that for some reason made him curious. Careful not to step into the quagmire, he looked at its source.

It was a small Asian man wearing a white coat. He sat in the epicenter of the blood pool. His head leaned to the side, his eyes staring blankly into nothingness.

Andrew paused. The first dead body, the one of the mercenary, had frightened him unspeakably. But this, somehow he felt different looking on this corpse. Maybe it was the fact that this man had been a target, someone he and the men had been sent here to get. Andrew didn't know but he was at the same time ashamed and thrilled by the sight. For a moment, he wondered who the man was until a heavy tug on his upper arm yanked him away.

When he looked up, the leader was staring at him from less than six inches away. Behind the usual blankness to his exterior features, he could see a hate there, a disgust of some kind. He wondered if it was for him, or his victim.

"Satisfied?" he asked rhetorically.

He started dragging Andrew toward the rear exit. From the look the man had given him, he judged that he should not fight the affront to his individual person.

"Clean up, Two," the man called as he shoved Tulley through the rear door.

Andrew went along for the ride. As he began down the concrete stairway, he suddenly caught himself yearning for a gun of his own.

Chapter Eighteen

"What the hell was that?" demanded Viejo as they tore out of the parking lot, fleeing the ambush.

Banks looked to DeGuello who sat next to him wiping blood from his eyebrow, the result of shards of wood or glass that had pelted them while under the withering gunfire from those horrible rifles. DeGuello was quiet but he returned Banks' look. He was thinking the same thing: They were officially off the reservation.

"We gotta get to 7-5 (Headquarters)," said Viejo looking out the rear window of their SUV and praying there was no pursuit.

"E, get the bag out of the back," DeGuello ordered the younger cop, trying to focus him.

Viejo did as he was told, stretching over the gear in the rear of the SUV, and returning with a black Tomahawk tactical bag. The bag flopped on the seat and Viejo ripped open the zipper revealing a few hundred rounds of ammunition and extra magazines. He started filling the magazines with rounds.

Banks watched the man work and felt ashamed of himself. Viejo and the others depended on him to see them through whatever they might face on the street. They depended on him every day and he'd just come within a hair's breadth of getting two of his men killed. To add to that guilt, he was a mess.

In over twenty years as a police officer, Peter Banks had never been in a gunfight. He'd been shot at; every now and then a round or two fired from bushes or shadowed alleys toward his passing cruiser. He was no stranger to the damage firearms did to people. He'd seen his share of corpses frozen in time where they'd fallen after an enemy had gunned them down. But he'd never before seen what he'd just lived through.

Banks gripped the wheel of the SUV to the point that his knuckles whitened from lack of blood flow just to keep DeGuello and Viejo from seeing his hands shake. He'd killed one for sure, possibly two men in a span of what could not have been more than five minutes. It all happened so fast, he recalled, shocked and still trying to wrap his mind around the events of the past few minutes. Not only what had just happened but it had occurred. The post incident fear and shock melted away as his mind drifted to how things had gone down rather than the why. Banks found himself chilled to the bone.

"What's the play?" DeGuello asked, shaking Banks from his dark thoughts,

"We're not going to 7-5. That's for sure."

"You think someone sold us out?" DeGuello asked.

"The only record of us going to Pak was on the sign out sheet at the evidence locker."

"Shit, think we were followed?"

Banks grimaced. "Don't know. We were there for a couple of hours before the shit went down. We need to get our bearings. Get the kids on the line and let them know that we need to meet up, somewhere out of the way."

DeGuello reached for his phone and paused, staring at it. "They wouldn't have been up on our phones? Think?"

Banks was quiet for a couple of moments as he fled the Charleston Peninsula heading west out of the city. "I'm glad we share the same level of paranoia," he told his partner.

Chapter Nineteen

Wyatt Friehurst slept his entire Saturday away. Well, he tried to sleep; it was more like he hid under his covers, locked away in his bedroom all day long.

Wyatt was scared. He'd never come close to going to jail in his life. Never even been around a cop when someone was getting arrested much less being chased through some ghetto by cops armed with machine guns. His mind raced between what his family was going to think about what had happened, if they even knew yet, and what that meant for law school. He had only a little over a year before graduation and after that was guaranteed a spot at his uncle's firm, one of the most exclusive in the country.

Wyatt thought of all that while replaying the indignity of being fingerprinted and photographed in jail. Then he sat in the dingy and dark jail that smelled of bleach and unwashed feet. He shuddered, a victim of his own mind. Like a life review, the events of the past day tortured him in repetition. If he was charged with a felony, his family would kill him, maybe even cut him off. When Wyatt considered the fact that he was arrested ultimately because he was trying to make a few thousand bucks off some ecstasy pills, his stomach twisted. He tried to burrow underneath his silk bed covers and hide under a stack of pillows and behind drawn blinds but it wasn't enough. No matter how hard he tried, he couldn't get away from the fears tearing his sanity apart from the inside out.

Eventually, Wyatt was able to drift off into a fitful sleep. He must have, he thought when stirred by the ringing of a doorbell. He lived on the second floor of a two-story Charleston row house just off Water Street in one of the more scenic parts of downtown. At first, he ignored the clanging sound that had so horribly disrupted his sleep. The person incessantly ringing the bell was persistent and after what seemed to Wyatt to be minutes on end of a ringing doorbell, he gave in and climbed out from under his covers.

Shuffling downstairs, he passed a couple sets of windows. The night was pitch black, telling him he had slept through the day and who knew how far into the night. Additionally, he figured it was not late enough for the bars to close since his two roommates were not at home. If they had been home, they would have answered the door and saved him the trouble of interrupted sleep.

The doorbell was still ringing when he finally descended the last step and made it to the door. By this time, Wyatt was incensed by the haranguing to the point he was considering whether or not to answer the door or simply shout at the visitor to go away and leave it at that. Years of etiquette and social norms that had molded Wyatt Friehurst won out against his frustration and as he pulled open the old wooden door, he immediately forgot about any ideas of shooing his visitor away.

It wasn't so much the flowing blonde hair, cutoff jeans, or the sliver of toned golden belly that Wyatt remembered so much as the straight predatory nature of the woman standing in his doorway. Her eyes, wide set on her face, greenish-hazel, and with just the slightest hint of an Asian slant. She was staring into his eyes the moment he opened the door. And held his gaze as nature took hold of Wyatt Friehurst and he soaked in every lustful detail of the figure filling his doorway. There was that hint of shame that came over him as he realized she had watched him drink in her body but it soon evaporated,

"Wyatt?" she asked.

"Un-hmmm," was his fumbled reply.

The smile that creased her plump lips was like that of a tiger when cleaning its maw of a fresh kill. At the same time she shifted her hips and her chest pushed out just so.

Wyatt was barely listening when she continued.

"Hey, Andrew feels really bad about what happened last night. He sent me by to see if I could cheer you up,"

"What?" Wyatt asked. *Did that asshole send me a hooker?*

She must have read it in his face, "Relax, prude, it's not that kind of party." She reached into the barest definition of a pocket of what was left of her jeans and removed a small Ziploc bag containing a trio of little white pills.

A sense of warmth flowed over him at the sight of the ecstasy pills. Wyatt had been in a terror when he was released from jail and had flushed his entire stash in a blind fury. His weed, his pills, even a dash of cocaine he'd forgotten he still had went down the toilet before he jumped into bed to hide under his covers like a little girl. It had only been an hour or so before he'd realized how much he wanted to change his outlook and quiet his mind. He had been empty of dope at that point and too afraid to call one of his roommates for fear they were working for the police against him. At the sight of the little baggie held out before him by an angel, he suddenly felt as if he would melt right there in front of her.

She handed over the bag and he let her in. The blonde was not three steps into the foyer before two of the little white pills were making their way down Wyatt's throat.

"Jesus, Andrew wasn't kidding around was he?" she said, watching Wyatt choke down the pills.

He looked at her as if he couldn't comprehend what she was saying.

"I've still got one in reserve," he told her. "A tune up for later,"

"Okay," said the girl.

Wyatt watched her hips slide back and forth atop golden, muscular thighs as he followed her further into his house and realized he could not let this girl leave. He had money, he wasn't the son of a congressman, but his family was well established. His uncle ran the most prestigious law firm in South Carolina. Suddenly, his internal dialogue thinking of the firm where he planned on making his own fortune and the events of the past couple of days collided and he silently urged the drugs to kick in. Paranoia was not his thing. Wyatt wondered for a moment if he was actually losing it.

"Do you have any wine?"

He heard and snapped back to the present where there was a solid ten wearing Daisy Dukes and an almost see through blouse standing before him, asking if he had any alcohol. There was something he could use to get his mind off the boulder perched on a toothpick over his head. He knew about wine. Showing random College of Charleston coeds his wine collection and talking them through several bottles on the way to his bedroom had been a staple in Wyatt Friehurst's arsenal.

"Sure," he answered casually as he noted the onset of a warm tingling in his extremities. "What's your pleasure?"

"Dry and red," she responded.

She slid her bottom up and over one of the bar stools under the window between living room and kitchen. Her legs spread apart just so as she leveraged herself onto the seat. Wyatt hoped he was being subtle as he strained to focus on that goal line between her legs. He wanted to cringe as she planted her glistening, pink polished fingernails directly in his line of sight.

Not dissuaded, Wyatt turned to the climate controlled wine cabinet in the rear corner of the living room and grabbed a French Cabernet Franc. He held it before her like any trained sommelier would.

"This is a 2008 Cabernet Franc that I found in the South of France while travelling before law school. Dry, red, and spicy, I think you'll like it." To Wyatt he sounded like a professional, words crisp and clean, and cultured. He hadn't realized, and did not pick up the indicator of the blonde's eyebrow arching as he muffled and slurred each syllable.

"Great, so what happened yesterday?" the blonde asked.

Wyatt worked the cork like a chimpanzee trying to drive a car. Finally, he wrenched the cork from the bottle, almost shredding it in the process, and filled two glasses.

"Oh, it was nothing," he said, "Just a misunderstanding. Wrong place, wrong time."

His slurs became worse but he was too in the zone to care.

"I bet jail was scary. Andrew said it sucked."

"Eh." Wyatt shrugged, he could handle anything at that moment.

"Did anyone try to get you to talk? Andrew said the cops were all over him when he was at the station."

For a nanosecond, Wyatt's curiosity tried to leverage through the growing fog surrounding his consciousness. Why was some piece of ass asking questions like this? The little voice tried to scream but could not make it through the din of narcotic white noise.

"Talk to me?" Wyatt retorted. "No, I don't snitch."

"So you didn't even talk to anybody about the gun?" she asked.

Gun? That little voice of alarm was further away now. Swept away under the sweeping currents of MDMA coursing through his bloodstream, it barely registered as suspicious that something was up with this girl. The thought was gone almost before the warning sounded. Wyatt did finally realize that his crystal goblet full of wine weighed a ton, and he was having trouble holding his head up. He also really wanted to close his eyes and pass out.

"What kind of stuff did you give me?" he spoke his words in slow motion.

The blonde was blurry in his dimming vision as she slid off the barstool. Only her alluring, almond shaped eyes remained in focus.

"The good kind," she answered.

After that, things got strange for Wyatt Friehurst. He'd been on plenty of narcotics induced rides in his time but none so funky as the one she took him on. He had to close his eyes, just for a second. He felt her take the crystal stemware from his failing grasp and help him stand.

Whoa, is this happening?

"Bedrmms thaa-waay," he told her.

"Thanks," he heard her say. "Now you just relax,"

When he did, Wyatt could not be sure but he might have pissed himself.

Regardless, he was along for the ride and he tried to help but his legs just would not respond as she carried/dragged him up the first flight of stairs to the landing. She set him in a sitting position on the landing. He leaned against the rungs in the railing and promised himself and her that he was good to go. He wouldn't pass out on her like that last time. He heard her giggle as she did something further up the stairs.

He sat there for what seemed an eternity waiting for her to gain her strength back or whatever she was doing when finally he felt her touch once again. Thanks to the ecstasy, her touch was like lighting dancing on his skin. She had his cheeks in her hands and when she let go with one he felt a ribbon of what might have been silk caress his head and slide down to his neck.

"Arr wi plyn drss-Up?" he asked her playfully.

"Sort of," was the now terse reply.

He felt the ribbon go taut and was excited, this girl was dirty. Wyatt liked it—right up to the point when she yanked on his ankles, dropping him three steps down from where she had tied off the other end of the silk scarf. The air was cutoff completely. Wyatt started to protest but she just held him there. Her hands on his ankles were like vice grips and there was no strength in him to fight. In one of his last fleeting moments, he was able to open his eyes and see her, his angel staring up at him as if fascinated by what she was watching.

God, she is so strong.

Chapter Twenty

"Poppy, Wilkes, and Thompson are on their way," DeGuello said as he shut off his phone.

Banks nodded. He was watching Viejo through the rearview mirror. The big Hispanic cop, a kid he'd pulled out of patrol just as he had handpicked the rest of his team, was staring blankly out the passenger side window. Though Banks had never been in a shootout before tonight, he knew the look. He'd seen it several times over his career from cops involved in shootings to cops who survived a knife fight, to cops who had demolished a car during a vehicle pursuit. That exhausted, robotic expression a person gets after experiencing that fine line between life and death. Even when the event only lasts a moment, the aftermath is the same, adrenaline dump and hyperactivity followed closely by exhaustion, slumped shoulders, and a thousand yard stare.

Banks drove out of the peninsula and headed toward Monck's Corner where he knew about a couple of quiet places to hide so the team could get their bearings. Deep inside, he was chastising himself for being so thick headed over being pushed around by the chief and that little shit prosecutor. Thanks to him, Pak was dead.

He and Pak went back a long time together. They'd met when he was part of an ATF taskforce working felony gun cases. Pak was known back then as a ball buster. The little forensic scientist was assigned to Charleston as part of an initiative through the ATF to speed up lab work at a local level. All over the country, forensic specialists had been assigned to ATF regional offices, and provided lab space to handle all but the most delicate of forensic techniques. When Banks had first arrived at the ATF, Pak was one of those people, every office had them, the guy or girl you only went to when you had no choice. Gruff and prickly to deal with, Pak had scared most agents away by fiercely controlling who could enter his sanctuary of equipment and white lab coats. He was a demon when it came to documentation and his demeanor when asking for an update to a case was a mix between a Marine Drill Instructor and a Honey Badger drunk on Cobra venom.

Banks remembered the first time they'd met. He had heard the stories, and heard the jabs and quiet insults thrown around the office behind Pak's back. But the forensic guys just like the evidence custodian, and the office secretary were more crucial to a cop's work than the gun and the badge. When he approached Pak, he did it following protocol. He knocked on the door to the lab and waited. After a minute, the heavy door swung open and the little Asian scientist peered out.

"Yes," he had snapped.

Banks had been holding a packaged AK-47, he remembered it so well. This AK-47 stuck out to him because he had found it leaning against a toddlers crib during a raid. The contradiction of seeing the little boy wearing a dirty diaper, with a pacifier sticking out of his mouth like a cutoff stogey and the automatic weapon together was one of those things that you can never truly get out of your head. Before Banks had a chance to speak, Pak had taken the box from him and held the paper custody form up for his inspection,

"Mr. Pak, right?" Banks had said,

"Um-hmm," Pak had barely responded.

Then Banks had snuck a look over the little man's shoulder to find his hook.

"Is that a comparison microscope?" he'd asked.

The question had brought Pak up short just as he'd hoped it would.

"It is," he said looking back over his shoulder at the scientific equipment.

That comment, and feigned interest, gained Banks entry into the inner sanctum of forensic science at the Charleston office of the ATF. For the next two hours, Pak had given him a tour of the laboratory and explained in detail what each item in his inventory could do. Additionally, the comment also bought Banks precedence in the eyes of the forensic scientist. In terms of backlog, it could sometimes take a week to get relatively basic scientific tasks completed through Pak's lab. For Banks, the longest he would have to wait would be maybe two days. And the delay would always come with an apology from Pak for holding him up.

What started out as a means of getting his cases to the head of the line with an ornery forensics Nazi who the rest of the task force was afraid of eventually turned into a steady long-term friendship. First he and Pak went out for a beer after a long day where both men had been locked under deadlines of herculean proportions. They had been the last two in the office and decided that a beer was in order before calling it quits. Banks took him to a quiet bar down on East Bay Street that was somewhat hidden from the usual tourist throng. There they shared war stories as most men in their line of work did, especially once alcohol gets thrown into the mix. What started out as one beer stretched to three as the men compared their pasts. Banks was surprised to find out that Pak had been a cop. The ornery scientist had pounded the pavement just as he did, but in New York City of all places. He got a graduate degree in Forensics from John Jay College and signed on with the feds. He talked in the same nostalgic way many cops turned feds did when they spoke of the glory days, pushing a cruiser on one adventure or another.

Eventually Pak's wife had called, ending what had all the potential of becoming a Tuesday night bender, which in no way would have been good for either man. That turned out to be the first of many meetings between

Pak and Banks. Even after Banks transferred from the ATF task force to move on in the ranks of the Charleston Police Department, they still got together for a beer every now and then. Pak was also on Banks' speed dial when it came to questions about firearms and other weapons.

That was how Peter Banks came to be in the possession of the last remaining piece of his evidence Pak ever worked on. The barrel of that converted AR-15 was sitting in his lap wrapped in a blood-smudged piece of loose-leaf paper. Banks unwrapped the paper from the barrel and looked at it in the dim light of the vehicle. It read Old South Armorers in hastily drawn free hand. Banks couldn't help but feel a hurricane of rage and guilt threaten to overcome the reserve he tried so hard to keep over himself. Not so much to keep his own self together but for that of his teammates sitting in the car with him. If they were going to get the people behind Pak's murder, they were going to have to have their act together.

Chapter Twenty-One

The Charleston Regional Office of the Alcohol, Tobacco, Firearms, and Explosives Bureau swarmed like an angry anthill. Ten minutes after Banks and his team fled the ambush, uniformed police were marking off King Street and the two surrounding side streets that flanked the tall government building. The original call went out as an active shooter in the vicinity of the building, which housed numerous state and federal government agencies. This meant that officers in groups of three searched the surrounding area outside while a special weapons and tactics team (SWAT) went floor by floor of the eight floor building in search of gunman they never found. When they finally reached the ATF office, the pockmarked walls and shattered glass of windows and doors eventually lead the team to the body of Yao Pak in the forensic lab.

The grim find at the end of an exhaustive and nerve wracking search through mazes of cubicles and dark alleys. Commanders on scene detailed security both inside and outside the building. The State Law Enforcement Division (SLED) crime scene unit was called to begin the survey of the events surrounding the death of a fellow law enforcement officer. The documentation of death was a given and often dismissed aspect of any given murder scene. Until that is, the crime scene surrounded another cop. It tended to bring mortality into focus for those left to watch as one of their own was photographed, measured, and studied before being shipped off to the morgue. The usual banter of dark and largely indecent humor, which served as an outlet for stress in saddest of industries, was not there when it was one of the their own. Largely, respondents to these situations were left to stew on the questions remaining in the wake of an officer's death:

anger, guilt, sadness, and fear all worried inside those responding, in hopes of relief after the longest of days on the job.

That was the general mood on the eighth floor as Tyvek suited crime scene technicians went about their duties photographing, sketching, and collecting whatever evidence caught their eye when Benton Schmidt, Special Agent in Charge of the Federal Bureau of Investigation Columbia, South Carolina Field Office stepped off the elevator. No one had even noticed the three-piece suit until he shattered the heavy silence of the scene,

"All right! Everyone, the bureau thanks you for your assistance in this matter but if you will please stop what you are doing and step away from the crime scene."

Charles Schwightz, the Resident Agent in Charge of the Charleston ATF office, and Special Agent Tom Burgess, lead investigator for SLED were conferring over a disheveled notepad on the other side of the main office area, the area least hit by the disaster that had resulted in the death of a fellow agent. Burgess looked up from his notes to see a mass of Tyvek hooded technicians looking at him. Under any other circumstances, it would have been quite the sight. The hoods covered all but their faces and plastic safety goggles framed their eyes. From his perspective, they all looked like confused Oompa Loompa looking for orders. At that moment, however Burgess was not feeling comical.

There were few hard and fast rules with Tom Burgess. By all accounts, he was the epitome of a down-home country boy. Normally quick to laugh, always fast with some slow drawled wisdom that could diffuse even the most intense of situations, and he was one of his chief's prized investigators—not only did he close big cases quickly, but he was able to work with anybody. That was right up until you messed with his crime scene.

Schwightz heard the notepad slap the floor where Burgess had been standing just moments before. The ATF man looked up to see Burgess, faded blue jeans, plaid shirt, and balled fists crossing the scene on a direct line to the FBI executive.

"You in the right place, pal?" he asked (Translation to cop speak: "Who the fuck do you think you are?") Burgess noticed Schmidt, who was four inches taller than Burgess's six-foot frame, and five inches rounder, stiffen then look down his nose at him.

"You are?" Schmidt asked, not extending his hand.

"Lead Investigator," Burgess responded.

"Oh, good." Schmidt reached into his breast pocket and produced a tri-folded single sheet of paper, which he handed to Burgess. "Thank you for your assistance in this matter. The FBI will be assuming lead in the investigation. Someone will be in touch if we have any further questions. Please have your people brief my evidence response team before they stand down."

Burgess was ignoring the FBI man and reading. The memorandum was on letterhead from the Governor's office, requesting assistance of the FBI. The governor, or one of his stooges, had taken his case away.

"Assholes," Burgess said under his breath as he handed the letter back to the smug bastard in the three-piece suit and stormed away from the scene.

The SLED agent had to round the building to the far side emergency exit since the elevator and the nearest exit were part of the crime scene. Burgess was fuming despite the voice of reason squawking in his head that it wasn't his problem. But he always ignored that voice. He slammed through the bar lock and started down the stairs only to become even further enraged. At the first landing, which was a mirror image of the stairwell that was taped off, he could see the blood pool in his mind superimposed over the dark concrete. A blood pool with no body, same as the blood pool in the cubicles. He could see that clearly in his mind as well. There was enough blood and assorted tissue at both spots to tell him that a body had been dropped there, however, no bodies save the forensic scientist had been recovered. Why police two bodies and leave the third? At the same time, there were no signs to tell him, the FBI he corrected himself, of what Pak had been working on at the time of his death. Likewise, the damn cameras and the monitoring station was a smoldering hole where the electronics had once been both in the building security room and the ATF's own security station. As Burgess descended the last flight of stairs, his gut was screaming that this was the biggest case he'd ever stumbled into, and he'd just been cut from the team.

He popped out of the emergency exit and scared the crap out of a uniform patrolman manning the perimeter. He held his hands up in supplication as the kid, the cop looked about twelve to the long time agent, instinctively reached for his gun.

"Sorry, Officer," he said as he walked past him.

"No problem Sir," responded the police officer.

Stepping into the alleyway between a four story parking garage and the federal building, Burgess saw the swarm of blue lights illuminating Meeting Street and sighed. He wanted nothing more to do with the circus, seeing all the activity just made him mad, knowing that he was no longer a part of it. The alley ended at Meeting Street and Burgess slid around the corner of the parking garage heading down the street toward his government car. He was going home to stew, no one takes his cases from him, or took, he reminded himself.

"Burgess!"

He heard the yell from behind him and cringed. Turning to meet whoever was coming to rub salt in his wound, he noticed the uniform with a silver cluster on the man's epaulets stomping toward him.

95

"Ch..." He was cut off.

"What the hell am I learning about murder charges against my team on the news for?" bellowed Assistant Chief Andrew Vaden, Charleston Police department.

The charge caught him off guard, "What?"

"This is your shit storm, isn't it?"

"Not anymore, I don't know what you're talking about."

"What the hell do you mean you don't know what I'm talking about?"

"I mean the Bureau just took over. What are you talking about your guys going up for murder? I've been in there for two hours and there's nothing pointing at a cop."

That caught Vaden off guard. The older man stepped back on his heel. "So then where is the news getting their reporting from. I just got my ass chewed out by the chief."

"Let's go see."

When Vaden and Burgess returned to the eighth floor, an FBI agent with a clipboard stopped them at the top of the stairway.

"Stop right there gentleman. This is a controlled area."

"Fuck off," Vaden blurted, pushing past the man.

Burgess followed, suppressing a chuckle as he watched the exasperated FBI agent try to figure out what to do next.

They rounded a corner toward the scene and found Schmidt and another suited executive consulting amid the scurrying crime scene technicians. Schmidt noticed their approach first and grimaced.

"I'm sorry, gentleman, but if we need your assistance, one of my agents will be in contact."

"Who put out the all points on my narcotics team," demanded Vaden ignoring the FBI man's attempt to dismiss him.

Schmidt sighed. "Your men are wanted for questioning in this incident. No charges have been filed as of yet."

"What's your evidence?"

"I am not at liberty to discuss the matter outside cleared personnel. The bureau thanks you for your cooperation in the matter. If you hear anything about your team's whereabouts, I expect your assistance in bringing them in."

Without another word, Schmidt turned on his heel and ended the conversation.

Burgess and Vaden were left standing in the darkened hallway, staring at the pompous prick's back.

"Doesn't look like we're going to get anywhere with him," said Burgess.

"We don't need him." Vaden growled and headed for the door.

Chapter Twenty-Two

They were all staring at him.

That was what Banks felt like anyway. In truth, his team was doing their best not to stare directly at him. He estimated that no one wanted to look desperate or scared, and he was thankful for that. If there was one thing you could always depend on with cops, it was stoicism and at that moment, he relished the bravado.

In truth, he really didn't know exactly what to do next. As it was he, DeGuello, Viejo, Wilkes, Thompson, and Poppy were all hidden in an old hanger in the far corner of an executive airport in Monck's Corner, South Carolina about twenty miles west of the city. He felt like one of the old desperados hiding out in box canyon in the black and white movies his father used to make him watch as a kid. His world had flipped on its head in the matter of day.

He began his Saturday in court, a rarity on the level of finding Bigfoot outside the internet. Threatened a judge, a congressman's staff, and a pissant Assistant District Attorney with media coverage of all things and won, or at least got a draw. Following that, he was more or less told he was keeping his job only because the chief could not fire him due to the aforementioned press coverage. On top of all that, he'd stolen evidence only to have that evidence stolen from him during an ambush inside a federal building that left a longtime friend dead. And he was now feeling about a hundred years old thanks to the adrenaline hangover as his body and mind tried to assimilate the effects of the gunfight he, Viejo, and DeGuello had barely survived.

Son of a bitch.

"What the fuck?"

Banks crouched and reached for his weapon instinctively as DeGuello's curse echoed through the corrugated metal building. The team was perched in front of a dusty box television, which was carrying the local news. Banks saw the Breaking News banner above and to the right of the anchor's head. The whole team looked at him for a moment, shock, and fear covering their faces before they all turned back to face the television.

He approached and heard the anchor, a forty-something black female he remembered from a crime scene years back when she was a beat reporter. She still had that non-descript sex appeal he'd remembered from back then but for the life of him, he couldn't recall her name.

She was talking about the shootout at the federal building. Then he saw his face and the others pasted up on the screen. They were the photos from their police identification cards, he could tell by the light blue background and that they all had dark blue uniform shirts on. They were posted like mugshots on some crime stoppers story.

'Wanted for questioning..." He heard the woman say.

"This is bullshit!" Viejo bellowed.

"This can't be happening." Wilkes dropped his face in his hands.

When the picture of Yao Pak was displayed on the screen, Banks froze. The frightening, heart stopping sensation that came over him at seeing his likeness with the caption of murder suspect had knocked him off balance for a second. The dark eyes of Pak staring back at him brought him out of it. That made him mad. Whoever those bastards were that killed him, they were gonna pay.

"Turn that shit off," he ordered. "Come over here."

Banks leaned over a rickety metal folding table, propping himself up on clenched fists. In front of him was the metal barrel he pried out of Pak's hand. He could see dark brown smudges of the scientist's blood smearing the cylinder. Next to it was the paper the barrel had been wrapped in, the same brown-red stains reminded him of how deep a pool of crap they all were.

The team settled around him and he could see each was drawn to the bloodstains. For a couple of them, this was the first time they'd been close to an officer involved shooting. That dark side of law enforcement that everyone knew about but only a few ever truly experienced. Banks wanted nothing more than to finish out his career without ever firing his weapon in anger. Now that that was no longer an option, he wished for nothing more than to see Poppy, Wilkes, and Thompson never have to have the same experience. Sadly, he had a feeling that was a long shot.

"We are far afield, guys," he said blankly. "Looks like the department, our own department, the feds, and whoever the hell tried to kill us is out to get us." He paused to survey each member of his team, "What do we do?"

The questions was rhetorical but he let it stand for a moment anyway.

"We've got a couple of choices. We can turn ourselves in, maybe face charges, maybe not. We can run and spend the rest of our lives looking over our shoulders, or we can work the case."

Out of the corner of his eye, he saw heads cocking quizzically.

"Before we get into this, I'm giving each one of you one more chance to bail. No hard feelings, this isn't what any of us signed up for. Any one of you wants to go turn yourselves in or take off, I won't hold it against you."

Banks was greeted by silence. Part of him was relieved. Part of him hated himself for getting them into their current mess. He let the silence hang for another moment then took a deep breath.

"We're in this, boss," Poppy finally said, breaking the silence. "We finish it together."

"That's right. So here we are. As it stands right now, we've gotten our asses handed to us. The evidence we had, which was the gun and the dope, has been reduced to this." Banks pointed at the gun barrel, "Pak was working on the rifling when we got hit. I managed to grab it before we had to run. In Pak's hand with the barrel was this." Banks pointed to the blood stained piece of paper, "Pak had taken some notes from the database search he'd done on the rifling. It looks like he was able to identify the barrel as coming from Old South Armory. It's in the upstate outside Greenville. It's a lead, not sure how much of one, but it's a place to start."

"Start what? It's not like we're going to be able to get a warrant on the place," said DeGuello.

"True, we are out on a limb, on our own. We are going to work the case and this is our case. We aren't trying to get a guilty verdict here. We're trying to clear our names. The only way to do that is to figure out where this weapon came from and who is moving it through our city. It's the same gun those assholes at the federal building were shooting. The crux of this shit storm is this weapon. No serial numbers, no identifiers, or even a manufacturer's stamp. This freaking thing is a felony simply due to the fact that it exists. On top of that, we've got a congressman's kid in possession of it with a known dealer."

"What do we do?" asked Thompson.

"We work the avenues we have. Poppy and Thompson, you guys are going to work your sources. Get down to the clubs and dredge the sewers. We need to know what Andrew Tulley's deal is as far as dope and money. DeGuello, Viejo, and I are going to Greenville to find out everything we can on Old South Armory."

Wilkes looked at Poppy and Thompson then back at Banks. "What the hell am I supposed to do?"

"You're going undercover, like you always do."

Wilkes' face was blank as was the rest of the team.

"We're going to need someone inside. I don't know what his deal was, but the Chief was all about bending over for the Tulley people. Not sure where Vaden stands but we need intel. If we do come up with evidence to save our asses, we need to know who, if anyone, we can trust. Go figure out who we can trust."

"Shit," Wilkes whispered.

"Neck deep." Thompson smirked.

Banks silenced Thompson with a look and all attention returned to him.

"We are in deep here, people, keep it tight, and watch each other's back. Once we leave here, ditch your phones, and get some burners. Send your numbers to this email address. I already set it up. Do it from public Wi-Fi so we can keep the phones as clean as possible. Then get some shuteye. I think we've got some long hours ahead of us. Any questions?"

When no one spoke up Banks figured it was fifty-fifty between keeping a stiff upper lip and not knowing what question to ask first. Under the circumstances, he figured that was as good a start to this disaster as they were going to get.

"Get some rest."

Chapter Twenty-Three

Marlon Hansfield was pacing. He was never much of a pacer, not one to let his emotions show, always conscious of his body language, but today he was pacing.

When he awoke on the fine Sunday morning that it was, he had been ready to maybe hit a round of golf or go to the beach. That was of course after lounging in front of the news with a cup of coffee for however long the urge suited him. He brewed his coffee, a finely ground Ethiopian import, and lightly toasted a bagel then slathered it with cream cheese. When all was ready, he sat down on his couch still wearing the t-shirt and shorts he went to sleep in and clicked on what should have been Fox news. Instead, the channel had been set to the local channel default and his eyes met with horror on the morning news. The caption above the greying anchor read: "Officer Down."

Hansfield immediately recognized the federal building on Meeting Street. The exact address he had informed Davidson of early last evening. With his heart caught in his throat, Hansfield turned up the volume so he could hear the baritone voice of the anchor's recount.

An active shooter at the federal building on a Saturday night. The building that housed the lab that Peter Banks ran off to with the rifle Davidson wanted so badly. Marlon noted that he was trembling by the way the black coffee was rippling in his mug. Suddenly it took effort to breathe normally. He felt like a spring, loaded and ready to pop. He had to do something.

That something included leaving his breakfast on the table and racing to shower and dress before fleeing to Kiawah Island. The guard at the security shack stationed at the front of the island held him to confirm his appointment with a resident of the island, so Hansfield knew Davidson was aware he was there. Still Hansfield felt as if the clock were spinning out of control as he paced back and forth outside the grand doors to the estate's beach house. Finally, after what seemed an eternity, an elderly black man arrived at the door. Dressed in a crisp white suit, the man had an expertise in his mannerisms that Hansfield failed to notice as he opened the door for him.

"Welcome," the butler said.

"I need to speak to Mr. Davidson," Hansfield demanded.

Hansfield jumped as a loud voice from deeper in the house announced, "Mr. Hansfield."

Davidson approached, his face implacable in his pressed expensive suit and tie. "I was not expecting you," he said as the two shook hands,

Hansfield took a suspicious look at the staff then leaned in toward Davidson. He gripped the man's hand like it was the only anchor keeping him from falling off a cliff.

"Did you see the news?" he asked.

Davidson stepped back and to the side to open the way for Hansfield. "Let's discuss it on the lanai," he suggested. "Can we offer you a coffee, or something stronger?"

Hansfield simply shook his head as he followed the man's gesture. He walked slowly toward the rear of the house like a child visiting a new grade school for the first time. He was timid as a field mouse. Hansfield took a seat in a plush smoking chair when it was offered and sat with his hands folded in his lap.

Davidson sat down next to him. "You have concerns?"

Hansfield looked at him as if he had sprouted a third arm in his forehead. "Of course I have concerns," he blurted, momentarily losing control of himself. When Davidson did not respond, he leaned in closer to the man. "I was at the police department, looking at the evidence.

The desk sergeant saw me. I'm the one who told you where Banks was."

His voice was quaking, which made him despise himself for letting weakness show.

"I can assure you the situation is under control, Mr. Hansfield. You will suffer no exposure of any kind on this issue. I would not risk your future. We see a lot of potential in you. We would not do anything to jeopardize that."

Hansfield heard the words but he still felt his hands trembling. All he'd worked for through law school: Clerking for the right judges, attending the right functions, all for nothing if he were tied back to that horror show at the federal building. The fact that he was tied to a murderer almost made him wet himself.

"I can see you're not relieved in the slightest."

Hansfield's head shot up to see Davidson standing on the other side of the room. He hadn't even noticed the man leave his seat.

"I think you need to get away and clear your head." Davidson gestured and the butler stepped to the doorway. "You put your trust in us, Mr. Hansfield, now let me show you that trust is deserved." Davidson turned to the butler. "Have Arthur show Mr. Hansfield to the Isabella. Advise Capt. Sowell that he is to motor down the coast until Mr. Hansfield is ready to return."

"What?" Hansfield could not believe what he was hearing.

Davidson stepped to him and put his hand on his shoulder. "I think it would do you well to get away. You put yourself at great risk for us. We recognize that kind of allegiance and reward it."

Hansfield nodded to the butler who gestured for him to follow.

Head bowed, shoulders slumped, Marlon Hansfield did as he was bid and followed the servant to the waiting limousine.

***

Davidson watched the Assistant District Attorney leave and made a mental note to advise the captain to cut communications from the yacht once it was in international waters. He looked up when another man wearing a polo shirt stood in the doorway, waiting for him to acknowledge him. He looked in his direction and the mercenary nodded.

***

Davidson walked casually but with a purpose into the conference room where Brigston, the Tulleys, and Brigston's mercenary, Dierks, were waiting. Davidson looked at the younger Tulley and was surprised to see a certain light in the young man's eye he had not noticed in previous meetings.

Perhaps making the boy take a little responsibility for his actions was not a bad thing. Davidson let the thought pass through his mind.

"Take your seats gentleman," he said and found his place at the head of the large rectangular conference table.

The assembled guests complied and soon the attention was on him, just as Davidson preferred when in a work setting. That was of course, all save for Congressman Tulley, who slouched in his chair and picked at his thumb. Davidson cleared his throat. "So, gentleman, where do we stand? Mr. Brigston."

Dierks spoke for Brigston, his words were choppy and efficient. "Recovery was completed as required."

"All of it?"

Brigston nodded.

"There is nothing that can lead an investigation back to your company, or to your men, Mr. Dierks."

Brigston nodded his head in assent.

"The casualties were processed, Sir," said Dierks.

"I do hope so, for your sakes. Mr. Tulley." Davidson addressed the congressman without using his title purposefully to get his attention. "Where do we stand with our new vector?"

"Vector?" Tulley asked.

Davidson kept his eyes locked on the doughy old aristocrat. "Mr. Tulley, it was you, using your son as a proxy, who lost Aleister Fitzpatrick when he was shot by the angry spouse of one of his employees. It was you again who assured me that Andrew could find a suitable replacement for Mr. Fitzpatrick so that we could get our product again through the port and off to our customers in Africa. Your son was then arrested in possession of a weapon that does not exist and which could land a great many people in prison or worse if it was to fall into the wrong hands. A rational man would not normally allow an employee to fail a third time however you still have a number of years in your term of office. As such, we still require your access and resources. You will have a suitable vector for the transportation of our goods by this time tomorrow. Or drastic corrections to our relationship will be instituted. Is that understood?"

Tulley squirmed in his chair and shot a self-conscious look at his son before answering meekly, "Yes."

"I have a..." Andrew Tulley blurted but was silenced by Davidson.

"Andrew," he said with only the slightest hint of a civil smile. "To this point, you have been allowed here as a means of cleaning up the mess you caused. According to Mr. Brigston and his man, that mess has been cleaned up. Once this meeting is adjourned, you will leave this place and never return. Do you understand me?"

"Bu..."

"Shut your mouth, boy!" his father snapped.

Though Tulley Jr. did not grasp the truth of Davidson's last statement, Senior realized he'd just seen his son's political career evaporate before it began.

"Perfect," Davidson stated. "Any questions?"

There were none.

"Good, we will meet again tomorrow afternoon for lunch. At such time, Mr. Tulley will have the final aspect of our system in place. Thank you for coming. That is all."

***

Davidson left the room without another word, leaving the rest of the assembly to file out in their respective groups. The Tulleys, without acknowledging each other, left for their waiting car while Brigston and Dierks loitered for a moment in the hallway. When Brigston saw that they were alone, he leaned in to Dierks.

"Get me that barrel."

"I still think we should have told Mr. Davidson."

"You don't work for Davidson; you work for me. Get your ass out there and recover my piece, move," Brigston whispered harshly.

"Yes, Sir," growled the paid assassin.

Chapter Twenty-Four

Wilke punched in the security code and entered the back door of Police Headquarters like he owned the place. It was one of the first rules the young cop learned when working under cover.

"If you act like you own the place, most people will think you do too."

That was how Banks put it to him before he bought his first eight ball of cocaine at an after hour's club down town. Wilkes remembered how nervous he was. He'd had that nervous energy, the kind that hurt when you were sitting still. He remembered his breathing had been ragged and his hands trembled at the thought of going into that bar and buying cocaine. Wilke still couldn't believe he was able to fake it long enough to do the hand-to-hand transaction with the bartender that night. He still remembered the guy's name, Arthur, a grad student at the Medical University. Arthur had barely acknowledged him then. Served Wilke powdered cocaine in a small plastic bag just as easy as serving him Pabst Blue Ribbon. Meanwhile, Wilke had felt like his insides were melting. He felt much the same way now.

He kept his gait casual and carried a file folder he'd found in the trunk of his unmarked vehicle while DeGuello and Viejo had scavenged all his surveillance and tactical gear for their trip upstate. Wilke carried the folder so it looked like he was working while at the same time clenching the thin file to keep his hands from shaking.

There was no one in the hallway when he walked past the roll call briefing room. The hallway led from the rear door to the office area adjacent to the desk sergeant's small glass enclosure. Between the roll call room and the door leading to the office space was a diminutive snack room with a table and chair. Wilke peered through the small window in the door and saw no one milling around. He was not surprised, given that it was the middle of a Sunday afternoon. Still, the emptiness of the large building added to his unease. When Banks had first told him the plan, Wilke had thought it seemed a little shady. Then again, again they were so far out on the edge after that debacle at the federal building that he didn't remember what normal was. Now that he was skulking around the department while being wanted for murder, the reality of the situation was hitting him. He had to get himself caught.

Wilke realized he had entered the lion's den playing the wrong game. He was there to collect and pass on intel, true, but how was he going to do that without first giving himself up. Stepping away from the office door, he slid into the snack room and slouched against the wall.

Shit!

The sudden announcement over the PA system made him jump out of his skin.

"Lt. Colonel Vaden, call on line 6."

Wilke tried to calm himself and come up with a plan. He had to get caught by his own department, but he also had to survive enough questions to convince the powers that be he had nothing to do with the Federal building. To do that he needed intel. Wilke couldn't imagine there was going to be much available in the databases yet but he figured it was his only shot. Unfortunately, the computers that were networked to the records database were either in the central detective's bureau upstairs, which was locked by badge access that he didn't have, or in the office adjacent to the desk sergeant, in full view of anyone walking through the main lobby or the desk sergeant sitting in the kiosk. It wouldn't be long before he was taken down once he made his move so Wilke posted back up on the door to the office and watched Sergeant Antonio who was at the desk reading the paper.

God.

Wilke watched the gray haired uniformed cop thumb through the pages of the Sunday paper. He guessed he maybe had ten, fifteen minutes tops before somebody came in that back door. He had timed it so that he had at least an hour and a half before the next patrol shift started and the roll call room filled up with uniforms. He tried to keep himself calm as Antonio casually thumbed the paper.

Come on.

Almost ten minutes went by, which on any given surveillance was a drop in the bucket. Unfortunately for Wilke, his only post was in the middle of a building where every occupant wanted him for questioning in the murder of a fellow law enforcement officer. He realized he'd rather be infiltrating ISIS than standing where he was right now. Just then, he heard the loud *SCHNICK* of the rear door to the building unlocking. On instinct, he moved, swinging open the door and sliding into the office like he knew what he was doing. He tried to keep his head down as if he was reading the file in his hands while watching Antonio out of the corner of his eye. Using the angles of the room as much as he could, he tried to hug the wall behind the desk sergeant to stay in his blind spot. Keeping his gait casual, he stopped at the first terminal he came to and logged in. He entered the PD's database using his assigned passcode and wondered if they had been aware enough to flag him and the rest of the unit for an alert if they accessed the system. He realized it didn't matter and that he was already committed, then he heard the door he'd just come through open.

Risking a sidelong glance toward the entrance, he met eyes with Assistant Chief Vaden. The second in command of the entire police department looked as surprised to see Wilke as he was to see his superior officer. The Assistant Chief's lips were clenched and his eyes were wide. Normally he was the calmer element of the command staff. If he didn't think the Assistant Chief would have killed him in that instant, Wilke would have laughed at himself.

So much for being sly.

***

Poppy unwrapped a stick of spearmint chewing gum and folded the rectangle once before tossing it into her mouth with a sigh. Thompson snored lightly in the back seat of her assigned Nissan Sentra. Every now and then, she would peek back at him through the rear view mirror and chuckle at the sight of the six foot three, muscular black man curled up like a toddler in the tiny rear compartment. He had taken first shift after they had decided to post up on Andrew Tulley's residence so now she watched the Lower Peninsula home while he caught some desperately needed rest.

They had all tried to sleep as much as possible in the old hangar they used for a hideout but there had been too much adrenaline, too much fear at the thought of being wanted by their own department, not to mention the feds.

Jesus Christ.

Just realizing that still made Poppy catch her breath in her throat. Everything else about her day after leaving the hangar had seemed so normal. It was any given day, even on a Sunday where she, Thompson, Wilke, or Viejo might sit on a house for one of their cases, or tail a subject around town. She was doing no different today save that as of now, they were doing it as fugitives, and their quarry had not made a move in over seven hours. They knew he was in There. They had already been sitting outside the house three hours before Tulley came home. Since then, they had checked on him every couple of hours through thermal imaging goggles. She looked at her watch and realized Thompson still had an hour of rest left. At the same time, she scolded herself for looking at her watch. That was the death knell of any surveillance. Once you start looking at your watch, the minutes start passing slower and slower until the second hand seems frozen on the dial. With another sigh, she slouched further in the passenger seat of her non-descript import, trying to get comfortable.

When Thompson groaned and started to move, she looked through the rear view mirror to see him itching sleep from his eyes.

"Any movement?" he asked.

"Last I checked through the thermal, he was rubbing one out. That was about an hour ago," she said.

Thompson chuckled. "Oh, the death of privacy."

"Unfortunately," responded Poppy.

She saw Thompson check his watch, a big, heavy G-Shock type monster and nod.

"I still got time," he said. "Wake me up if anything happens, 806, out," he said signing off with his issue call sign.

He probably figures that we're on the lam.

Poppy returned her eyes to the building that Andrew Tulley called home. She watched a black Lincoln pull up in front of his place. Tulley walked out of the apartment a minute later. He wore a light blue polo shirt over khaki's and boat shoes.

Looking in the rear view mirror, she said, "You've got like an hour right?"

"Mmm hmm." Thompson sighed.

"Wrong. He's on the move. Wake buttercup," she said with a grin as she fired up the car.

Thompson somehow managed to leverage his huge frame between front and rear of the little sedan while Poppy drove. She felt the car pull a little to the right when he plopped down beside her and started putting his hiking boots on.

"I know right," he said tying his shoe. "I didn't think I would fit through there either."

Thompson finished tying his shoes and popped a piece of gum in his mouth to wake himself up.

They followed as Tulley, riding in the back of the Lincoln, was driven along the battery. After a little over five minutes of winding around the peninsula, the vehicle stopped at the harbor marina. The car came to a rest in a parking space near the Salt Water Pub. Tulley exited and walked inside. Long shadows cast by a fading sun in the west cast everything in an orangish hue.

"You want to try and tail or hold what we got since there's only two of us?" asked Poppy.

"Don't know, let's give it a minute, and see if he's in there for a drink or if this is some quick stop."

Chapter Twenty-Five

Banks, DeGuello, and Viejo were still in the car. It was Sunday night in Pickens, South Carolina, a tiny speck on the map near the North Carolina border. A stark contrast to the low country whose flat marshes and beaches could cause one to forget there were such things as hills in the world. Pickens stood as an outpost in the foothills of the Appalachian Mountains. The roads were winding and framed in steep cuts and valleys. Lakes and streams wound through the rocks. The GPS led them to the Old South Armory, an otherwise legitimate appearing firearms manufacturer. Banks was driving and leaned back as much as he could in the seat as they slowly rolled past the outer fence that bordered the property.

"Looks pretty busy for a Sunday night," said DeGuello.

"Sure does. What've you got, Viejo?"

Viejo had been burning through his data plan scouring as much public information as he could from local, state, and federal databases. He was actually amazed at the amount of information anyone could get from public records on the internet. Silently, he had warned himself four times in the last hour to figure out how to have stuff deleted from the internet. If he survived the next week without going to prison.

"According to the Secretary of State's site Old South Armory is an LLC run by a guy named Brigston, he's the CEO anyway. They report about three million a year in revenue. There's not a whole lot else there that can help us. Locally, the Pickens county information gives us data on the company's holdings, the buildings here, and looks like a residence a little further up in the mountains. The LLC is listed as the owner of both properties. The sale of these places was last listed in 1997 when Old South took over from a local. The GIS (geographic information systems) is just as good as the one in Charleston though. We've got some imagery and the reported layout of both properties."

"Psst, that internet shit scares me," DeGuello whispered.

"That's cause we're dinosaurs," responded Banks.

"It's not all."

"What?" asked Banks,

"Might be nothing but I've got an old civil suit from a couple of years ago. It made the papers. Seems two guys filed a lawsuit for hazardous workplace after they were injured when a lathe went haywire. One guy lost an arm, another lost an eye. Gotta keep digging but the lawsuit was thrown out at the state level and the two guys got nothing."

"Keep on that," Banks told him. "Might make a good source if in a pinch."

"Copy that," Viejo said.

"All right, find us some food," Banks ordered. "We need to get our thinking caps on."

**

The pub Andrew Tulley had disappeared into started filling up about an hour into their watch. The clientele was a mix of retirees, tourists, and what looked like pastel flavored young professionals. As on all stakeouts, the two cops started getting antsy. The little voices in their minds whispering that he snuck out the back, left the driver as a decoy, and so on and so on til it was Poppy that broke first.

"Think we need to go in and check it out?" she asked.

"It's only been an hour," replied Thompson who was slouching in the passenger seat.

"I know," she replied. "I just hate sitting here doing nothing."

"Now I know why it's me and DeGuello that draw all the surveillances."

"I thought it was that we work better when you guys aren't around," Poppy retorted without missing a beat.

"Maybe," responded Thompson blandly. "Let's give it another half hour."

The half hour dragged on as the sun slowly faded, leaving their world illuminated only by passing cars and the lights of the parking lot. From their perch, a couple of hundred yards away from the building, they could see the main entrance but if there was another exit opposite them, they were screwed. That possibility, however slight, was driving Poppy crazy. She was about to voice her concerns again when Thompson bolted upright.

"North side door," he said in a tense but controlled voice.

She was drawn to a sudden pie slice of light opening from the bottom floor. A skinny white male in khaki's and a polo, though it was too dark to know the color, stumbled clumsily out the door. He was quickly followed by another male wearing a white t-shirt and black pants, maybe an employee.

"How did I not see that?" she asked.

"Drifting," Thompson responded.

She nodded her head. *Guilty.*

"That's him right," Thompson muttered.

"Yeah, he looks hammered."

Tulley was swaying as he spun on his heel to face the guy who had all but tossed him out the back door of the Salt Water Pub. The food service worker, if that's what he was, was laying into him about something.

"I don't give a fuck!" they heard him yell through the slits of their windows.

Poppy and Thompson rolled their windows down further and strained to stretch an ear toward the opening.

Tulley was mumbling something that they couldn't quite get but the other guy was agitated and raising his voice.

"Yeah, but don't bring this shit to where I work man. Gawwdamn! Come on, let's do this so you can get the fuck outta here."

They watched Tulley fumble in his pants pocket while at the same time dropping back a step to steady himself. It was too dark to see who exchanged what but the two men did a hand to hand of some kind. When it was over, Tulley was studying his new possession while the other guy dropped his take in his pocket.

He turned to leave Tulley outside the door but before he went back inside, they heard him say, "You better get a hold of yourself, man, otherwise I won't be here for you again."

Tulley mumbled something as light from the closing door dimmed. They could still see his silhouette as he stumbled to the Lincoln and climbed in the back.

"Did he just serve or buy?" Poppy asked. "I'm guessing he picked up."

"I thought he was the man though."

"Maybe with the pills. Tonight I guess he has another taste."

"Maybe," Thompson agreed.

The Lincoln pulled out of the parking lot. With the increased nighttime traffic, Poppy and Thompson struggled to follow.

"Surveillance sucks when you have to follow the traffic laws," muttered Poppy.

"That's funny," Thompson responded.

"Wouldn't be funny if some patrol unit blue lit us for running a red ball or something."

They were both quiet for a moment. Just a second ago, they were on mission, chasing their prey wherever and however. It was strange how easy it was to forget that they were wanted in connection with the death of another cop.

Their reality cast a sobering quiet over the vehicle. Thompson grimaced at the thought that all he had worked for was being unraveled simply because they took the wrong politician's kid to jail.

Thompson grew up on the streets of Charleston, less than a mile away from the Citadel. Dad, as much as his father could be considered a dad, was a long haul trucker and Mom was a Medical Assistant at the Medical University of South Carolina. She did what she could while he stayed on the road for weeks at a time, chasing more tail than paychecks. Eric was left most of the time to raise himself and his two sisters. When the parents were not around, he tried with his sisters, but there was only so much a twelve-year-old boy could do, and the allure of the streets was something not everyone could deal with. It was much the same for Eric Thompson.

He started staying out late with his friends. When his mother confronted him for breaking curfew, he would stay out later the next night just to spite her. She could only do so much when working seventy hours a week to pay the rent. He became one of the faces on the street corners, a professional loiterer, waiting for when night came, bringing with it excitement, the potential for something, anything to happen. That's when the older guys took notice of him and he of them. They were amazing, driving awesome cars, jacked up and painted bright colors, always with a handful of cash in their pockets. He knew they were drug dealers, everybody knew they were drug dealers, but none of that mattered.

"Hey lil man," they would say. "Want a job?"

There was no money at home so, hell yes he wanted a job. The older guys would have him stand watch on the corners to keep an eye out for 'One time' or the 'Po-Po,' the street designation for the police department or whatever the dominant music or movie on the streets was from one month to the next. Eleven-year-old Eric Thompson was more than happy to oblige them. He started calling out whenever a marked unit would come around the corner, giving the older kids time to run or hide their stash before getting roused by the police. At first, the police didn't take notice of him, just another little thug running the streets. But when Eric began standing on the corner where business was being done, he started making his way onto the police radar.

Marked units would come around and put all the guys on the nearest wall or fence and pat them down for the dope or guns. Little Eric was fast as a kid and when the older boys realized that, he was promoted from lookout to rabbit. When the police would come by, he would run as soon as they approached.

"Don't let them catch you," the older boys would say. "They catch you, you goin to jail."

So Eric would run, to avoid the threat of imprisonment. He didn't even have any drugs on him most of the time. Everyone just knew that if he ran from the police, they would immediately chase him, especially young cops, giving everyone else the chance to get away. The police would never catch him. Eric was fast and small framed. He could fit through the holes in the fences; he could hide in the crawl space under a porch.

Young Eric was useful and he was willing. The older boys on the street told him how to act, what to do, and they paid him. He had a little bit of money for himself. It was a game he and the others played. Like keep away from the police, at least that's how little Eric thought of it.

Then came the night he turned twelve. His mother tried to tell him he couldn't go out but as had become routine, he ignored her and spent most of the night on the street. That night he got to the corner just in time to see Mikey punch another boy in the face. He didn't know the other boy but he could tell he wasn't from around the neighborhood. Mikey was the biggest and strongest of the boys he hung out with. He was always threatening or hitting someone who stepped out of line, or tried to hold back money they owed him. Eric couldn't hear what was being said, or understand why Mikey was beating the other boy but the fight didn't last long. The boy was bloody and stuttering when Mikey finally let him run away. Eric had just stepped up to the corner as Mikey turned toward the stoop they all sat. He was wiping blood off his knuckles with a rag he kept dangling from his back pocket.

"You see dat lil man?" Mikey asked. "That's what happens when you try to step on someone else's block."

Eric didn't know what to say. He just nodded and sat down on the step in his normal place near the railing so he could skip under and run if need be.

"I'm a get me a burger. I be back," Mikey said and walked off.

Eric was listening to one of the older boys named Desean talking about this girl he knew when Mikey came back around the corner carrying a McDonald's bag. Eric remembered thinking how hungry he was at seeing the familiar bag and wishing for a Big Mac like the one Mikey chewed on as he walked back toward the group. He reached in the bag and pulled out a hand full of fries and Eric could smell them. It made his mouth water. Mikey was only a little way from the stoop when a car came around the corner. Nobody paid it any attention. It was just another car going down the street. Then Eric heard his first gunshot.

BANG! Then more: BANG! BANG! BANG! BANG! BANG!

It happened so fast no one moved. It was the squeal and smoke of tires that snapped Eric back to reality. He looked up to see the boy Mikey had been fighting hanging out of the rear driver's side window of the car as it sped down the street. The rest of the boys were yelling, screaming, and hiding while Eric sat on the scoop unsure what to do.

Should he run? Should he hide?

Then he saw Mikey. He was at the foot of the steps staring back at him. Only he wasn't really looking at him. In fact, he wasn't looking at anything. The older boy was simply staring up at the streetlights still as a rock. He had half-chewed French fries in his open mouth. Eric saw the pool of blood spreading quickly away from Mikey's head. His eyes were drawn to the pink chunks of meat spilling from the huge hole in the side of Mikey's skull. Little Eric started screaming, and running.

He ran home as fast as he could. Bursting through the door, he found his mother sitting in the corner of their living room, reading. He almost knocked her out of her chair he hit her so hard. He just wanted to be safe. He couldn't think of anywhere safer in that instant than in his mother's lap.

She rocked him without question as he cried and shivered in her lap. He curled his lanky twelve-year-old frame up into her chest and tried to hide from the world. Hide from what he saw. He felt he had been hiding in her bosom a lifetime when the doorbell rang and he leaped like a prairie dog popping out of his hole to look for wolves.

His mother tried to soothe him as she extricated herself from his gangly arms and legs. He watched her intently as she answered the door. Eric saw the policeman, a tall black man, standing in her doorway. The spoke softly for a couple of minutes. Eric heard his mother gasp and look back at him. He saw fear in her eyes.

"Come here, Eric," she said to him.

He was trying to keep from whimpering as he approached. His eyes cemented on the imposing figure in dark blue. The metal insignia on his chest and collar glinted in the darkness of the front porch. The cop's name plate read Fuller. Fuller shared a look with Mom then looked back at Eric.

"Come out here, son," he said.

Eric did as he was told. His head was bowed. He was shaking.

"Have a seat, Eric," Fuller said.

They both sat down on the rickety wood of his front porch. Eric looked at his feet while he felt Fuller studying him.

"Mikey Benson was a friend of yours?"

Eric sniffled at the name. He wanted to jump up and run away as the memory of the gaping hole in Mikey's head tortured him. He nodded.

"Yeah, mine too," said Fuller.

That surprised Eric.

"Me and Mikey met a long time ago when he was just a little bit younger than you are now. His mom used to fight with her boyfriend every now and again. I would catch the calls quite a bit. It was tough on Mikey so we would walk and talk sometimes."

"He never said anything like that."

"No, he wouldn't have. It was a long time ago like I said. And me and Mikey lost touch."

Eric didn't say anything in response.

"Yeah, so what happened tonight? You seem pretty shook up. You saw it, huh?"

Tears welled in Eric's eyes. His lips quivered so much that he couldn't talk so he just nodded.

"It's not an easy thing to see."

Eric rubbed his eyes.

"It's okay to cry, kid, I've seen grown men cry, cops like me, when they see something like that. Don't be ashamed."

Eric took a deep breath.

"Do you go to school?"

Eric nodded.

"What are you going to do tomorrow?"

Eric looked at him confused. "Huh?"

Fuller swiped at a piece of grass that had stuck on his pant leg, "Well, you've been on the block for a while now. People out there, Mikey's friends, are going to want to go after the kid that killed him. They take that as an attack on themselves and will want to kill the boy that killed Mikey."

"I don't want to kill anyone." Eric whimpered.

"Good, now what about the street corner. Am I gonna see you there tomorrow?"

The idea of going back to that place made Eric want to retch. The realization that there were no other options made him even more scared than he already was.

Fuller must have seen it. "How old are you Eric?"

"Twelve."

"Twelve... you have a job? I mean outside of what Mikey and the other boys were paying you?"

Eric shook his head.

"What if I told you I could get you a job every day after school?"

Eric shrugged his shoulders.

Fuller shrugged himself. "Well think about it. You had a pretty close call tonight. You're a very lucky guy."

Eric didn't know what to say.

"Think about that job. In the meantime, try to get some sleep and hug your mom."

The statement took a minute to hit Eric, but when it did, it felt like a punch in the stomach. Mikey seemed so much older, like he was a grown up. The idea of Mikey having a mom didn't even register in Eric's mind. He turned from to porch to see his mother watching from behind the screen door. He wanted to run to her.

"Are you going to arrest me?" Eric finally asked, wanting nothing more than to run back to his mother's arms.

Fuller stood up. "Why would I arrest you, son?"

"For being on the corner, for hanging out with those boys."

"You knew what they were doing, dealing drugs, and so on, right?"

"Yeah."

"And you hung out with them anyway?"

Eric nodded.

Fuller sighed. "Tell you what, you meet me at the station tomorrow after school and we'll see if we can't find another option." Fuller handed him a business card with his name and phone number. "Now go see your mother. She's worried sick about you."

Eric dashed into the small house and wrapped his hands around his mother in a bear hug. He didn't see Fuller disappear into the night.

***

Thompson wanted to both laugh and curse as he remembered the four years of washing patrol cars, mucking out stalls at the police stables, and doing whatever odd jobs people around the department found for him to do. He didn't know it at the time but Fuller and the other cops paid him out of their own pocket for the various tasks he did for them. It wasn't until he came on the job himself, after graduating from the Citadel, that he realized those cops who barely made enough to get by as it was still took money out of their own pockets to watch out for a stupid ass kid from the hood. The idea of unraveling all their effort and caring going up in smoke pissed off Eric Thompson off to no end.

They followed the black Lincoln carrying Andrew Tulley through the peninsula. They noted that they did not seem to be heading back toward Tulley's residence. The vehicle headed down Calhoun Street toward the nightlife area of Charleston known as the Market. When the Lincoln made a right at King Street, they followed. The Lincoln passed by the cut through street leading to the Market.

Their minds began to run with different scenarios of where they were going.

What was Tulley up to? Was he dealing? Was he using? Or was he just heading to some place to get a piece of ass?

Thompson and Poppy followed Tulley's vehicle in silence until the Lincoln made a left turn onto Broad Street. The black car came to an abrupt stop and Poppy had to drive past it to pull over in a less obvious location a block away. Luckily, it was Sunday night in downtown Charleston and the tourist traffic was light.

Chapter Twenty-Six

"You sure you wouldn't rather be home, Sir," Timothy Radner asked his passenger.

Andrew Tulley was already halfway out the rear compartment when he paused just long enough to look back at Radner through the mirror. His eyes were blood shot and his face was flush after a hard hour of too much drinking and a quick hit of a potent strain of marijuana. Radner was sure it would take a year to clear the passenger compartment of the sickly stench; however he was paid handsomely to keep an eye on Mr. Tulley.

"I'm fine, Timothy, take the night off. And if you ask me if I want to go home again you're fired."

"Yes, Sir," Radner responded.

Tulley slammed the door shut and jogged across Broad Street, oblivious to the traffic that had to slow for him to pass. He walked north on Broad Street for about a half a block and ducked into an alley that led to a nondescript door with a red light shining above the frame. Tulley swung the door open and disappeared.

***

"He went to Vince's," Poppy stated.

She had the best view of the street was able to see their quarry pass through the door that lead to the quiet little bar.

"Interesting," Thompson responded

She instinctively slouched in her seat just a little as the Lincoln passed by. All the windows were down and she was able to see the driver, dressed in a dark suit and talking on the phone.

"That should make Andrew a little easier to follow huh?"

"Let's hope so," commented Thompson.

Poppy stared at the unmarked door at the end of the dimly lit alley. She had to know what was going on behind that door. She nibbled on her lip as she weighed the merits of the gamble she was about to take.

"I'm gonna go in," she said.

"Huh?"

She grabbed her make up kit out of her purse and touched up as best she could a face that had been sitting in a car all day and was running on about three hours sleep in the last twenty-four. She dabbed a little concealer here and there to even herself out and applied a fresh coating of eyeliner and mascara. Her hair was in a ponytail so there was not much she was going to be able to do about that. She adjusted the mirror to look herself over. Tank top and jeans was never the classiest of get ups when working the clubs downtown. She reached inside the low neck of her tank top and propped her breasts up in her bra doubling her cleavage. It never ceased to amaze her what a little cleavage could do for a girl whether dealing with drug dealers, college professors, or other cops. Poppy was not the kind of woman to ignore a weapon that was so easily in reach.

Thompson whistled, "Breaking out the big guns tonight huh? They don't stand a chance."

"Just playing a hunch," she said.

"What are we gonna do for comms? Not a whole lot of places for concealment there."

"How about I just leave my phone on and kill the screen?"

Thompson shrugged. "It's not a great safety net."

"It's not a great plan but we can't follow this asshole all night with just the two of us in one car. Even his driver will figure that out eventually."

"He just kicked his driver loose."

"Yeah but he just pulled back up a block behind us."

"Andrew needs a babysitter."

"Apparently, I saw him cut his lights when I was fixing the girls."

"They look ready for the show," Thompson teased her.

"All right then." Poppy opened the driver's side door and skipped across Broad Street, following in Tulley's footsteps.

***

Andrew Tulley caught himself on the bar as he stumbled through the door of Vince's Pub. Steadying himself, he looked up to see that hulking form of the bartender, Hank, scowling at him. Though Tulley considered himself to be in relatively good shape, all the alcohol and THC flowing though his system hurt his stamina. It took him a moment to catch his breath after the climb from street level. As he looked around the small bar, he saw only one couple seated in a booth in the far corner. They were quietly chatting with each other and clearly not interested in whatever was going on around them.

Perfect.

"Three fingers of Maker's, Hank," Tulley told the bartender.

"Seems like you started without me tonight, huh, Drew?"

Tulley hated it when he called him that. He nodded, took the tumbler full of bourbon as it was offered, and moved down the bar to collapse on a stool.

He was in no mood for the regular back and forth between he and the various bartenders he knew around the city. He had tried to hide in his house and disappear after the last meeting with Davidson and his men but the images of the night before played on a loop over and over in his mind. He realized he couldn't be alone in his house. All the blood and bullets from the ATF Lab and the viciousness of Brigston's goons haunted him.

He needed to get out of his head and was out of any good weed so he went to Jack. Jack was the best source for pot in the city; he was rolling in the cash he brought in. But Jack thought he was smart keeping a menial day job scrubbing dishes at the Salt Water Pub. Tulley figured he would have a drink or two as he waited for Jack to see him. Four shots of Patron in ten minutes created a very brazen Andrew Tulley who stomped into the kitchen twenty minutes later looking for Jack. Jack told him after throwing him out a side door that if he did that again, he would break his legs and Tulley believed him. Jack still sold him an ounce and Tulley knew he would have anyway. Money was money, and Jack depended on Tulley for good ecstasy just as much as he depended on Jack for good weed.

Andrew smoked a bowl in the back of the car as Radner tried to take him home. Tulley at first thought he would concede to his driver/chaperone but as they drew closer and closer to home, he couldn't bear the thought. The walls and the ghosts of three dead men staring back at him made his hands shake. When he realized they were passing near Vince's, Tulley made Radner drop him off.

The weed was making Andrew feel better, slowing him down just enough to keep him sane. But he couldn't go home. He took his first sip of the biting Kentucky bourbon. It was like a burning blanket he could wrap himself up in, further pushing the world away. It still wasn't far enough. He made it through his first round before the ghosts found him, and now they were using a different tactic.

It wasn't so much the blood and the gore that he had waded through with the imposing and horrifying man, Dierks, pushing him along. It was the guilt, a sudden onslaught of regret. Not so much regret that the men had died but that he had enjoyed the moment at first. He remembered the adrenaline spike. The way his heart was beating in his chest as he crouched in the hallway while they assaulted the office space. They wouldn't let him have a weapon; Tulley had never shot anything more than a shotgun during skeet shoots at his father's hunting club. The concussions and the noise, the smoke, and the smell of cordite in the atmosphere had been intoxicating. He had been swept up in a whirlwind of violence and went home that night wanting more.

It wasn't until after the meeting with Davidson the next day, after he had returned home to his family's house on Legare Street of which he was the only resident. His father normally stayed in their second home on the peninsula, the Legare Street residence was where Andrew lived while attending law school. The quiet home, its two stories, and stillness had opened him up to reality. In retrospect, he was horrified by what he'd been a part of.

They killed a cop, tried to kill more, and two of Dierks' men had been killed right in front of him. How could they get away with that? Dierks made him and another surviving member of his team carry the two dead mercenaries out of the scene to the whole building. They burned down a government office, and he helped destroy evidence. He didn't kill anyone himself but if they were ever caught, no one would care what he did or didn't do. His life would be over. His life?

Suddenly Tulley thought of Davidson, Dierks, and Brigston. Would they let him be arrested? Would Davidson above all let any of them be arrested?

Davidson scared him even more than Dierks did. Where Dierks was clearly a violent man, he wore the chiseled features and barely controlled rage in his quiet indifference. Davidson was a calculating machine serving... who? Tulley had no idea who the real power was behind the guns. He hated his father for getting him involved.

"It's the family business," he had scolded him, embarrassing Andrew in front of the staff like he always did. *"Now man up or move out."*

Tulley had manned up, he had found a new intermediary for the shipments in Anton Tate after Aleister Fitzpatrick was killed, or he almost did. Andrew was about to seal the deal before those cops had showed. Tulley scoffed to himself over his drink as he realized that this whole shit storm was the result of a pervert who couldn't resist banging the help at his own strip club. If Fitzpatrick could have just kept his pecker in his pants, that asshole wouldn't have shot him for banging his wife. And Tulley would be nowhere near the death of a cop.

Fuck!

Panic started rising in his chest as he imagined himself being splattered all over the news as a cop killer. The embarrassment to his name and the death of his political career before it even got off the ground. That was only if he lived long enough to be arrested.

He knew in his heart that Davidson wouldn't let that happen. He wanted to run but he had a feeling he wouldn't get too far. Tulley wasn't sure if it was the combination of weed and alcohol spurring his paranoia but he felt like a fly in a spider web. No matter what he did or where he went, the spider was behind him, waiting. He had to get out of there. The musty atmosphere of Vince's was beginning to smother him.

Tossing a twenty on the bar, Tulley spun the seat around and took a step before looking into the wide set crystal blue eyes of a petite but rock solid blonde. She was wearing a tank top and pair of jeans. She held his gaze and demurely stepped around him, sitting down next to the stool he just vacated,

"A Cabaneret Sauvignon, please?" she asked Hank.

The bartender nodded and set to task.

Tulley stood only a couple of feet away from the woman whose tight pony tail kept her hair off her shoulders exposing petite ears, a tight jaw line, and a curving neck. He followed the trail to the pert but not overbearing amount of cleavage squeezing from the tight tank top. The girl was tight but that wasn't the thing. Tight was a pre-requisite for any female wanting to approach Andrew Tulley. It was something else, a confidence or something like it just in the way she carried herself. She had him curious.

"I'll cover that, Hank," Tulley said, resuming station at this bar stool.

"Not necessary," she told him blankly.

Tulley looked at her for a moment and tilted his head.

"Do I know you?" he asked.

Poppy felt her breath catch in her chest. She wasn't around him most of the time during his arrest. During the search, she and Wilke had been upstairs tearing through the place while he was detained downstairs. She squinted just a little and tweaked her nose.

"I doubt it. I just moved here," she said.

He studied her for another few seconds then seemed to slouch inwardly and threw up a hand. "Maybe not, anyway, I insist," he announced in practiced fashion. "Andrew Tulley."

He offered his hand and over enunciated to make sure he didn't slur his words.

"Debra," Poppy said. Debra was her go to name whenever she did undercover work. It was a name she hated.

Being pretty when you're a rookie cop guaranteed you two things. At least half of the men and a couple of the other females in the roll call room, to include supervisors, would try to hook up with you; and at some point you were going to be on a street corner or in a hotel room impersonating a prostitute.

It was no different for Poppy Montague. Her field-training officer didn't try to mess with her. He was tough on her and treated her like any other recruit, which included doing pushups in the lobby stairwell of police headquarters when she messed up her reports. He had her shaking doors up and down strip malls in the driving rain, and had to be first to go hands on when trying to arrest a rowdy drunk. Jerry Hardison was a career street cop who only dabbled in the detective world before realizing his place was in a cruiser chasing calls and facing the unknown every time he went to work. He didn't care who she was or what gender; he was a field training officer for the simple reason of building a strong core of street cops. And if she couldn't hack it, he would have cut her loose the second he got the chance.

Poppy hacked it, sometimes only by the skin of her teeth, but she did it and kept asking for more whenever Hardison could pile it on her. He made her in his own image and she took to the mindset that a cop's place was on the street and in a uniform. By the time she was cut loose at the end of training, she didn't give the plain clothes life a thought. She soon realized that what she wanted to do was not in her control. Poppy wasn't a month into life on the street when her lieutenant pulled her aside and detailed her to vice. The detectives needed a prostitute and all eyes fell on her.

She fell in and did what she was told. The first time some fool rolled up and stopped his car in front of her, she almost threw up. He propositioned her and she froze. The guy wasn't even suspicious, he just asked how much for a blow job. He was driving a minivan with two empty baby seats in the second row. She remembered that the wedding ring on his finger seemed to glow. That ten or so seconds between doubting she could fool anyone into believing she wasn't a cop and looking at that gleaming ring on the John's hand was all it took for Poppy to figure out the game. She hopped in the van and had the guy wrapped up in handcuffs a mile later.

It was confidence the Vice Sergeant had told her two weeks later when she asked why she was permanently reassigned from patrol. A good undercover knows people, knows themselves, and knows how to put themselves aside and become what their target wants. According to him, it was a rare quality and Poppy was a natural.

She hadn't been in a uniform since. Half the department couldn't pick her out of a lineup, and she had been who the subject wanted for so long and on so many different occasions, that slipping on a new personality was like putting on a different pair of shoes. She gave a sideways glance at Tulley as he looked her over and read him in an instant.

"So what are you doing in here on a Sunday night, Debra?" Tulley asked, a slight slur to his words.

"Fleeing an empty apartment." She sighed then looked at him with a sheepish smile. "I just moved in and all I have are boxes and an angry cat at home."

"I know the feeling," Tulley said, taking a fresh tumbler dripping bourbon from the bartender.

"What about you?" she asked.

He seemed caught in the question for a moment. He looked at her and then stared at his drink. His face changed. The veneer of drunken playboy fell off like the nose of the Sphinx and was replaced just for a second by what... Fear?

He cleared his throat. "Just needed a minute out."

"Wife driving you nuts?"

He scoffed. "No, no wife, no kid."

It was like watching a single wave heading for shore, crest (happy go lucky), trough (scared little kid).

There's something wrong here. Poppy tried hard to put a finger on her feeling.

Not the kind of wrong where she needed to bail but the kind of wrong in that she wasn't selling and he wasn't buying. There was no build up or transaction to pull off here to get an arrest. It was more like an interrogation. She realized she had never done an interrogation before, not in the strictest sense of the word. Interrogations of drug dealers are more like a business negotiation. Everyone in the room knew the score. It was simply a matter of settling on how many people the dealer needed to sell out before they get to go on with their life. This was her against his demons and the question was—what was she going to have to do or say to get him to let his guard down. She chose the lowest common denominator and threw back half a glass of wine.

"That Makers looks good," she said then tapped the bar. "Another round."

Tulley looked at his almost full glass and the two shared a grin. He drained his own glass.

Atta boy. She worked hard to hide a grin.

Hank gave them both a refill and she suggested they get a table. The second round was more intimate. Just the two of them outside the hovering attention of the bartender, Hank. She watched as Tulley settled in and started his game. On the job or off, Poppy seldom made it much more than a day or two without some guy dropping lines on her and he was no different. It took him less than three minutes to point out that his father was a United States Congressman. Another five to get to the fact he was in his second year of law school, and another two to mention that he had his own place South of Broad Street in one of the richest areas of Charleston.

"Beats my digs," she replied. "I'm in a one bedroom up East Bay. A medical residency doesn't pay much."

"You're a doctor then?"

"Will be, hopefully. Always fear the future, know what I mean?"

That triggered him. He shied away for just a moment,

"What was that?" she asked.

"Huh?" Andrew responded.

"You just went somewhere else there for a second. Like something was bothering you." She quarreled with herself. Trying to keep in role on the outside while the excitement built within.

He took a drink and shrugged. The booze and whatever else he had put in his system was getting to him. The slurring was gaining on his enunciation and his eyes had a sleepy air to them.

"Just personal stuff," he said, looking again at his drink.

"It's all personal," she said.

He remained quiet and wouldn't look at her. She watched as he started shriveling away.

"Hank, another round," she announced.

Tulley looked up and the hint of a grin spread across her face. When he looked at her, the overconfident drunk was gone replaced by a broken, scared little boy. It only lasted for a split second before he was able to repair his veneer. Poppy Montague had no idea what a motherly gesture was but she tried her warmest, most inviting smile, the shift from sex appeal to maternal nurturing almost made her head spin but he responded. His eyes seemed to open back up just a little, not inviting so much but not a closed off defensive posture.

"Thanks," he finally said.

Poppy reached over the table and took his hand. She batted her eyes just a little and squeezed softly.

"No problem," she whispered.

Ten minutes later, when he started to cry, Hank let them out on the fire escape. They sat on the metal grate landing with their legs dangling over the side. She leaned against the railing, resting her cheek on her forearms, and watched as he rolled a joint. It was the sloppiest roll she had ever seen, even by people more hammered than he was, but he finally was able to seal the delicate paper into some semblance of a cigarette. He sniffled and tried to offer it to her.

"Can't, drug test, medical school remember."

"Sorry," he said quietly as he sniffled and put the marijuana to his lips.

"So this guy that you know who runs... sorry ran a strip club got killed by the husband of one of the dancers and somehow this is your fault?"

He shook his head as he breathed out a lungful of sweet noxious smoke, "Yeah. My dad had told me to find someone in town we could work with and I found him. When he got killed, I had to find someone else."

"What did you guys do together?"

"Doesn't matter now."

"So that's what has been eating at you? Your friend getting killed."

He looked at her with a crooked grin. "No," he wheezed, "That guy was a piece of shit. But I'm in trouble now because the last guy I found to work with us got arrested the other day and with him was something very important. The people my dad and I were working with did something and made me help."

His voice was cracking.

"What happened, Andrew?"

"They killed somebody."

"What?" Poppy sounded shocked.

He shook his head like an eight-year-old finally coming clean for blaming his sister when he stole a fresh a batch of cookies.

"They did it, they killed him, and now if we get caught they'll kill me. I know it."

"You need to tell someone. What about the police?"

He shook his head and took another long drag.

"They know the police, they have the police working for them too."

His voice was so desperate, so helpless that Poppy actually felt for him for a moment. It was a brief moment. He leaned his head against the railing of the fire escape and closed his eyes. She watched as after a moment his breathing started to slow and lengthen.

Oh, shit! She stared at him in disbelief. *He's about to pass out.*

***

Andrew Tulley had no idea how great it was going to feel when he finally told someone what was going on. He felt like he could breathe again for the first time since the shooting when he told this girl what happened. He was so exhausted, just spent. As soon as the words were out, he felt his eyes closing.

Rest, just for a moment.

That sounded so good to him.

"No, no, no." He heard her say. "Come on, get up."

He did as he was told. She was pulling him up by his shoulders.

She's really strong.

The thought flitted through his skewed mind. He clumsily grasped one of the rails and helped her get him to his feet. She had him by the elbow and guided him through the door where Hank was smirking.

"Put it on my tab, Hank," he slurred, his speech was bordering on incoherent but he didn't care.

He felt her trying to steady him and he went with it. Once he got some food, and back to his place, he knew she was a sure thing. Tulley felt her breasts rub innocently against his shoulder and grinned.

He took his steps absentmindedly, letting her guide him as she went.

"I have to call my driver," he told her when they exited into the alley.

"I've got a car," she said.

He noted a little more stoicism to her voice, almost abrupt in her answer but he ignored it.

There was a little sedan waiting for them at the intersection where the alley met Broad Street. As they reached the car, she opened the back door and before slumping into the rear compartment, he heard another car door open. Andrew Tulley looked up to see a large black man staring back at him from across the roof. He recognized him immediately.

"No!" he said, his mind now clear as a bell.

The nurturing, soft hand on his elbow suddenly turned to steel and he felt her fingernails dig into the underside of his arm as he tried to pull away. He looked at her and she was looking at him. She wasn't laughing but he recognized an amused smugness that hadn't been there before. The empathy and quiet maternal air about her was gone.

"Andrew Tulley," she said, "You're under arrest for the murder of..."

Squealing tires interrupted Poppy's well-practiced reading of rights to Andrew Tulley Jr. They were frozen for a moment as they watched the smoking black SUV round the corner a block away. Thompson moved first.

"Get in!" he yelled.

Tulley was frozen in the headlights of the approaching vehicle. Poppy snap kicked the back of his knees, buckling him, and threw him in the rear compartment of the Nissan. She leaped in on top of him and yelled.

"Go!"

For a small car, the Nissan had a little pep. Thompson burned a layer off the rear tires as he peeled out into Broad Street. The SUV was less than a hundred yards behind them when he got up to speed.

"Hang on," he warned, dive bombing onto Meeting Street, throwing Poppy and Tulley in a tangled mess across the back seat.

"No!" Tulley cried.

"Shut up," Poppy retorted shoving him hard against the rear door to clear herself from his legs.

"You don't understand," he yelled. "He's going to kill me."

She took a worrying look out the back window toward the SUV. In the deepest part of her mind, she prayed they had panicked and the SUV had just been some drunk college kids in daddy's ride.

She was wrong. The maneuver had gained them some distance on the heavy vehicle but it was again gaining on them. A thought occurred to her and she checked to make sure her phone was still in voice record mode. There was a green bar across the top of her screen showing it was still active.

"Who's going to kill you, Andrew?" she demanded while at the same time reaching for her go bag for extra magazines of ammunition.

"Davidson and Dierks." His voice failed just a bit when he said the word Dierks. "He was the one. He was the one who killed that cop; they made me go with them. He does what Davidson tells him. Davidson is going to kill me."

"Who's Davidson?"

Tulley went blank for just a split second. Poppy wanted to slap him but held back. When the instinct returned, she was blocked by a torrent of shards when the rear window of the little car blew in.

"Who's Davidson?" she screamed.

"He's the one... he's the one in charge of everything," Tulley said softly.

His eyes fluttered and Poppy thought he might pass out.

"Hang on," Thompson announced again.

She braced as he dove around the corner onto Calhoun Street. Normally these streets would be crowded with tourists or college kids but at three o'clock in the morning, not even the college kids still had it in them to be out and about.

"Time for talking is over, Pop!" Thompson shouted.

Poppy turned off the voice recorder and faced the rear window just as a swarm of rounds peppered the trunk.

They must be using suppressors.

The lack of a report before the impact of the rounds was an utterly horrific experience. Like being sucker punched. She responded with a barrage of her own, though it was only from her .40 caliber Glock. She might as well have been throwing rocks at them.

"What's the plan!" she yelled.

"I'm going for 75. It's our only chance." Thompson yelled back.

Though the move might land them all in a jail cell, Poppy couldn't argue with the logic. Her phone beeped and caught her attention. The message on the screen requested she share her recording. She thanked God at that moment for the social media revolution. Every smartphone was now hard wired to share every aspect of the user's life, regardless of the format. She hit yes, and rapidly started entering in a number.

"I'm..."

They were passing the intersection of Calhoun Street and Coming Street when the entire world stopped with a sickening crunch and a massive impact. The little Nissan bounced like a disintegrating pinball off the front grill of a reinforced Toyota Land Rover. Spinning madly Poppy blacked out when she banged off the sides of the car and tumbled with Andrew Tulley.

The stillness was horrifying. Her survival instincts were screaming before she fully regained consciousness.

Blinking glass and debris from her eyes, the world was dark, and spotted light danced through her vision.

A sudden *Pop!* jolted her awake, and she instinctively reached for her right side, her gun side, to find nothing but belt loops and her waist.

Shit!

She scrambled against the protestations of her aching body and fought to free herself from the limp form of Andrew Tulley. A smattering of heavy splats of weapons fire impacted the body of the crumpled up Nissan and she moved more quickly. Where was her gun? She had slipped it under her leg to send the message too...

"Get out of here, Pop!" Thompson screamed.

Eric?

Poppy looked up to see her partner still in the front seat. He was still seated as if nothing had happened. He was firing his own department issued sidearm and hers out the shattered windshield.

"Eric?"

"You gotta..." Thompson shuddered under the impact of three rounds when they breached the windshield and made his t-shirt jump across his chest.

"Eric!" she screamed.

Her gun clattered to the front passenger seat and she grabbed it.

"No, no, no," she whispered then spat as she opened fire on two shadowy figures she could just barely see out of the spider webbed windshield.

Poppy fired five rounds before the gun went dry. Even through smoke and cordite filling the compartment, she could still see them coming.

"Fuck you!" she screamed, no longer thinking about Thompson, or Tulley, or the fact she was about to die.

She scrambled around the car for a magazine, a knife, a stray round to throw in the open breach. She didn't care; she just wanted to kill one of them before her time ran out.

When the door next to her was wrenched open, it caught her by surprise. Letting herself fall to primal instincts, she charged as much as any charge could be mounted from the back of a Nissan Sentra. There was a bright spotlight blinding her but she attacked anyway. Hoping for anything, a grasp of clothing, a throat, an eye to gouge—it didn't matter.

She made it out of the car but before she could attack the figure closest to her. A heavy blow to the side of her head dropped her to the street unconscious.

Chapter Twenty-Seven

Burgess watched his suspect through the one-way glass and tried to make sense of what he was seeing.

"He's a good kid, Tom," Vaden said, "Twice decorated when he was in patrol. He is one of the smoothest operators we have in the Special Operations Bureau."

From Burgess' standpoint, he was looking at a scraggly twenty something in faded jeans, hiking boots, and a button down flannel. The kid stared at the handcuffs ringing his wrists with the same look a wolf gives his paw when it was stuck in a trap. That was a good thing. The kid was put off by the sensation of confinement; the distraction would knock him off his game.

"I'm sure he is, Andy. They all are right up until things go sideways." He reached for the door to the interrogation room.

"I'm just saying, keep an open mind."

Burgess was mildly offended by that but it was not the first time he'd heard something similar. He paused and turned back to Vaden.

"That goes without saying, Assistant Chief. We don't dictate how a case goes. They do," he said nodding to the room.

Vaden nodded. There was the slightest hint of a grimace to his face. He didn't want to be a part of what was about to happen. Burgess understood that all too well. This was his officer. No cop wanted to treat another cop like a suspect. No one more than Burgess himself. But the job was the job, the case was the case, and the kid cuffed to the interrogation table was the only lead they had at the moment.

Burgess stepped through the door. He and Ben Wilke made eye contact. Burgess held the stare as long as the kid would play it. The gesture gave him his first instinct as to where they were starting.

All interrogations were at their core a negotiation. Each party had their side, their story, and their secrets. That information each wanted to hold from the other. That piece of evidence the cop had to leverage the suspect into cooperation or that info the suspect held back from discussing in the hopes the cop on the other side of the table hadn't done his homework. Each player had their hole card. During the interaction in that small suffocating room, each player would decide how best to play out their resources.

Burgess didn't see any wrath in his subject. No judgement toward him for interrogating a fellow cop. When it came to internal investigations, there was always that inference if not a flat out accusation that the investigator was a rat and that the subject was being persecuted rather than prosecuted. He saw none of that in Wilke's eyes. Wilke was studying him the same way he was studying Wilke. Burgess kept his face placid and calm. Inside, on the other hand, he was intrigued. However it turned out, this was going to be interesting.

He and Vaden approached the two chairs opposite Wilke. Before sitting, Burgess lay a manila folder down in front of him. As he sat, Wilke reached up and scratched behind his ear. The movement brought Burgess up short. He watched as Wilke's right hand, free of the steel constraint make the gesture of scratching behind his ear.

Wilke noticed him watching and returned his hand to the table. He then slipped the other ring that was not cinched off his left wrist and slid the handcuffs across the table. Burgess felt his face reddening and fought the urge to lunge across the table. Wilke read him like a book.

"What?" he asked. "You SLED guys don't carry a spare handcuff key? Nice search technique by the way. While I'm..."

"You think this is a fuckin game, shitbird!"

Wilke's eyes darkened, "I'm not sure, all I know is that I come in to check out a lead in the system and next thing I know I'm handcuffed to a table. If it is a joke, it's a bad joke. How about that?"

Vaden interrupted Burgess before he could launch into a tirade. "This is a serious matter, Detective. Where are Banks and the others?"

Wilke shrugged his shoulders. "Don't know. Haven't seen anybody since Friday night. We had a drink after doing a warrant. That's the last I've seen any of them."

"Bullshit," muttered Burgess, "Your squad is wanted by the FBI for questioning in a murder right now. Banks is in the wind, you know it, and I know it. What do you think happens if the Bureau geeks get to him first, huh? You sitting here playing dumb doesn't help anyone."

"I don't know what to tell you. Whatever they were into the other night, I'm damn sure they didn't kill an ATF agent and both of you know it too. So I should ask you now... What is really going on here?"

Shit.

Burgess hated going into an interrogation without having a hammer in his back pocket to crush his subject. Some damning evidence that would force them to talk or some carrot to dangle in front of them to caress their cooperation. Sometimes things dropped in your lap and you had to roll with what you had, which in the case of Detective Ben Wilke wasn't shit, and the young cop knew it. They had no angle. Had no video footage to show him at the scene. They had nothing to go on and Wilke knew it. Burgess could tell by the way he was looking at him. He was smug, almost gloating...

"Hold on," Burgess blurted. "You're a fuckin spy."

"What?" Wilke looked at Vaden then back to Burgess.

"He sent you here didn't he? Hoping you would get close and feed him whatever we had. What's his angle?"

"Chief Vaden, I don't know what this guy is getting at. If I'm under arrest, I want a lawyer. If not, I would really like to take off."

Vaden's eyebrows were furrowed as he looked from Burgess to Wilke and back again. "What are you getting at Tom?"

"Banks," he said. "Banks planted the kid here to keep an eye on whatever investigation we had going. He would only do that if he had something of his own in the works. What's he up to, kid? If he is on the up and up like you say, we can be working together right now instead leading a manhunt after him."

Wilke was quiet then. He studied Burgess then looked at the Assistant Chief.

He's weighing his options, trying to decide whether or not to trust us.

Burgess watched as Wilke's eyes flashed back and forth and finally came to rest on Vaden.

It's his own people he doesn't trust.

Burgess could see it in the way Wilke wasn't looking exactly at Vaden but more at the brass, the badge, and the rank. Burgess made a mental note.

"I wish I could help you," Wilke finally said. "But like I said, I haven't seen them."

"Then where were you all weekend. No news travels faster than through cop channels. Your unit is involved in the death of an ATF agent and you're nowhere to be seen, not even to get the story for yourself?"

"I had family in town."

"Uh-huh."

Just then, Burgess' breast pocket started vibrating. He swore. Wilke cringed when he produced the phone. The name on the screen read "Mom." Burgess held the phone up for him. He had a voice message.

There it is! Burgess suppressed a grin. Wilke all but leapt back when he saw the phone.

"Speak of the devil," Burgess said. "Mom's always there when you need her huh?" He looked at his watch. "Even when it's almost four o'clock in the morning."

"She worries," Wilke said.

"She should," responded Burgess. "Open it."

Wilke chuckled, "I don't think so, Chief, are we done here?"

Vaden looked at him. "Why don't you want to share the message, Detective?"

Wilke didn't answer but Burgess had already put the phone down and opened the manila folder that had been resting in front of him. In it was Wilke's personnel record, which only showed that he was a solid cop. Burgess had only held on to it because he didn't like going into an interrogation without something in his hand. It got the subjects thinking. Wondering what he had on him. A subject wondering what was in the file took his mind off his circumstances. In this case, the file was only a prop but suddenly it held the source of a bet Burgess was taking with himself. He found what he was looking for and held up the locked phone one more time.

"Four digit code," he said. "You going to open it?"

"No."

"Okay," Burgess started entering the kids badge number. "One-zero-eight-one."

The phone blinked and unlocked. He smiled.

Wilke's shoulders slumped.

"Remind me to change my passcode, will ya?" he asked Wilke as he put the phone to his ear.

Burgess listened as a stuttering, panicked voice filled the air. There was a lot of background noise making it hard to hear everything that was said. After a moment, a female voice prompted a frightened male for information, peppering him with questions. He didn't recognize either one. He grimaced as heavy banging on metal made both voices shout in alarm. The message ended and he dropped the phone on the table. He hit replay and set the sound to play through the phones speaker.

"What the hell is this?" Burgess asked.

Wilke heard Andrew Tulley's voice, at least it sounded like him from the other day at the warrant. He was frantic, not the smug douche bag that had flaunted the fact his father was a congressman in all their faces. His chattering, wild voice was hard to get over the din of the background noise. When Wilke heard Poppy's voice on the line, his eyes widened and his breath caught in his chest. He could tell by her inflections, her voice just a tick higher than normal and her words coming faster than the normal laid back, unenthused Pop that he knew. She was pinging Tulley for a name. What the hell was she doing with him anyway? They were just supposed to keep tabs on him...

The sound of banging in the background and the way she yelped just before the phone went dead made Wilke want to leap out of his skin. He had to do something; that was a cop's first reaction. Attack the problem, whatever it was, and get it resolved. He looked at the heavy steel door over Burgess' shoulder and felt like a caged animal. He looked at the phone again. He had no idea what happened, where they were. Thompson was with her. What were they doing with Andrew Tulley in the middle of the night? His mind spun in circles until Burgess' words stopped him cold,

"You ready to get on board now, kid?"

The question was infuriating. Wilke struggled to keep from swinging at state investigator.

"Who the hell is Niles Davidson?" Wilke responded.

Chapter Twenty-Eight

Monday

The clock on her dashboard read 6:00 AM.

Only an hour and a half to go, Myra told herself.

The sun was a vague blue haze to the east, promising to bring triple digit temperatures suffocating humidity for the day. Luckily, she would be asleep for the majority of the worst part of the day.

Myra had been cruising neighborhoods on the west side of Charleston since five o'clock in the morning in an effort to stay awake. It seemed to her that if she was on a thoroughfare where she could drive for miles in a straight line, she had to fight to keep her eyes from closing on her. If she snuck around the tight cookie cutter neighborhoods that seemed to sprout up like dollar weeds around the outskirts of the city, the relatively constant motion of turning and weaving around block after block helped keep her awake. Besides that, there were at least three mornings in the last month where someone was caught doing report after report for overnight car break-ins sometimes up to twenty or more in one night. She half hoped that she would get lucky and catch the guy in the act. She hoped as she yawned but knew catching a criminal hot in the act was easier said than done. It was kind of like finding a needle in a haystack, when the needle had infinite places to hide, and watch and wait for the police to show themselves so the needle could go where the police were not.

She couldn't help it and looked at the clock again to see that it was only 6:02. Myra grimaced. She knew she was going to be looking at that damn clock every five minutes until day shift checked on. She needed something else. The pop music station she had playing was on the third replay of their song list that night, and the droning bass and mindless lyrics were starting to work against keeping her awake. Talk radio wasn't her thing but the local morning show would be starting and she figured they might touch on whatever was going on with the Narcotics unit.

She didn't know any of them personally but she had seen them around now and then. No one could believe what was going on, that cops from their own department could have killed another cop, much less a fed. None of it made sense. And the department wasn't helping any, since none of the brass had said anything about what was happening. All the line knew about the Narcotics unit was what the public knew: that the FBI wanted them in connection with the death of that ATF agent. A commercial on the AM station ended and the local show came back on. The first comment out of the speakers was that the police were out of control. It was the chief's fault and the mayor's fault. Rogue cops were running the street, and now they'd killed one of their own.

Great.

As she guided her cruiser around a corner, something caught her eye. It was still dark, just a flash, a shadow against a garage, less than nothing. But it had what her FTO called her spidey sense tingling. She slowed without hitting the brake and swung around at the next intersection.

Coming back around on the quiet neighborhood street, she arrived at the house where she thought she had seen movement and turned on the bright alley light mounted on the side of her cruiser's light bar. The entire front facade of the house was lit up as if it were noon. She passed slowly, creeping along the driveway where a Toyota Four Runner and a Honda Odessey were parked. Morning dew gleamed in streaks and spots along the cars. Her light cast shadows as it bounced through the interiors, subdued by the low-level tint on the vehicles respective windows. She squinted and leaned across the compartment of the Crown Victoria she drove, straining to see what it was that had caught her attention. Her light was passing from the Odessey to the Four Runner when she saw movement again. A quick flash, a bump of a shadow moving across the hood of the Toyota. Her light followed and she focused, zeroing in on the source of her curiosity. The alley light cleared the Toyota and illuminated the side of the house where a figure was fleeing toward the back yard.

It all happened so fast she almost couldn't believe what she was seeing. Without thinking, she threw the cruiser into park. The vehicle, still in motion, stuttered and the gears ground against their sudden halt. She was out of the car and barking into her shoulder microphone,

"Control 426! Foot pursuit High Moss Estates, Parker and Holt!" She felt out of breath. She was charging after the shadowy figure who had managed a good thirty or forty yard head start,

"Stop! Police!" she ordered.

The suspect didn't turn back toward her. All she could see was the back of their dark clothes and their feet bouncing as they ran.

Beach, Pluretti, and Corporal Wayne, the shift supervisor, were each signaling over the radio that they were responding. Wayne called for the dispatcher to hold all traffic on the channel.

"426," Myra called again. "Suspect wearing black sweat shirt, black pants, black tennis shoes." She could barely make out the light colored soles as the suspect sped ahead of her.

The neighborhood was new and populated by a several dozen open lots. There were very few trees or shrubbery that had been left by the developer when the lots were cleared. Myra was barely gaining on the suspect if any but luckily, thanks to the geography, she was able to keep him in sight. That was of course until he came upon a row of houses and dodged in between them.

Myra could hear sirens in the distance and growing closer. The audible tones competed in her head with the sounds of her breathing and pounding heartbeat. She came upon the house, a two story vinyl sided structure, and slowed. She kept her distance from the corner where she had last seen the suspect and, gun in hand, she slowly arced her way around the bend, slicing the pie, was how they described it in the academy. She cleared the area and the suspect was gone.

Moving cautiously in between the houses, she reached the next street and now she could hear the subdued whining of cruisers as her squad flooded the area. She reached for her microphone and was about to put out her location and the last where she'd seen the suspect when a cry off to her right stole her attention. She started running while barking into the microphone,

"Suspect last seen on Connor Lane." She snatched a quick look at the road sign and the house beside her. "114 Connor Ln, possibly traveling south on foot."

She ran toward the sound of the scream and saw an overweight elderly woman wearing a billowing nightdress and cloth slippers pointing further down the street toward a stand of trees that bordered the neighborhood.

"Suspect heading for the trees at the end of Connor Lane," she relayed through her microphone.

Continuing down the street, she was passing 118 Connor Lane when there was another flash of movement out of the corner of her eye. There he was, cutting back off the street,

"Stop! Police!" she ordered again with no response.

Giving chase, she again reached for her microphone.

"118." She stopped her broadcast when she found her suspect.

It was a white male. She could see his face in profile while he tried to stumble over a six-foot privacy fence. He was only twenty yards away. She stopped cold in her tracks and raised her gun,

"Don't move!" she yelled and almost choked as her voice quaked. She found herself shaking.

The suspect stopped for a moment and turned to look at her. They stared each other down for a moment. She could see him weighing his options. His eyes darted back toward the street,

"Get on the ground!" she ordered.

He looked at the ground, then at her, then at the street.

"On the ground now!"

He bolted, running for the street once more.

"Son of a bitch!" She gave chase, following him in between the houses.

As she rounded the corner, she saw him silhouetted in the early morning light and the flashing blue lights of the police cruiser blocking his path. Without looking back, he spun and retreated. Myra realized too late that she was moving too fast to stop. They collided.

The suspect swung at her wildly and missed. She ducked and kicked at him, pushing him off her more than doing any damage. He was in a crouch. The man had the look of a wild animal trapped in a corner. She stood between him and the potential freedom of open ground.

"Get on your knees!" she yelled but even to her it sounded more like a yelp than an order.

He looked her in the eye again, then his eyes flashed to the gun in her hand. She instinctively tightened on the grip and trained the front sight of her Glock model 21 on his heart,

"Get down!" she ordered one last time.

His hands slid out to his sides. His fists lengthened and his fingers spread. Slowly, he started lowering his body.

Then Beach, moving like a defensive end with an open lane to the quarterback, hit him with a full body block. The large cop rammed the suspect so hard the man flew three feet before banging off the vinyl siding of a pastel green home. He landed in a heap.

Beach stood and looked at her briefly before planting a knee in the suspect's spine and yanking his arms behind his back to be handcuffed. The kid—he seemed no more than eighteen or twenty, a white male with the ash-white look and pallor of a meth addict—started babbling that they had the wrong guy and that he was going to sue each and every one of them.

Myra watched with a sense of helplessness while Beach ratcheted the steel straps down on the suspects wrists and started to pat him down. She didn't notice Wayne coming up from the street until she saw Beach's stern facial features look past her. She turned to see the supervisor coming her way. He watched Beach retrieve a clear plastic bag with rocky flake and a broken off car antenna from the suspect's front pocket.

"Nice catch," Wayne said. "What made you start circling around here?"

"We've been getting hit with B&Es up this way, Sir. I just thought I would take a look."

"That's what I was hoping you were going to say," Wayne said.

He was older than Beach or Pluretti, into his forties or so as far as Myra could tell, and she sure wasn't going to ask her corporal his age. Beach and Pluretti were a couple of years older than her too. Made her feel like a kid playing around the adults more often than not.

She watched as Beach rolled the guy from his stomach to a seated position then support the suspect as he kicked his way to his feet. The kid was complaining about police abuse while Beach guided him passed Wayne. Wayne ignored the meth monster but she could see him share a look with Beach as they passed. She also detected a sigh of sorts from Beach.

When Wayne looked at her again, she could see the doubt in his eyes.

"Tell me what happened?"

"I was rolling the neighborhood just to see if there was any movement. We did have a bunch of break-ins here in the last month."

"And?"

"Something caught my eye. When I got turned around, I observed him fleeing from the residence across the field."

"And?"

Myra hesitated for a moment. "I gave chase, which ended here when Officer Beach cut off the man's access to the street."

"How'd you feel about going after a suspect one on one? Your first time right?"

Another pause. "I was fine."

He looked at her like he wanted to believe her.

"I pursued the suspect on foot. When I rounded the corner here, he was retreating from Officer Beach. We ran into each other then I began ordering him to the ground."

"Ultimately, it was Officer Beach that brought him down."

"Yes but I had him. He was complying."

"You didn't feel the need to go hands on to make the arrest?"

"I would have but his posture changed and he started complying."

She could feel heat rising in her neck, and her words were coming out faster. He didn't believe her.

Wayne nodded his head and looked at the ground for a moment.

"Well you did a good job. Good initiative following up on our hot spots. The L-T is going to be pleased. Write it up then get some sleep." He turned and started a casual stroll to his cruiser.

Myra was rooted in place as she watched him go. Her squad didn't trust her. She knew it but had held out some hope that Wayne was different. He thought she was scared just as Beach and Pluretti did. But she wasn't scared... was she?

***

Viejo adjusted the mosquito netting surrounding him and settled in as much as he could against the wide oak tree. He was nestled back twenty feet inside the tree line on a ridge overlooking the Old South Armory. He had a set of binoculars, two liters of water, and a bag of beef jerky to keep him company while he sat in the pre-morning darkness, listening to the sounds of the woods around him. As a Hispanic kid from the most inner of the inner city of New York, he found himself wishing he had traded spots with Wilke. Walking into the lion's den like Wilke did would be a hundred times better than sitting in some dark woods waiting for a bear or something to eat his ass. And Wilke was one of those granola eating hippies anyway, he would love this. Viejo preferred concrete to leaf litter under his feet any day. The idea of critters and things running through the woods all around him creeped him out.

"This blows," he muttered to himself, and to the bear that he just knew was sneaking up on him out of the darkness.

In the dark of night, Viejo's binoculars were all but useless. He hoped to God that he would not be there long enough to need them during the daylight.

The small manufacturing operation below him was lit relatively well with spotlights at the corners of the two buildings on the premises. The main building was a large single story square with a loading dock on one side. The second looked more like an office complex, small and squat, toward the front of the property and just inside the fence line, eight feet of chain link topped with barbed wire. He saw no sign of security or any movement on the site. There were plenty of cameras though. Viejo clicked his radio.

"No movement. I see cameras facing the front gate and doors at both buildings. It's too dark at the loading dock to see if there are any eyes there or not."

"What's our approach?" DeGuello asked.

"Come in from the tree line, best guess."

Viejo received a double click in his ear, noting that DeGuello had received the message.

Viejo scanned the building and the surrounding area for anything he may have missed until two shadows crept into the lower right portion of his vision. Though he knew not to watch Banks and DeGuello directly but to keep an eye out for threats in front and around them, the movement of the two men drew his attention, distracting him for the moment. He saw them crouching at the fence line and then Banks snipping the lower links until he and DeGuello could crawl through it.

Once they were moving on the other side of the fence, Viejo resumed scanning around the compound. It bothered him that he was limited in the darkness. Just being a firearms distributor meant that this place had some form of beefed up security, if not personnel then some security system Banks and DeGuello might or might not be able to beat. The more his mind ran with the possibilities and the odds against them in this scenario, the more nervous he got. Viejo concentrated on slowing his breathing and focusing on the building in front of his teammates.

"Gonna try this window," Banks whispered in his earpiece.

160

Viejo double clicked the microphone on his radio.

***

Banks was on point approaching the window. Staying out of the line of sight from the dark frame, he flattened himself against the concrete building and studied the frame. It was metal with two panes. The frame met in the middle where he could see a latch on the inside. He looked to DeGuello who was doing the same from the other side. DeGuello made a gesture of snipping wires and pointed toward Banks' side of the frame. There was a wiring system of some sort that DeGuello had spotted. Banks grimaced.

He hated security systems. Though one of the benefits of working dope meant that you were sent to learn things like lock picking or circumventing various types of security systems, that didn't mean you became an expert after three days or a week of training. It had been years since Banks or DeGuello had gone through the ins and outs of building security; much less had actually done it.

Banks took one last look around the frame and stepped in to face his obstacle. He retrieved a small set of tools from his back pocket. It was completely dark on the interior of the building. He didn't see any telltale red dots in the blackness that would give away a camera or motion detector. He studied the wiring DeGuello had spotted for a long moment. Banks leaned in as close as he could get without touching the glass trying to observe what he could about the security system.

He opened the small kit and retrieved what looked like a small spatula and a shim. Before attempting to circumvent the security, he shared a look with DeGuello. His longtime partner was not great at hiding what he was thinking. It wasn't so much as a frown on his face as it was a mix of a frown and a smirk.

Thanks for the vote of confidence. Banks grimaced.

Following the wires to where he thought they stopped, he delicately slid the flat head of the spatula between the upper and lower frames. He hoped, and if the training rang true, this was where the sensor was for the security system—two plates on opposing sides of the window frame that if separated improperly would set off the alarm. Once he had the spatula between the frames, he slowly slid the flat metal shim between the spatula and the frame. The shim was little more than aluminum foil. Once he had it between the tool and the window frame, he bent it under the frame and took a short length of duct tape from DeGuello. Securing the small piece of metal with the duct tape, he gently slid the spatula out of the space between the frames and took a deep breath.

His next move would determine whether they were going to commit first degree burglary this morning or run for the hills. Banks paused for a moment and shook out his hands. The stress of the operation was causing him to unconsciously strangle the small tool in his hand and his palm was cramping up. After a moment, he reached up with the small spatula again and slid it in between the panes, this time in the center of the window where the latch should be. The spatula slid through the panes and he moved it to the right until he met resistance. He stopped then and with as little pressure as possible, he pushed ever so slightly against the resistance until he heard a quiet click.

The sound surprised him; the sensation reminded him of years back when he was at the police academy. The firearms instructors preached the slow squeeze of the trigger. Just a slow squeeze, let it surprise you when the weapon fired. Banks had been dreadful with the gun during his time at the academy and had never forgotten the lessons he'd learned trying to pass weapons qualifying. He let out a long slow breath and looked again at DeGuello, who now appeared surprised, if not shocked that he'd managed to pull it off.

162

Banks got his fingers under the upper portion of the lower window frame and pushed. The window rose slowly and he was greeted by a cool breeze from the air conditioning unit. Even better than the A/C was the lack of flashing lights and blaring alarms.

"We're in," Banks reported through his radio to Viejo on watch.

He was greeted by two clicks of the microphone.

"Let's go commit a felony," he whispered to DeGuello before hopping through the open window.

***

The inside of the Old South Armory looked like every other machine shop Banks had ever seen. Workbenches and various metal working equipment was scattered throughout the large open space. The smell of various chemicals and lubricants spoke of a long history of work going on in the building.

"What are we looking for?" DeGuello asked.

"A: More of those rifles, B: paperwork and names connected to them."

"That shouldn't be hard." The sarcasm flowing from DeGuello was suffocating.

"I like your confidence," responded Banks.

The two spread out across the machine shop, searching the area for anything that could tie the company to the illegal rifle they had confiscated. Banks concentrated on finding an office or even a computer to look through. He carefully studied each door he came to for security sensors before opening them. He was lucky enough to find the breakroom, janitor's closet, and a bathroom before his ear bud squelched,

"Shit! Incoming!" hissed Viejo.

Banks and DeGuello met in the center of the machine shop. They half froze in fear of being caught.

They looked around for hiding places like a couple of cockroaches caught in the open when the lights come on.

Then the wide roll up door leading to the loading dock slowly started to rise.

"Shit," DeGuello hissed.

He dove around a workbench.

Banks watched the door rise higher and higher, stark white light from the lamps outside filling the growing gap between the door and the concrete. Finally, he backed away and slid into the janitor's closet. He held the doorknob in a death grip, keeping the door open just a fraction of an inch so he could watch the activity.

Voices filled the quiet expanse of the workspace. Two men.

"We gotta get this thing loaded and gone. They moved up the time frame."

To Banks, the speaker was no more than a silhouette in the darkness.

"What's the big freakin deal?" another male said as he hopped up from the loading dock.

Banks could not make out features but saw the man stretch and heard a yawn.

"The deal is they tell you to move, you move. Christ, come on."

Banks held his breath when he saw the two men walk directly past the workbench where DeGuello was hiding. The two walked directly past where he hid and somehow the big man was able to elude them.

He shifted as far as he could to watch from the tiny crack in the door as the two men walked past the open window without looking at it and stopped at the rear wall of the machine shop. The smaller of the two, the one who was not happy about being up at the early hour, tripped what looked like a light switch at the end of the room. There was a sharp clank of a heavy lock being thrown then a whir of a small electric motor. Slowly, the wall folded in on itself. In the darkness of the shop, it was hard to see what was behind the false wall.

You've got to be kidding me. Banks stared at the opening.

He looked over to where DeGuello was hiding and could see the top of his dark head just peeking up from the workbench. He could barely make out when DeGuello turned his head toward him. He might have gestured somehow but Banks couldn't tell. The two men could be heard speaking again, approaching the loading dock. DeGuello's head abruptly disappeared like a whack-a-mole.

Banks shifted his attention back to the direction of the voices and saw the shadows of the two men. They were returning to the loading dock. It appeared they each were pushing a large crate. It was too dark to see what they were pushing. A sudden clang was followed by a surprised yelp that made Banks flinch in the darkness.

"Son of a bitch!" one of the men shouted. "Goddamned rednecks!"

"What?" the other one asked.

"They keep moving their benches. I can't get through. When the crate hit the damn thing, it knocked over a dip cup. I got that shit all over my pants."

His partner started laughing.

"Not funny!"

"That's disgusting," the other one managed while scoffing.

The second man shoved the workbench out of the way of the crate he had up on a dolly and moved toward the dock. Banks followed him as he went shoving each workbench that was mounted on caster wheels out of the way. They clanged into the next row of equipment as he passed. Banks instinctively reached for his sidearm as he watched the man approaching DeGuello's hiding spot.

This is not happening, Banks told himself.

The guy was two benches away from DeGuello. Not losing steam, he shoved the bench out of his way. One away from DeGuello. Banks' unsnapped the safety strap on his holster.

What was he going to do, shoot these two? He was the one committing a first-degree felony by breaking into a place at night. What was worse was that he'd dragged his oldest friend along and now one of them was about to be discovered. These two were just doing their job for all he knew. The man reached the workbench where DeGuello was hiding and shoved it to the side. He strained for a moment before the workbench slowly slid out of the way,

"Goddamn." The guy strained harder. "Whatta they got an anvil in here?"

He cleared the crate.

The two of them passed DeGuello's hiding place and loaded their shipment onto the truck. Banks let out a slow breath, believing it was over then held it when the two returned past him.

"Come on," he heard one say. "We gotta be out of here before anyone starts showing for work."

"I know." The other one paused at a dispenser to retrieve a shop rag. "This is gross," he muttered.

His buddy cackled.

***

DeGuello was playing a hunch. He had managed to extricate himself from the tight under shelf of the bench as the two passed. He crept slowly around the workbench and studied the dock as well the truck beyond.

It is pretty dark. He risked a look toward the two men.

They had disappeared into the darkness of the workshop. He looked toward the janitor closet where Banks was hidden. He could see the door cracked but couldn't see him to communicate. The crates were in the far back of the trailer parked on the loading dock.

So close.

DeGuello took a tentative step toward the trailer when he heard the quiet whirring of the wall sliding back into place. Leaping back into the darkness he watched as the men pushed two more crates his way. This time he could actually get a look at them from his perch.

The crates were long molded plastic, like Pelican cases they held their own equipment in. What he thought was one large crate maybe five feet high, four across was actually a stack of four smaller crates each equal in length. DeGuello felt a twinge of excitement, a familiar one he knew well, the same he'd felt the first time he'd searched a car and found a gun. The feeling one got when that single piece of evidence showed that made the whole case. He'd been on the job almost twenty-five years and that excitement had never faded.

Out of habit, he started working out the details of the bust. These guys were pushing cases that looked plenty large enough to contain several of those Godawful rifles each, and they were walking right past him. In a second, they would be contained in that trailer. He and Banks would have them dead to rights. When he finally caught himself up with reality, he was confused.

In all his excitement, he'd forgotten that he was way off. He and Banks were committing burglary in the first degree. If they were to snatch these guys up, no matter what was in those crates, it would never make it to trial. Not to mention the fact that they were currently the faces circulating on the freshest BOLO (Be on the Look Out) forms the FBI had printed. Wanted for questioning in the death of Yao Pak, ATF Agent.

DeGuello held his breath as the two men pushed their respective crates past and loaded them into the trailer. He heard what sounded like straps and heavy ratchets being cinched while they secured their load. DeGuello felt his face flushing at the idea that he might be letting clear evidence of his and the rest of the team's innocence drive away. Another minute passed and he heard the door to the trailer shut with creak and a whine. The loading dock rolling door slid closed. He heard the truck rumble and drive off.

Damn it.

"Was that what I think it was?" Banks asked, appearing right beside him.

"Gonna feel like an asshole if our only evidence just drove away."

"You and me both. We gotta see what's behind that wall." Banks keyed his microphone. "Viejo, you have eyes on that truck?"

"Affirmative."

"Get me all the identifiers you can."

"Done," Viejo responded.

"Taught him everything he knows," said DeGuello,

"Poor guy," Banks retorted .

It was hard to see from their vantage point where exactly the two men triggered the false wall. They felt around in the general area until DeGuello finally tripped a light switch and the electric motor activated. He was surprised by the sudden activity and jumped back as if the switch had been electrified. In moments, the wall slid out of the way.

Banks watched with keen interest, the seams were almost invisible between the permanent and mobile walls. He had seen plenty of false compartments in vehicles before but never a false wall and hidden room. It was impressive.

Inside the room were more workbenches with assorted parts containers and some partially constructed weapons. Banks and DeGuello spread out, trying to find any evidence that would tell them the modified rifles came from there.

Toward the back of the room, Banks found an old metal desk and file cabinet. A boxy out of date computer sat on the top of the desk. When he flicked the mouse, the screen flashed. He sat down in the creaky old chair that strained to hold him and played a hunch. They weren't going to have much time to look through the place before the normal shift showed up. He just hoped taking time to get through the computer would pay off. When the screen flicked on, he was surprised to see that the computer wasn't lock or logged off. A basic Windows graphical user interface stared back at him. None of the icons on the screen leapt out at him so he clicked his way through to the computers main drive. He started searching through files looking at spreadsheets and Word documents. The data didn't mean anything to him. Flipping from folder to folder, he stopped when his eyes caught a file extension, .CAD.

What is it about that fuel? Banks stared at the screen for a long moment wondering why that extension had triggered his interest.

"All this shit looks alike," DeGuello hissed from across the room.

Banks didn't look away from the screen. "Try and grab a little bit of everything," he said. "Maybe there is some other way to match the pieces to the barrel we've got."

Banks heard the clanging of metal pieces hitting each other. That's when he got it. Cad, AutoCAD.

Shit.

He minimized everything he had up and went back to the home screen, where he found an icon with the caption AutoCAD. He clicked on the program and realized on first look he had no idea how the system worked. He only remembered the term CAD from a case he had a few years back where an architect had murdered his partner for stealing his design for a downtown building. The subject's partner had stolen the design and outbid his subject for a waterfront project. Banks remembered the designs had that

.cad extension and had been drafted on his subject's computer and then stolen by the victim. His subject had beaten in his former partner's head with a hammer for the betrayal and was currently serving twenty-five to life at Lieber State Correctional.

He double clicked the file and a diagram of various pieces and parts of a weapons system appeared.

"Incoming, Boss," Viejo said, startling Banks.

"How far?" DeGuello asked.

"Three minutes at best."

"Shit." DeGuello swept the parts on the bench in front of him into a backpack he had brought. He went for the switch for the false wall.

Banks yanked the cable out of the back of the computer and slung it under his arm like a football. He ran for the exit as the wall started sliding closed.

"Jesus," he said when the wall closed on him,

"Come on, you old bastard," DeGuello barked.

Banks pressed himself against the opposing wall and slid past the closing wall banging the case of the computer as he went. In the stillness of the empty shop, the collision sounded like a bomb going off

"Asshole." He tossed the computer to DeGuello who was already waiting outside the window.

DeGuello chuckled and ran for the underbrush behind the building.

Banks slid the window closed and saw a column of light shine through the building as someone entered through the front door. He ducked and scurried away from the building. Meeting DeGuello ten feet inside the tree line, the two crouched and waited to ensure they hadn't been seen. Holding post for five minutes, they watched two jacked up 4X4 pickups and a Hyundai rolled into the parking lot. The sun was growing in the sky as Old South Armory opened for business.

Chapter Twenty-Nine

Marlon Hansfield thought he must have died in his sleep. Never much of a believer and even less of a church going man, unless there was a power player there he wanted to get close to, he was perplexed. He found himself on the luxurious cruiser Niles Davidson had sent him off on for much needed rest and relaxation. After the events of the last couple of days, Hansfield now found himself pampered at every turn. The crew had run the boat through the smooth swells of the Atlantic Ocean, off the coast and into international waters. A blonde beauty named Biannca, the type of young fit work of living art, made her uniform of polo shirt and mid-thigh length shorts look like lingerie. She'd made him a stiff Manhattan when they left the marina and ensured his glass hadn't run dry since. Hansfield had only stopped drinking to eat five star dishes prepared by the staff chef or to partake in the potent strain of marijuana that Biannca expertly rolled for him at random intervals. The day had drawn to a close and he didn't remember how long into the night he'd made it sitting on the aft lounge watching the stars with Biannca before passing out.

When he woke it was daytime again, the sun shone through the curtains bathing his stateroom in a soft orange glow. Consciousness came to Marlon Hansfield in a slow ecstatic wave, a rhythmic dance around his pelvis that was at once intriguing and overwhelming to his clouded senses. Once he blinked the blur out of his eyes, he realized he must have died in his sleep and this was his reward. The young tight mate, Biannca, was straddling him. Her back to him, she gyrated on his steel hard cock, the tensing muscles of her back and shoulders dancing to her sporadic moaning. The curving apple shaped cheeks of her ass jiggled just

171

right and he found himself hypnotized. He reached out to make sure she was real. As his hands danced across and grasped her waist, she didn't even break stride.

"Good morning," she hissed.

"Uh-huh." He moaned.

He pulled her down harder onto his cock. She picked up the pace, grinding on him.

"Oh my God," he gasped, praying to hold out.

She sighed and a yelp of excitement escaped her.

The phone rang.

The shock to Marlon Hansfield's system was like a sudden splash of ice cold water across his soul. He leapt up just as he was about to finish.

"Hello?" she asked after grabbing her phone.

She looked at him, oblivious to the incredulous pain on his face.

"Uh-huh, understood. What about him?" she asked.

"What the hell?" Hansfield blurted.

Her eye slid toward him and she turned away. Her ass caught a sliver of light coming through the cabin window. He wanted to cry for her to come back.

"Okay," she said and ended the call.

She gathered a robe from where it was draped over a chair and covered herself, heading for the door.

"Where do you think you're going?" he asked, exasperated.

She cracked the door and looked back at him as if he were asking her directions to the library. She reached back and tossed him a towel from a shelf next to the door.

"Clean yourself up, sweetie," she said. "We gotta go."

And she was gone leaving him alone, confused and utterly crushed.

Twenty minutes later, Hansfield showed on the deck. He had showered and, sadly, finished himself off. Still feeling abandoned and unsatisfied, he didn't say a word as he passed the two male deck hands, heading for Biannca who was standing next to the starboard side rail. A twenty foot Boston Whaler was tied to the larger cruiser.

"After you," she said in that ever present cheerleader's tone that was now the equivalent of hearing a cat coughing up a hairball in the middle of the night.

He could barely look at her while he passed from one boat to the next. He looked out over the ocean and couldn't see the mainland in any direction. They had to be almost thirty miles off the coast. He'd been out in boats before and been able to see the Cooper River Bridge from almost twenty-five out. The water was bright blue out there and deep. He looked over the side and studied the abyss below him. He wondered how far down he could see before the light from the sun no longer penetrated the water.

"It's almost four hundred feet deep here," Biannca said.

He heard her leap into the boat behind him.

"Hmpf," Hansfield grumbled. He couldn't believe this girl had the gall to try and keep up a conversation as if nothing ever happened. After what she pulled? He heard her banging some gear around in the small boat.

"Can you give me a hand with this?" she asked.

Bitch.

Hansfield turned her way and put his hands out expecting her to hand him her bag or something. He felt a cold slap across his wrist and the ratcheting sound of a tightening handcuff.

"Huh?" he asked, looking up into those chipper blue eyes.

It was like the girl didn't have an off switch. She was a full-time pageant queen ready for the next question from the judges. Her eyes still sparkled as he looked from her to the handcuff then to the weight belt. It was attached to the other end of the handcuffs. The gleam never left her perfect blue eyes when she tossed the weight belt over the Boston Whaler's gunwale.

Hansfield couldn't understand. His brain was not fast enough to realize he should be screaming before the fifty-pound weight dragged him overboard in an uncoordinated flop. The weights pulled his light frame under with little challenge. His last image was of Biannca, blonde hair shimmering through the blue water, waving goodbye with just the tip of the fingers of her right hand.

By then, it was too late to scream.

Chapter Thirty

Ben Wilke tried to keep his calm while he pushed through the mass of police uniforms and scrambling medical staff crowding the emergency room of the Medical University of South Carolina. Vaden and Burgess were in tow when he rushed into the building. He saw officers looking at him. Some were scared. To a young cop, the job was an adventure, action, excitement, the whole bit. Not until they saw what could happen on the street to one of their own did the reality of the game they played start to sink in.

Some of the expressions were respectful but also contained an air of pity. Some expressions were of contempt, the look a cop gave a random stranger when they crossed under crime scene tape or stumbled onto an accident scene. There were a lot of newer cops on the street that didn't know Wilke or the rest of the Narcotics Unit. To them, he looked like some redneck barging through what was hallowed ground. A cop was fighting for his life behind a closed cloth curtain. Who did this guy think he was?

Wilke found Sargent Ferris, a friend of his from when the two worked patrol together. She had called it in. She and another car were first on the scene to what they had thought was a random early morning traffic accident. She recognized Thompson, still strapped in the front seat, and immediately put out a code 46 (Officer Down) over the radio. In the ensuing madness, she had rendered aid to Thompson as much as she could before handing him off to paramedics. She hadn't left his side, riding in the ambulance, planting herself outside the curtain when the doctors pushed her away from his bedside. Wilke noticed dark splotches on her uniform and heavy red stains on the cuffs of her sleeves. Her hands were discolored in a shade of rust from where she tried to clean Thompson's blood off them. The sight of his friend's blood covering another cop sent lightning through the deep primal predatory part of his brain.

"What happened?" he asked.

Ferris started to speak then noticed Vaden come up behind him.

"Sir," she snapped, instinctively straightening to attention, "We got a call for a T/A. When we rolled up, we found Thompson still strapped to the driver's seat. He was unresponsive. Looks like three rounds in his chest. Still had a pulse when we transported. They're working on him now."

She was trying to keep her voice calm and professional so as not to excite the crowd of uniforms, and some in plain clothes surrounding them. The emergency room was a madhouse. No matter what time day or night, if a cop was injured or worse, other cops flooded the hospital. Even if they were off duty and the only thing they could do was give blood or be there to support the family. Cops came out of the woodwork when one of their own was struck down.

Wilke tried to process what he was hearing. Staring at the curtain, he couldn't believe it. Not Thompson. Where was Poppy?

"There were rounds all over that car, Sir."

He heard Ferris reporting to Vaden.

"Expended brass, impacts in the rear and sides of the vehicle."

"Where's Poppy?" Wilke interrupted.

"Who?" asked Ferris.

***

Poppy had a ringing in her ears. It was the first sound she could identify when she came to. Her eyes were scratchy and blurry when she finally opened them and

176

realized she was in an empty room alone with Andrew Tulley Jr. He was sitting in a corner on the floor holding his head. Her arms and ankles were bound to a chair and her mouth was dry and coarse. Her first instinct was fear— overwhelming, paralyzing fear. She took a couple of deep breaths, which caused a sharp stabbing pain in her ribs. Breathing was also made difficult by the way her arms were pulled and tied behind her. The breathing calmed her despite the pain.

Fear and panic don't help, she told herself. The feelings were a reaction not a solution.

As far as she could tell, she wasn't injured to the point of immobilization. She wiggled her fingers and her toes to get the blood flowing under the tight confines of her restraints. She figured she maybe had a concussion and a cracked rib or two. That wasn't enough to keep her from getting out of wherever she was. The room was so plain that it would make beige paint bored. The off white tile floor barely contrasted with the off-white walls. There were no bearings to get—no sounds outside of the ringing in her ears. She turned her attention to Tulley.

He was slouched in the corner. His head hung low in his palms and his fingers were buried in the messy curls of his brown hair. He didn't seem to be any worse off than she was, maybe a little banged up but nothing visible. She hoped he was feeling all the booze he'd been shoveling past his lips prior to... what? She couldn't remember how she got there. She remembered they were in the car being chased then it seemed the whole world had decided to flip on them.

Where is Thompson?

Another conflagration of fear threatened to take over. She swallowed it down.

Wherever he was, he isn't trapped in here tied to a chair, she told herself, *at least that was something good.*

She realized she was still staring at Tulley when he looked up at her. He appeared beat at first then he must have realized she was awake. He shifted his position to look at her and grinned.

"Not feeling like such the badass now. Are ya, sweetheart?" he chided.

She didn't answer. She watched him while testing the restraints pinning her to the back of the chair.

"Not quite so talkative anymore." He rose to his feet. "Don't bother with those ropes. These guys are pros. You're not going anywhere."

She tried squeezing her palms together to get some slack. When that didn't work, she attempted to release the tension in one hand and pull against the ties. Whatever they had done back there just seemed to tighten the knots the more she struggled. She felt her limbs starting to tremble and swore at herself to keep it together.

Tulley was halted in his approach when a voice was heard from outside. She watched his expression change from cocky to cautious.

"I understand, Sir," the voice said, "The situation is very close to being resolved. The shipment will be on its way no later than this afternoon." There was a pause. "Yes, Sir, I agree. I have identified several opportunities to revise the current process and maximize our efficiency. This will not happen again. You can assure the gentleman that the delivery will suffer no further delay." Another pause. "Yes, Sir, thank you."

The door opened and in walked a man in a crisp, tailored suit, with razor sharp edges. He placed his phone in his breast pocket and shut the door. When the door closed, he spun on his heel and studied both her and Andrew Tulley.

The new arrival was relatively good looking in a pristine sort of way. He looked as if he shaved with a laser and there was not a hair out of place where it rested close to his scalp. He wore wire-rimmed glasses that seemed to shine as much as the rest of him did. She guessed he was maybe mid-thirties give or take. His features were sharp and his expression was alert and unemotional.

The moment stretched and she could see Tulley suffering under the silence. He was nervous, scared of this man who looked to Poppy like a bank president.

"Mr. Davidson," Tulley blurted.

Closing the distance between the two, he extended his hand. Davidson looked to Tulley's hand then to his eyes but did not return the gesture.

"Thank you, Sir," Tulley said looking to Poppy.

Davidson continued to stare at Tulley. The quiet killed him; Poppy could see it. Tulley apparently had no further interest in engaging the man he was so afraid of so turned back to her. He took two heavy strides toward her but wouldn't look her in the eye.

"See what you get bitch!" he shouted. "Now you'll see who..."

Davidson closed the gap between him and Tulley with the quickness, agility, and grace of a Golden Gloves boxer. He kicked out Tulley's feet with a fluid sweep and stayed close on him when the young man fell. Tulley could not have registered the impact with the tile floor before Davidson started delivering an onslaught of blows to his face—one after the other in a staccato barrage of fists. When Tulley tried to curl into a ball and put his arms up to defend his face, Davidson would adjust target to his ribs and beat on him until his hands dropped, and he would return to his face. The assault was relentless until Tulley went limp on the tile. Poppy watched the beating with a surreal and distant feeling. Davidson was so precise in his movements, so vicious, but his expression never changed. His breathing never increased. He never made a sound. He delivered one of the most merciless beatings upon another human being she had ever seen. And he did it with all the passion you would expect from a librarian stacking a shelf.

When he was finished, he stood straight and adjusted his tie. Davidson turned toward her. Before turning his attention away from his attire, he froze. His pearl white, heavily starched shirt was splattered with blood. Only a couple of flecks, Poppy could barely see them. He examined them with the attention of a mineralist inspecting the quality of a diamond. He finally looked up at her.

"I apologize, Ms. Montague," he said flatly. "I fear that unfortunate event has negatively affected my appearance and I have a meeting scheduled a short while from now. Please excuse me."

With that, he turned on his heel and exited the room, leaving her perplexed. Tulley moaned pitifully with a slimy drool of bloody spittle dripping from the corner of his bloodied mouth.

Poppy was having trouble keeping calm now. She watched Tulley moaning on the floor for what seemed the blink of an eye before the door again opened quickly and in walked Davidson. His suit was new though just as crisp and gleaming as the prior one had been. He was trailed by two men wearing khaki pants and polo shirts. They lifted Tulley's limp form and dragged him out of the room. Davidson watched them go. When the door closed, he turned to face her.

"I apologize for the incident earlier, Ms. Montague. There are some things one must tolerate in business and some things one cannot tolerate from one's associates. Mr. Tulley's behavior as of late has grown... intolerable," he said.

Poppy stared into his eyes but did not respond.

Davidson studied her for a moment in a detached, clinical way. "Now, I'm sure you have an idea of why you are here. I am hoping we can come to a quick resolution.

You and your colleagues have become involved in a very sensitive project that I oversee. It was an oversight by a particular member of my team that brought about your involvement, however that is neither here nor there. You see, I and the people I represent, put a very high value on security and the quiet nature of the project. I am sure you understand and have the same appreciation when it comes to your investigations. You wouldn't want sensitive details related to an active case to be leaked would you?"

Poppy shook her head slowly. "I would not."

"Yes, of course not. See where our dilemma comes in is that the information you and your colleagues have gained is a major breach of our protocols. Specifically, the item you seized from Antwan Tate's residence. We have reacquired the majority of the material, however we are missing a very sensitive item—the barrel of a specific rifle. I need to reclaim that piece of property in order to ensure the safety of the project."

"You're the one who killed Agent Pak. Tried to kill my friends," she stated.

"Well not me personally, no. I employ specialists for that kind of work."

"Regardless," Poppy said. "You're under arrest as an accessory to the murder of a police officer."

The statement half surprised her. She was no longer frightened of the man. She wanted to kill him.

If Davidson was surprised by her statement, it didn't register. He did pause for a moment to study her further in that stoic style of his. She wondered if she had ever come to hate a person so fast in her life. She imagined that being held against her will probably nurtured her rage.

After a long moment he spoke. "I need you to tell me where your Lt. Banks is. You and your colleagues have gotten involved in something you have no business in."

Poppy scoffed. "Untie me and we can talk."

Davidson checked his watch, "Ms. Montague, I would really rather keep this transaction civil, however, I am on a tight time schedule. Tell me where your fellow officers are. Tell me where the rifle barrel I require is."

The fear was like a smoldering campfire just below her consciousness. Poppy felt it like a tendril of fire licking up out of the ashes. She swallowed.

"No."

Davidson sighed then turned on his heel and walked out of the room.

Poppy watched him leave. That smoldering fire in her gut was gaining in strength. She fought to control her breathing while squirming against her restraints. She thought she felt a little give around her right ankle. When Davidson returned he was again followed by one of the polo shirts who carried a chair similar to the one she sat in. She froze when she saw a black box Davidson held in his hands.

He carried the item like it was a cigar box and he was going to flip the lid at any minute to offer her one. The polo shirt dropped the chair in front of her and Davidson waited next to it while the guard left. Once the door closed, he sat down facing her and rested the box on his knees. She tried to keep her eyes on him and not the box but she couldn't help herself when her gaze continued to drift back to the object. He looked down at the box.

"Ms. Montague, please understand I do not want to take this step. Before I open this box, I implore you to give me the information I need."

Poppy fixed him with a stare that she hoped hid her fear. At that moment, she was more scared than she had been in her entire life. She did not respond to him.

"I understand," he said quietly then flipped the latch on the box.

He kept the box in full view while he worked. Under the lid was a series of vials and syringes lined around a small square box with a row of light emitting diodes (LED) lining one side.

From a slot in the foam lining of the box, he produced an alcohol swab and a small finger stick device. Poppy wanted to jump out of her skin if only to free herself to kill this man with her bare hands. She squirmed in her restraints when Davidson leaned over and sanitized a patch of her forearm with the alcohol. Following the cool sensation of the alcohol swab, he pressed the sticker to her skin and she heard the plastic click and felt a pinch. Placing the swab and stick on the floor next to him, he retrieved a narrow tube from the box and she watched as he placed it against the blood bulging from her forearm. He only retrieved a small droplet. She kept her eyes fixed on the small tube while he returned his attention to the box. He positioned the small tube with her blood into a socket in the cube in the center of the box. After a moment, the first LED in the row across the cube glowed green.

"This is a fascinating system, Ms. Montague. My organization over time has come to refine the science of elicitation to the point of perfection. Years of experience and a library of scientific research have shown again and again that the greatest impediment to an interrogation of any sort is motivation. What is that key piece of information? That essential knowledge needed to cause a person to provide their interrogator with information they would otherwise never disclose. As you know well, the methods of elicitation have varied over time, everything from hacking off body parts, using loved ones as leverage, even the current preferred method of utilizing water to simulate drowning. All of these forms can work in one way or another with varying degrees of effectiveness."

Davidson paused a moment and patted the cube gently. Poppy noticed the second LED now glowed green.

"Now this... this streamlines the process of identifying that motivation. It saves one time. Whereas we once had to research or experiment with various forms of interrogation in order to find that one weakness hidden by our adversary, this device takes all that away."

Poppy noticed the third of five LEDs had turned green.

"The tiny amount of blood taken from you is analyzed by the device. The analysis will study your DNA, blood factors, etcetera, I am not fully versed on the biochemistry involved. In simple terms, what the device does is identify the most effective chemical correspondent to your genetic makeup and creates that solution on demand."

Even under duress, Poppy had a hard time following that. Davidson seemed to notice.

"This will create a solution customized to your biochemistry to create the optimum motivation for you to provide the information I need. I would prefer however not to resort to this. I ask you once more, Ms. Montague. Where are your colleagues?"

Poppy took a steadying breath. She had to keep her voice steady.

"Say I tell you what you want to know. I walk out that door?"

Davidson did not respond. He looked on her with a form of... pity maybe? Poppy couldn't be sure but it infuriated her.

"You're gonna kill me anyway. I'm not telling you shit," she said.

Davidson sighed and looked to the device, as the final LED turned green.

"Before we start, Ms. Montague, please consider this. Sometimes it is not how long we live but the comfort or lack thereof in which we die that really matters."

A vial of clear fluid slid from the side of the cube.

"Let us begin," said Davidson.

He filled the syringe with a dose of the clear fluid. There was only enough for three doses in the vial. The organization had found in Iraq and Afghanistan that if a subject were to require over three doses, the survival rate dropped to less than five percent. Something having to do with the synapses in the brain losing cohesion. The brain would still function though the synapses would fire randomly, no longer connecting with corresponding nerve endings. The brain's electrical communications system turned to static as one neurologist put it. Kind of like corrupting a hard drive, the data was still there just inaccessible.

***

Davidson held the syringe up before his subject. She was scared but tough. He respected that. This was a far cry from some mountain hole in a country no one cared about. This was different; this was the simplest of operations requiring nothing more than common sense to succeed.

Yet here he was administering a dose of the lethal customized chemistry to a police officer. They were by all rights on the same side. He'd administered the dose to five subjects since the treatment went into the field. Three had broken after the first dose. One required the use of the second dose. And one had gone all the way.

The first three had survived relatively unscathed and provided him the information he needed. The fourth was non-responsive last he saw him, the man had been laying in a pool of his own bodily fluids. The last had died badly. Davidson remembered seeing the moment his subject's body gave up, when the brain faded to static. It was in the eyes. Not only was there a vacancy to them but they seemed to drift out of sync, one sliding up and one down and to the left. He remembered it being very unsettling.

He hoped for the officer's sake, it did not come to that. Unlike the majority of his subjects, she had done nothing wrong.

Davidson sank the syringe into her arm and depressed the plunger. The effect was almost instantaneous. Poppy Montague shrieked; it was the animalistic scream of a person whose rational mind had been overcome by the most basic of human sensations… pain.

Her entire body shook, arms tensed and feet pointed toward the ground, spasming as each muscle fiber attempted to flee the agony, only to struggle against the nylon ropes she had been bound with. Davidson saw the muscles and veins on her neck bulge under the strain and her back arched while she shook. He hoped she would see the light.

After an exact thirty seconds, her body shrank in on itself, head and shoulders drooping against the restraints binding her to the chair. She heaved deep, tired breaths. A dribble of spit slid out from her lips. Her shoulder length hair now fell over her face.

When she looked up at him, he sighed. There was no acquiescence in her eyes. Her hair hung over her face and her eyes seemed to blaze in the shadow. She had the look of a feral animal. Before he could ask her a question, she interrupted him.

"Was that it?" she hissed, "A lot of hype, asshole."

"That was the first dose," he explained. "Designed to stimulate nerve endings throughout your body for a brief moment to cause a large degree of pain while not causing any permanent damage."

He paused, to let the importance of his words sink into her brain.

"How do you feel?"

"A little tingly," she said.

"Will you tell me what I want to know?"

When the girl grinned, she surprised him. He had performed this treatment on battlefield-hardened men in some of the grimmest places on earth and a couple them had soiled themselves after the first dose. He found himself both impressed and intrigued while he filled the syringe again with the prescribed amount. While it was true part of him had no interest in harming this woman, she would in no way be the reason his operation failed. There was no room at the executive level for a case officer who could not complete a simple domestic operation. All his past exploits, all he'd worked for be damned if this were to fall apart. He could not allow that.

He approached with the second dose.

Her lips crinkled and she squirmed against her restraints. She mouthed the word "no" when he grabbed her forearm and again set nerves firing all across her body.

He stood back and watched while her head turned toward the blank ceiling above as if beseeching whatever higher power might make the pain stop. Her mouth wide in a silent scream as there was no breath in her to make sound. He could see her ribs pushing against the fabric of her tank top and the sinew in her shoulders looked as if they would snap. She strained so hard against the pain, trying to pull away. Her bound arms stretched to a nearly impossible angle for her shoulders to bear.

When it stopped, she went still. He waited. The moment stretched and he began to wonder. After a minute passed and there was no movement, he reached under her sweaty mop of hair to feel for a pulse against her neck. He didn't notice a hint of movement until he felt teeth catch the gap in the second knuckles of his index and middle fingers. She bit down. Before he could fight her, she shook her head furiously back and forth.

"No!" He howled, pulling away.

He felt a pop and a tear, then release. He reeled back cupping his right hand. Davidson looked at his mangled fingers.

Maybe she ran out of steam, maybe he was able to free himself on his own merit. Regardless, she had managed to use her only weapon against him. He looked at his fingers. The index was the worst of the two. The knuckle she had bitten into was completely destroyed. The digit was not amputated fully, but it only hung from the remainder of his finger by a bulbous chunk of flesh. His middle finger was severely damaged on the outside of the knuckle and he could see bone, white against the blood that ran from his hand in a steady flow.

"Bitch!" he yelled, feeling his temperature rise when she looked back at him ginning and licking at the blood dribbling from her mouth.

She loosed a tired chuckle. "Tastes like chicken."

Davidson charged at her in a white rage but was able to catch himself at the last instant. She was watching him while he gathered himself back up and it embarrassed him.

Control was his greatest asset. Calm and clear under even the most difficult of situations was how Niles Davidson had trained himself to be. It was a practice he learned from watching and learning from the terrible lack of control his family showed under even the simplest of situations. Lack of personal control had cost his family and himself everything at one point in his life. He had worked and sacrificed all to gain the position he had come to enjoy. He would not be undone by this animal or his own lack of self-control.

Holding his damaged hand away from his clothing, so as not to cause another change before his meeting with the senior Tulley, Davidson straightened his tie and adjusted the wire rims of his glasses. He was able to fasten a single button on his suit coat with his left hand. His right hand throbbed an angry hot pain with each heartbeat. He focused on the sensation; it helped him clear his head. He cleared his throat just a little and straightened in front of her.

"I imagine that felt good, Ms. Montague," he said.

He could see a lack of confidence in her eyes. Fear simmered just under the surface.

"It's the little things," she whispered.

"Yes, I understand you have to use the assets at your disposal. However, this incident has not changed your position in any way. I will offer you this though. Tell me where your unit is and I will spare you the third dose. In my experience, the third dose tends to have rather permanent side effects."

To her credit, Poppy Montague was able to smile once more at him. "Hasn't this been a permanent sort of situation all along?"

He smiled slightly offering a simple nod.

"Have at it." She sighed.

Chapter Thirty-One

No one spoke when DeGuello took the off ramp from I-26 toward Huger, South Carolina. A Love's truck stop seemed to grow out of nothing but fields and brush. The angular buildings and wash bays stood in unflattering contrast to the rest of the surrounding rural landscape. Pulling around back, Banks, DeGuello, and Viejo kept an eye out for a setup, looking for cars that didn't belong or were sitting off by themselves, maybe with one too many antennas to be just some good old boy or tourist passing through. When DeGuello piloted the vehicle behind the store in a round sweeping arch, Wilke, Vaden, and another man could be seen leaning against a black Chevrolet Suburban. Banks felt his chest tighten while he studied his fellow officers. One was his, the youngest member of his unit. A kid he'd plucked out of uniform patrol. It was the way Ben Wilke could talk to people on the street that drew his attention.

They were in the middle of a round up. The unit had spent three weeks doing low-level street buys at various hot spots around the city. They had let the warrants stack up until they had about thirty bodies to arrest. The mayor and the chief liked a good show of force every now and then, usually right before summer arrived. The hot low country summers always seemed to bring violence with the rise in temperatures. It became sort of tradition to do a big operation in late spring.

During this particular round up, Banks and DeGuello were on the East Side out on foot with a number of officers, including Ben Wilke. Walking down the street in their tactical gear and stopping at various houses to query residence or arrest suspects with known addresses. They would lock up those on the list and put them in a paddy wagon that trailed them. Wilke was out in front of the group by about fifty yards when a well-known crack dealer named Charles Middiean rounded the corner. Banks and DeGuello spotted their quarry at the same time and prepared themselves. Nesmith was infamous for running on them, be it in a car or on foot. Arresting the career criminal was something of an adventure every time he came into contact with law enforcement. Nesmith looked up and they locked eyes. The crack dealer froze in place, tense, as if deciding on which yard to dash into.

"Charlie!" Wilke called out.

Middiean turned and his eyes fell.

"We've got paper on you, man," Wilke said, approaching him.

"Nah, come on, Wilke, not me."

Wilke walked up to the man and the two shook hands.

"Yeah man, they got you on film. pal," he said.

"Shit," was all Middiean said in protest before he allowed Wilke to cuff him.

DeGuello and Banks watched the action take place. A rookie acting with the rapport of a thirty-year veteran. Banks saw the talent immediately and had him transferred to his unit within a week.

As they approached in the car, Banks did not see the usually casual and sarcastic young detective. He saw a man on the edge between rage and collapse. He knew that he had put the young officer through the ringer, sending him into headquarters the way he did. Wilke was one of the fastest people mentally that he had ever met. He'd doubted the kid would have any trouble talking circles around Vaden. He hadn't expected Wilke to be the point man for the phone call he'd received an hour and a half earlier. Wilke was a young cop. He hadn't seen what the job was truly capable of doing to a person. Not up close the way he had when he arrived at the hospital. Seeing one of your own go down in the line of duty has an effect on a cop the first time they see it. The reality that they aren't just playing cops and robber or cowboys and Indians hits them like a Peterbilt. Add on to that the fact that Poppy was MIA, and Banks was truly unsure if Wilke would be able to keep going. Banks wasn't supposed to know about the two of them, but everyone knew; he just never let on. Maybe he should have put a stop to it back when DeGuello first told him.

The car stopped and the three cops exited the vehicle. Viejo and Wilke immediately shook hands and Banks could hear Viejo asking for an update. DeGuello and Banks studied Vaden and the unidentified cop Banks suspected of being a fed of some kind.

The guy looks hard. Banks was looking at him the way he himself stared down criminals on the street. He felt heat rising on the back of his neck.

"Who's this?" he asked.

"Special Agent Tom Burgess, SLED," Vaden said.

"Any word on Thompson or Poppy?"

Wilke spoke before Vaden had a chance.

"Thompson is in an induced coma. He made it through surgery to remove the rounds okay but they are keeping him under until they can repair his internal damage." Wilke's voice trailed off.

Banks turned to Vaden, "Where's Poppy?"

"Everybody is working on that from state, local, and federal. We'll find her."

"The feds want to put us away," Banks stated.

"All the feds except the bureau," Vaden corrected. "We're working another angle. On the bureau."

Banks turned to Burgess. "Your people got eyes on that truck?"

Burgess nodded without dropping the hard exterior. "My people have it. You sure this is what you say?"

"As sure as I can be," answered Banks. "What now?"

"I've got people tracking the owner of Old South Armory, guy named Brigston. Trying to find a link between him and Congressman Tulley. Waiting on a call."

"Always," Banks grumbled, "We still wanted or what?"

Vaden sighed. "Technically, yes, you and your team are, but..."

"But what? Kind of tough to be kind of on a wanted poster. Sort of like 'kind' of having freakin AIDS," Deguello interrupted.

Vaden put his hands up. "The bureau is still circulating the BOLO. There's no paper on you though. We're going to sort this thing out, then we'll see where we stand."

"Easy for the guy not looking at a jail cell to say," DeGuello quipped.

"It's what we got," Vaden said.

"Best I can offer. You know that was a good move despite what is going on," Burgess interjected.

"What?" said Banks.

"The armory, going on the offensive instead of just going to ground. Threw everybody for a loop."

"Beats sitting around being hunted by your own," DeGuello added.

"Technically, that good move was first degree burglary," Banks said.

"Yeah, we'll handle that if this works out. I do have a question though. Why drop the kid in the meat grinder? He just walked into the station."

"Had to know what was going on," Banks responded.

"I wasn't fooled," said Burgess.

"Sure you weren't," Wilkes said, he and Viejo stepping into the conversation.

Chapter Thirty-Two

She was trembling and her breathing was ragged but her eyes, though tired, were firm. She watched him while he prepared the third dose.

Davidson couldn't help but appreciate her strength and above that her loyalty. She didn't deserve this, he reminded himself, however she was not the priority. Not to mention she had bitten clean through his fingers. Instinctively, he wanted to beat her to death with his bare hands but his rational mind thus far had managed to keep him on point. His focus was getting the final batch of product into international waters and clearing out of this bug infested swamp. How much could he blame her for taking her one shot at him and making it count. Part of him admired her for that.

He manipulated the plunger to ensure he had the proper dosage, an operation made almost unbearable given the burning numbness radiating through his hand. He had to prop the vial just so between his arm and chest in order to manage getting the fluid into the vial. He held the needle in front of her one final time.

"Please, Ms. Montague. I promise it doesn't have to be this way."

Her eyes were burning with an impressive maelstrom of what he estimated were equal parts of hate, fear, and regret. He often wondered what his subjects had thought about in their final moments. Those closest to them? Words left unsaid? She managed to shake her head weakly then straightened against her restraints and looked him in the eye. She struggled and a strangled whimper escaped her brave façade when he plunged the needle into her arm.

She screamed again, only this time there was a feral aspect to the cry. As if all the rage and fear accumulated over a lifetime were blasting through her lungs. Davidson watched patiently when the tremors started. Her body had gone rigid as the serum took hold. When she screamed, she had looked like a tortured statute, completely still but for the bulging veins in her neck.

He watched for the tremors that always began in the extremities. He wondered if it was a byproduct of the brain drawing in on itself as body systems do during hypothermia, or if the signs were just a consequence of the brain losing electrical cohesion. One of their researchers in Afghanistan had tried to explain a theory on the symptoms once but he had a hard time wrapping his head around the devastation this procedure could cause without bringing on death.

The tremors turned to outright shaking similar to the convulsions during an epileptic incident. Her legs and arms fought against her restraints, and her spine stiffened and shook as the muscles governing her body struggled without direction. When her eyes let go of their spark, Davidson felt a tinge of pity for the girl. Whereas most of his subjects were true enemies or at the least foreigners, she was an officer of the law simply doing her job.

The clinical fascination that the transformation always brought on was still there, however, with Poppy Montague, he would have preferred giving her the dignity of a clean death over what was soon to be left of such a strong and vibrant woman. Her eyes lost focus and her head sagged toward her chest. A string of drool soon followed. Her eyelids fluttered here and there, as the convulsions slowed to a subdued tremor that would be the only future Officer Poppy Montague would know.

Her eyes stared listless and devoid of consciousness at the floor beneath her. Davidson knew it was over.

Eerily similar to wiping the hard drive on a computer. He studied her.

She refused to be broken. Davidson respected that despite the ongoing trouble her refusal to comply presented.

***

Brigston was waiting for him when Davidson exited the room, leaving Poppy Montague strapped to a chair drooling on herself. He pulled a cloth from the breast pocket of his suit and wrapped his hands.

"That was unfortunate," he said.

Brigston sounded surprised. "She didn't break?"

Davidson ignored the ignorant question and drew in closer on his colleague. Niles Davidson and Davis Brigston, or at least the men known as Davidson and Brigston, no one affiliated with the organization used their true names, met for the first time in Baghdad, Iraq during the invasion. Niles was running an operation aimed at identifying potential political leaders in the chaotic aftermath of Saddam Hussein's rule. Leadership had determined their chosen replacement for Hussein would be more likely to be accepted by the population if those that held sway over public opinion were not given a chance to voice their opinions positive or negative. Brigston was a team leader running the paramilitary segment of the operation. He and his team were to extract and dispose of those Davidson chose to target.

Those anarchic days in Iraq allowed some feats of planning and daring that Davidson prided himself in pulling off. The operation in Iraq had led to similar operations in Afghanistan, Yemen, and other locations before he was ordered home to take over as lead officer for the current project. Through all those operations, Davidson had requested and been granted Brigston. Brigston was a standout as far as running a tactical component was concerned. His operations were crisp, quiet, and never without a hiccup… until now. Davidson fully put the bulk of the troubles with the operation on the Tulleys.

Congressman Tulley was a narcissistic pig solely focused on the bottom line and how much of that made it into his pocket. That kind of man was easy to deal with. The problem with the Tulleys was the sudden insertion of Andrew Tulley Jr. Congressman Tulley held enough sway with the leadership to leverage his wishes despite the protestations of Davidson. Tulley Jr. was arrogant, a drug abuser, and had demonstrated no ability to think critically or strategically when Davidson's people vetted him on their annual personnel surveys. The man was a juvenile who had never had to function on his own in his entire life. Yet, somehow, his superiors granted him special access and an active operational role in one of the most sensitive operations Davidson himself had ever been a part of much less in the lead. Instinctively, he studied his scuffed and bloodied knuckles while the thought of Andrew Tulley Jr. floated through his head.

The Tulleys were at fault for a large majority of his current operational setbacks. However, there had been actions by Brigston and his men of late that had provided cause for concern. Davidson trusted Brigston with his life, and had on several occasions, literally put his future in Brigston's hands. There was no one more he would trust with sensitivities such as they currently were working. As he stepped in to look Brigston in the eye, he spoke with a low, even voice.

"That girl is dead because your team did not do the job when they had the opportunity."

"Yes, Sir," Brigston stated, straightening.

"You hid the fact the most sensitive part of the entire weapon, the weapon that is not meant for public knowledge, the weapon that does not exist, has been in the hands of local law enforcement for the last two days."

"Yes, Sir."

"I don't want to hear how or why, or what you are going to do to rectify this situation. Until now, we have shared a mutually beneficial professional relationship. This happens again and that relationship becomes null and void. Is that understood?" Davidson could see the meaning of his words raking across the mercenary's soul.

"Yes, Sir."

"Good. I want to plan for contingencies. I want Dierks covering me during this meet. I want that shipment crossing the Atlantic by sunset, and I want this place sterilized. We might be changing venues after recent events."

"Yes, Sir," Brigston said though the man looked at him like a four-year-old waiting to speak by holding his hand up to the teacher.

"What else?" Davidson asked.

"The congressman is here. He's with his son."

Davidson grimaced and smoothed out his jacket.

***

Tulley was red faced. He paced back and forth in front of the sofa where his son lay, holding an ice pack to his face. Davidson entered the room, and slowly and casually walked toward the congressman. When Tulley saw him, he charged forward,

"Are you out of you mind, you son of a bitch?"

Davidson did not flinch when the heavyset old man huffed in his face. Tulley's eyes burned like a madman though Davidson knew he would not raise his hand. The lack of reaction on Davidson's part further fanned Tulley's fire but still he would not attack him.

"I will have your head for this, you motherfucker!" Tulley pointed at his bruised and battered son.

"You will do nothing of the sort," Davidson said, sidestepping the old man and surveying the work he had done on Andrew Tulley Jr. "Your son has been responsible for the continuing downward spiral of this enterprise.

Normally, the punishment for such failure is exponentially more severe." He paused and flashed his eyes at Brigston. Through the brief exchange, Davidson was sure that his colleague had received the message, "You know this."

"This is unacceptable!" Tulley raged, circling the room.

"I agree, Congressman, this has become unacceptable. First, you disregard my chain of command within this operation and go above me to get your son a role. You want to get him involved, show him how the world really works. Excellent. Your son is given the task of finding a fresh outlet for our shipments to West Africa. Who does he put forward but the drug abusing owner of a strip club."

"You killed Fitz?" was the weak mumbled question from under the ice pack.

"Didn't have to, Andrew. The other animals in the zoo did it for us. Though, despite the horrid lapse in judgement shown by your son, I am again countermanded and he is given another opportunity to show his worth with the recruitment of Antwan Tate. A man who also doubles as your partner in crime selling pills of all things. Greed and immaturity bring the police to our doorstep. You had one of the samples at the very house where you were arrested." Davidson delivered his diatribe smoothly, like a physics professor explaining Schrodinger's cat.

A weak hiccup belayed Tulley Jr.'s burgeoning excuse but Davidson has no time for it.

"Since then, we have had to show ourselves more than we ever have while operating in this environment. We have had contact with local authorities and suffered casualties. This is unacceptable," He pointed at Tulley Jr. "If I ever see this man again, I will put a bullet in his head."

Tulley Sr. started blustering, trying to get his words together. It occurred to Davidson while he waited patiently that it had probably been a long time if ever that this doughy fool had ever had someone threaten him or a member of his own family. He chose not to wait for the supposed orator to get his act together. He retrieved his cell phone from his breast pocket and with a swipe, navigated to a particular file. He held the phone to Tulley's eyes. The man froze. All the rage and redness in his face drained, and his face paled.

"That girl is fifteen years old. Just about out of your range as I understand it." Davidson deactivated the screen and replaced the phone in his pocket with smooth grace. "I have archives going back two years. If I am ever queried on what has happened here, every news outlet in the country will receive my files, even the outlets we don't control. You should be more careful when a billionaire invites you to a private island he calls The Playground."

Tulley was swaying just so on his feet. The man's shoulders slumped. He stared at the ground.

Davidson let the quiet build in the room until he finally said, "I see we understand each other. What is the ETA on our truck?"

Chapter Thirty-Three

Banks and Viejo were riding with Burgess and Vaden a little less than a mile behind the target.

"We've got two SUVs with four men apiece from the Incident Response Team on point," Burgess said, filling Banks and Viejo in on the operation they had just handed off. "We've got another six agents from the Charleston ATF Regional Office on standby just outside Charleston County. They'll fall in once we get a better idea of where we're going. SLED is going to handle administratively since both your department and the ATF have been implicated in the investigation."

"I don't care who gets the credit," responded Banks. "I just want them locked up."

"What happens afterward?" asked Viejo.

"We see what we've got and keep going," answered Vaden.

"No I mean with us," Viejo blurted.

Vaden turned in his seat. "Funny thing about that BOLO on you guys. The bureau put it out before they even completed the initial survey of the crime scene."

"And it was put out by the SAC himself," added Burgess. "I've got a subpoena in to dump his phone but it takes time. I have a buddy in the Columbia Office who told me the SAC up there is real chummy with the Tulley machine down here. We'll see where it goes." Burgess' phone rang. "Hold on."

The other three cops waited while he stared straight ahead.

"Lead on Brigston. He's got a property on Kiawah Island. 447 Beaumont, it's on the water."

"Get that to DeGuello and Wilke," Banks said, but Viejo was already on the phone relaying information to the car behind them.

"They got it," Viejo said, "Wilke's calling to get a warrant now."

"It's not much but it's the best we've got right now. We already had units canvas all of the properties and businesses we could link to the Tulleys in the low country and got nothing. It's a long shot but it's worth a try."

The desperation to find Poppy Montague alive was palpable between the four men. No one gave voice to the feeling.

"I'm going to have Team Three and the Tac Unit link up with them when they go. This case is starting to give me the creeps," said Vaden.

"I know what you mean," added Burgess. "Never had a case this big where I didn't have at least an idea of who the players were."

"All we've got at the moment is some dumb shit congressman's son and a locked up dealer. They don't have the juice to send a hit squad after us," said Banks.

Burgess corrected him, "At the moment all you've got is a dumb shit congressman's son. Antwan Tate died in his cell the night you got jumped."

"What?" Viejo asked.

"Yeah, and the other guy, Tulley's buddy. He's dead too. Units found him this morning. They're thinking auto-erotic asphyxiation. As if this shit wasn't weird enough."

"Beginning to wish we could bring the 101st on this bust with us L-T." Viejo said.

"You and me both, kid," Banks said while he watched the sedan carrying DeGuello and Wilke blow past them at over a hundred miles an hour.

He watched them go. Despite the fact he was charging into his own hornets' nest, he felt a little tinge of guilt for not going after Poppy himself. Never one to enter a church outside of a funeral, Banks found himself saying a silent prayer.

Chapter Thirty-Four

DeGuello listened while Wilke tried to coax a verbal warrant out of Judge Carol Patrick.

"That's what we've got, Judge. It's circumstantial but it's our best bet and the property is in the name of someone who will potentially be a co-conspirator." Wilke paused. "No not yet..."

The kid was exasperated as the judge was pushing back on his probably cause.

DeGuello grabbed the phone from Wilke's ear and put it to his own.

"Hey Carol," he said, "Yeah, DeGuello. It's Poppy." He waited. "Yeah someone snatched her. We need in that place." He waited again. "You got it, gentle as mice, thank you." He hung up the phone and handed it back to Wilke who was watching him with a mix of rage and helplessness.

"Poppy got her niece out of an abusive relationship. Broke the guy's jaw. Judge has a sweet spot for her," DeGuello said and crushed the accelerator beneath his boot.

***

Davidson and Brigston watched the congressman shuffle to the black Lincoln Town Car that would take him and Davidson to their meeting. The man was deflated. His slouched shoulders and slow, small strided gait made him seem as if he had aged a decade in the preceding half hour. Brigston handed Davidson a small inner ear transceiver, which he placed inside his left ear canal.

"Comm check," he stated.

"Copy," Brigston answered.

"Copy," came the deep rumble of the mercenary, Dierks. "On the heavy."

"I'm here," was the final answer and the response Davidson had been waiting for.

"How are things on the boat, Biannca?" Davidson asked.

"Heading back to port," she answered. "The passenger was delivered to the continental shelf."

"Copy. Are you in position?"

"Just about."

Before joining Congressman Tulley in the car, he turned to Brigston.

"Have the men clean this place up then exfil. We're going to have to reassess before moving forward. There's been too much exposure here. We may need to consider a different venue before the next shipment."

"Will do."

***

Biannca, wearing a tight muted purple sweatshirt and matching yoga pants, crested the top of the stairway and exited to the roof of the tall condominium. The location overlooked the Charleston harbor and several warehousing units abutting the port. She had a rolled yoga mat under one arm and a light string strapped backpack over a shoulder. At the doorway, she crouched and on her stomach low-crawled to a hole in the low wall at the roof's edge. Fifteen feet away, she noted the long form of Dierks wearing grey camouflage to blend in with the stones covering the roof. He lay behind a monstrous fifty-caliber rifle, which like her own perch peered through a hole in the short wall. He retracted himself from the reticle for a brief moment so the two could share a look. They locked eyes like two wolves from separate packs staking out the same water source. Biannca held his glare until he slowly looked back to his eyepiece.

Moving slowly and methodically, Biannca unrolled her yoga mat and gathered the long rifle barrel, which had been hidden inside. She then opened the pack and retrieved four pieces, which she assembled to a lightweight rifle. She attached a scope almost as large as the rifle itself, snapped it onto its quick release mount on the receiver, and then lay prone on her yoga mat. Cozying up to the eyepiece of her own scope, she began surveying her field of fire.

***

When the truck passed Summerville, the SLED surveillance team handed over the operation to the ATF. The dark SUVs of the state agents fell back as the smaller sedans of various colors meant for undercover work took up position around the target vehicle. They drove toward the peninsula of Charleston where there were several options for access to the ports. The Wando terminal on Daniel Island, and downtown Charleston itself held options so the multi-agency team of officers and agents continued to follow, hoping their luck would not run out and that they would not be spotted. When they passed by the I-526 exchange continuing toward downtown, Burgess got on the shared radio channel.

"They passed up the exit for the Wando terminal. SLED roll on and set up off East Bay Street, and at the Rutledge Avenue exits. ATF will keep the eye. I know this isn't much by way of briefing but this is kind of a fluid situation. Keep your heads on a swivel when this thing jumps off. We've seen what happened downtown the other night, and we think this same group has taken one of our own hostage. These guys have some very sophisticated weaponry at their disposal, and they won't hesitate to make use of them. Don't slip out there, cause they won't.

"One more thing, I want to thank everyone here for the trust. I know there was a leap of faith in buying in on this for everyone and we appreciate it." Burgess replaced the microphone in its dash mount as the various units involved in the operation relayed acknowledgement of the broadcast.

***

When Wilke and DeGuello arrived at the parking lot near an abandoned self-storage warehouse on John's Island, there were two marked units, an ambulance, and three unmarked cars waiting for them. He was out of the car before it was at a full stop. He had a notepad in hand, which he slapped on the hood of one of the marked units.

"Detective Ben Wilke, Sergeant Max DeGuello for those of you that don't know us. Gather around." He paused for a moment to let the assembled group huddle around the hood of the car, "Detective Eric Thompson is in critical condition at MUSC right now. Detective Poppy Montague is missing in action. Both are the result of the same incident. They were ambushed in their vehicle late last night. With what little investigators have had to go on, we have ruled out almost a dozen potential places where Montague could be save for one—this property on Kiawah Island. The property is owned by a party suspected to be a connection to the incident, which resulted in the death of Special Agent Pak of the ATF.

"We don't have a lot to go on as far as who is inside or what kind of numbers we're going to be facing. I was able to pull a rough sketch of the house from the county database. Three story, almost three thousand square feet. We're going in no-knock. Team Three will secure the perimeter and ground floor. SWAT, you will take the second floor. County, you guys will take the third. DeGuello and I have the first floor along with part of Team Three. EMS, hang back. We'll call you if we need you. Any questions?"

There were none as Wilke looked at each of the cops standing around them. Like any tight knit community, police took it personal when one of their own went down in the line of duty. Only unlike most tight knit communities, cops were armed and willing to burn down the whole world to bring those responsible for harming one of their own to justice. A grim stoicism had settled over the assembled police.

"Remember, guys, the group that hit us the other night had weapons we've never had to deal with before. They were fast and they were lethal. Be ready when we hit that door. Don't give them a chance to put us on our heels," DeGuello added. "Let's go."

Chapter Thirty-Five

The ride to the meeting with Tulley's contact was understandably quiet Davidson reflected as he watched marshland pass by. Crossing John's Island heading for the Charleston Peninsula, he could not help but dwell on the events that led them to this point. It was bad business, bad operational security, for either himself or the congressman to be anywhere near the payload before it left American shores. In the past, this had not been an issue using various mechanisms from longshoremen, truck drivers, or cut outs like that idiot Fitzpatrick to be the only part of the organization suffering exposure. This minister Tulley had in his pocket was a new avenue. Change in a smooth operating machine was never without some degree of failure. Some failure improved the process and was small, something to grow from. In the case of running an illegal major arms propagation operation, failure at any point in the operation could be fatal. He understood the risks associated with the work he had chosen. Lately, however, Niles Davidson felt more and more like he was plugging a failing damn with his fingers and hoping he wouldn't run out of digits.

There was no backup for him if things turned. There was no trust among the various entities from the front company in upstate South Carolina run by Brigston, or the congressman who had for years, since long before Davidson took over the operation, used his political machine to open doors or smooth over rough edges. Without looking at the haggard old man, Davidson considered the congressman.

Everyone gets complacent, was his first thought.

Perhaps the congressman was integral to the mission at one point. He must have been for the mission to have been so successful over a long period of time. But now, with his insistence on including his idiot son in the operation, he had slipped. He could no longer see the big picture. All he saw was legacy and ensuring that his family kept power in the state and at the capital in DC. Like an old, sick, feudal lord hoping his moron offspring could carry on the family name, Tulley had lost focus and it not only threatened the operation but also Davidson's career. Davidson would not allow that. They were changing venues.

The machining operation and manufacture of the new weapons design would not be impossible to transfer. Maybe Mississippi or Louisiana and they could ship out of the Gulf Coast. Davidson knew the reputations of the political leaders in that area and at the least, they were worth taking a look at. He had come to realize in his fifteen years of government service that everyone had a price and politicians especially sold out for less than most. If they couldn't be bought, then they might have a few exploitable skeletons in their closet. In most places, you couldn't rise to high political level without crawling through the sewer with your hand out. The idea of restarting the vetting process, rebuilding the operation, and with the added pressure of customers in the third world who had real intractable timetables, the powers that be would not want the operation stalled. This made Davidson sick to his stomach. More precisely, it made him furious, and the man sitting next to him was the sole cause.

Maybe it would just be easier to take him out of the equation, Davidson wondered.

He looked at the old fool, staring at his hands, in the seat next to him. It took a lot of pull to get clearance to remove a sitting politician. His superiors would not be swayed easily, and Tulley had pull. Davidson tried to weigh the dilemmas between starting over or excising a festering wound. Neither option truly seemed efficient.

"How long have you known?"

The question snapped him out of his strategic mind experiment. It took him a second to absorb the context,

"The pictures?" Davidson clarified.

His response was but a weak nod.

"Long enough," he answered. "Honestly, I hope I never have to use such an extreme mechanism. We had a very prosperous arrangement. Regardless, I can't help but wonder, given all the time you have spent with us, that you would believe we would never find out."

The congressman remained silent.

Davidson let the silence grow. A message appeared on his phone, requesting a report.

"Appears to be normal traffic flow around the area. There is a black Cadillac sedan inside the target area with heavy tint. Hard to tell if there are any occupants. No counter surveillance or other activity noted," Biannca said through the transceiver.

Davidson typed 10-4 into his phone as a response.

"How much further do we have to go?" he asked.

"Approximately fifteen minutes out, sir," was the answer from the driver's compartment.

Chapter Thirty-Six

"Wilke, how far out are you?" Banks asked over the radio.

"About five," was the reply.

"Hold until we execute on our end. I hate it but we can't have this part of the deal blown by you guys letting them know the gig's up."

"Copy," was the response.

Wilke slammed the radio down on the dashboard while DeGuello pulled off the causeway leading to the exclusive island community.

"You know it's the right move," he said to the younger officer.

Wilke didn't answer.

***

"Target vehicle is approximately two miles out, East Bay Street." The report came from the lead surveillance vehicle.

"Copy," responded Burgess. "We're going to let the truck roll in and send an unmarked through to get eyes on the target location before we initiate the take down."

Banks shifted in his seat. He hated giving up the reins on an investigation, even if it was the right thing to do. In the seat next to him, Viejo patted down his tac vest in an unconscious act, which dissipated nervous energy. Banks could relate.

It was a cardinal sin in policing to raid a place without knowing everything you could about it and the occupants before entering. They didn't even know where they were going, much less what kind of place the takedown would happen in. Banks thought of the various cops from the ATF, SLED, and his own team he was supposed to look out for who were following him on a hunch into God knows what.

In fact, the only detail of the action they were about to take that was even remotely static was the fact that this group had access to some of the most destructive small arms he had ever seen. Banks thought of Pak for a brief moment. He could see the man sitting motionless against that workbench, blood pooled in a lake of sticky red around him. They had all been fighting for their lives in that instant but Pak was the one who fell. Banks wondered what those last moments were like for the man. He had presence of mind to try and staunch the flow of blood from his wound, and courage enough to protect that one piece of evidence, the barrel, that led them to this moment.

Banks wondered if Pak had realized the end was coming or if he had just fallen away as he succumbed to the loss of blood. Either way the memory of his friend dead on the floor enraged Banks. Not simply because these assholes had killed a fellow law enforcement officer but because he had been the reason his friend died. If he'd have just let it alone, not pushed the limits with the department, with the pricks running the show, and let the system do what it always has—as fucked up as that might be—Pak might still be there intimidating agents, and torturing them with evidence requirements.

But Banks knew he couldn't do that. He'd made a promise once, a long time ago, that he would never let himself be pushed around just because the bad guys had juice. The city deserved better. Allie Vandrein had deserved better.

It was so long ago but Banks could still see her clear as day sobbing and shaking on the witness stand in state court as thousand dollar an hour legal sharks put her life on public display. She was raped and he had pulled the case. Like a lot of rapes he had little to go on, except her foggy recollection of what had happened to her. Allie had been slipped a rufie at a club off East Bay Street after flirting with the first son of one of South of Broads most elite families. Old money, the kind that can make things disappear. The kind of money that makes people believe they are not part of the same shared society as the rest. According to Allie, the subject, Everett Paine, bought her a drink while they talked. He was charming and witty, and seemed to her like the rare guy that wasn't trying to get laid but rather just wanted to talk. One drink turned to two, then three. After the third, the world went sideways and last she could recall, he was carrying her out of the club. She woke up the next morning, laying on a park bench near the waterfront covered in bug bites. She was sore and had injuries denoting sexual assault but whatever evidence Banks may have been able to collect was washed away when she jumped in the shower, frantic when she finally was able to get home.

He got a statement from her and was able to follow up at the club but staffers noticing the two people together was as far as he got. The case came down to Paine's word versus hers, which translated into the state's attorney leaving the girl hanging on the stand while defense spun their assertion that the sex between Annie and the high roller had been consensual, and that they had mutually parted ways after the act. They even managed to imply both that Annie may or may not have been a prostitute and that she was making the vicious accusation simply because of the defendant's net wealth. Banks had to watch the whole thing helpless as she looked at him, eyes pleading while she cried that the attorneys were lying. All the while, the state prosecutor never raised a finger in objection. The case was lost before it ever started.

Annie Vandrien left Charleston shortly after trial and never returned. The moment that sold it for Banks, leading him to take that oath, was when the judge dismissed the case. When Banks saw a shared look between the prosecutor and the defense attorneys, congratulating each other on a job well done, was when he made a simple promise to himself. He would never again allow a corrupt system to serve the rich over the poor, the powerful over the helpless. Besides that, Pak would have kicked his ass himself if he'd known he had laid down on a case.

"Target vehicle turned left onto Portside Road," the surveillance team reported over the radio, snapping Banks back to the here and now. "Slowing, looks like it's going to be a left into one of the warehouse lots."

Burgess snapped up the radio from its cradle and keyed the mike. "Don't follow, we're going to take a look," he said, pulling out of the line of police vehicles that were staged a mile away.

He piloted the car as Vaden guided him to Portside Road The street was little more than a collection of cracked, battered pavement lined with storage facilities in various states of disrepair. Opposite the warehouses was a group of six level condominiums—an attempt to repopulate a portion of the marsh front with luxury residences. Burgess kept the pace as normal as he could while still getting a decent look at the target as he drove by. The property was bordered by a rusting chain link fence that had long ago been covered on the inside with a torn and decaying tarp. The only clear view of the location came when the unassuming sedan cruised by the still open gate. Watching from the rear seat, Banks and Viejo studied as much of the location as possible when they passed. The truck, two black luxury sedans, three men, two white, one black, all wearing suits. It looked like a temporary storage facility with littered containers in different states of repair scattered about the yard.

This is it, Banks told himself. *This is the best look we're going to get.*

Burgess relayed the observations over the radio while they continued down the waterfront to find a place to turn around.

Chapter Thirty-Seven

Davidson saw the small sedan pass by the narrow gap in the chain link fence that surrounded the lot. He looked at the truck with the attached container. Inside was the product, the next generation weapons his superiors agreed to provide specific men around the continent of Africa. Weapons were a commodity, always had been and always would be. By supplying them to warlords scattered around the continent, his superiors were fostering goodwill with strong men, which in turn gained them access to the resource rich landmass.

"As I said, Mr. Davidson, we have an understanding at both ends of the transportation process. Your goods will be taken care of and delivered safely."

Davidson had almost missed the Minister, Dixon Schuster, of the Southland Baptist Outreach addressing him. He glanced at the middle-aged black man and studied his wide grin and dark eyes for a moment. Then he looked at Congressman Tulley, who had taken a complete one hundred and eighty degree turn the moment they pulled into this rundown staging area for Schuster's charity. The grin Tulley wore across his face was only slightly superseded by Schuster.

Car salesman, holy men, and politicians. Davidson sneered. *They're all cut from the same cloth and all focused solely on separating their marks from their money.*

"I thank you for your assurances, Mr. Schuster," Davidson said words that were not deeds. "When will the shipment be in the hands of my associates?"

"Ten days." Schuster wanted to continue but Davidson cut him off.

"And the payment is sufficient?"

"Yes, Sir. Your contribution was quite generous."

I'm sure it was. Davidson had to hold back an irritated snort. *Tulley brokered the deal.*

He wondered how much the congressman's cut was as he looked on the two professional conmen.

"Incoming." Davidson heard in his ear.

The word froze him in time. He glanced at the gate and could hear a speeding engine in the distance. He looked to the back of the lot for an exit.

"What is it?" he heard the congressman say but ignored him.

"Three black SUVs approaching the front gate," reported Biannca.

In an instant, he saw the first of the SUVs bounding over the curb, the front tires of the heavy vehicle bouncing off the ground. It had barely landed when a heavy crack sounded and a split second later the hood of the vehicle shuddered when a large caliber round slammed through the engine block. The black SUV sputtered for a moment then rolled slowly to a stop, partially blocking the entrance.

Davidson watched with a sort of curious detachment when a second vehicle, mirror image of the first SUV, slammed its wounded comrade and began pushing it out of the way. A second crack preceded a spray of blood smearing the interior of the windshield of the second vehicle. Simultaneously all the windows of the second truck blew out as if a tornado had struck inside the cabin.

Davidson turned on his heel and ran when the third SUV screeched to a halt behind the second. He knew what the force accompanying a fifty-caliber bullet could do to the occupants inside the cabin of a vehicle. It was the shockwave that accompanied the heavy projectile. The speed and force caused an overpressure that had devastating effects on victims within the enclosed space as it passed through. The congressman and minister squawked behind him as they tried to follow, pleading for his help.

There was no help now. Not for any of them. Davidson felt a staggering mix of fear and rage burning inside him. There was only one option if he was to escape. Though it meant the death of everything he'd worked for his entire life. He dashed toward the decrepit old warehouse in the rear of the lot, leaving the old men in his wake.

"Wildfire." He grimaced, as if saying the word caused him physical pain.

***

Biannca heard the order and blinked. It only took her a second to get her head back in the game but the gravity of the decision Niles Davidson had just made gave her pause. Looking at the growing swarm of law enforcement vehicles below, she could understand his call. She returned to the scope atop her rifle and took aim at the two old men chasing Davidson.

The minister was first. She shot him through the heart from three hundred yards away. The overweight black man had barely hit the ground when she hit him again through the back of his head. The force of the round splattered the contents of the man's skull in a fanning arc around the upper portion of his body.

The congressman was a very bold decision on Davidson's part. Assassinating a politician was seldom sanctioned. Even when it was, the act always came with a price. Someone always had to fall on their sword in front of leadership. She wondered what Davidson thought he had to gamble with to make this call on his own. She drew a bead on Tulley and fired hitting him in the back. The old man fell in a clump, half obscured behind a row of fifty-five gallon drums preventing her from taking an insurance shot.

***

Banks and the others had turned around and made their way back to the lot when they heard the horrible crack of a high-powered rifle even through the closed windows of their unmarked car.

219

"Son of a bitch!" yelled Burgess when the third ATF SUV in line slammed into the rear of the second, blocking the gate.

"Scatter!" Vaden ordered when more weapons fire sounded from above.

Outside the car, the rifle fire was crisper in the open air. Banks tracked the sound to the condos above them while he hunched behind the engine block of a car parked in the street. Toward the lot, agents from SLED and the ATF were taking cover while the radio plug in his ear squawked frantic voices calling for medics and trying to identify the location of shooters pinning them down. Viejo bounded next to him and trained his AR-15 on the building across the street.

"You see anything?" Banks asked.

"Roof I think, off cover though. I can't see a thing."

Several more shots rang out from above. The men could hear bullets banging off the bodies of vehicles trapped in the kill zone.

"Come on!" Banks ordered.

He dashed from behind cover and toward the building. He had never been in a situation like this in his life. In all honesty, he had no idea what to do. What tactics did you employ when facing a sniper on an American city street?

Shit.

That wasn't in any book he'd read. He fell back on instinct. He was in a fight and the bad guy was inside the building in front of him. He was going after the bad guy.

***

Biannca fired at any cop that tried to get inside the fence line. She was impressed with their courage when they dared to pop out from behind the vehicles. A couple even tried to retrieve a fallen comrade. Some of them were kind of cute too, she realized studying them through the scope.

She thought it was too bad when one in particular she thought looked like Chris Pratt tried to make it to a downed agent. She shot him through the right femur and left him to writhe around on the ground in front of his co-workers. It would be distracting and a discouragement to any other hero that wanted to try and earn himself a medal.

She only needed to buy time, anyway. Davidson needed time to get clear and Dierks was still trying to root the drivers of the Old South Truck out from cover. She watched with one eye when he dropped one of the two as the target panicked and tried to flee toward the rear of the lot. Dierks' weapon was overkill on the human body. He hit the target running for the warehouse in the right shoulder. Biannca watched as the man's upper body separated from his shoulder to his corresponding lower rib cage burst off his body. The remaining employee from Old South was hiding under the massive frame of the tractor-trailer.

That won't be a problem.

Movement to her right caught the corner of her eye and she looked at Dierks. He was holding a small basic cell phone in his left hand. He looked at her and she nodded. He turned to enjoy the show while he hit send on the little phone.

***

Viejo joined Banks just outside the door to the building and covered Vaden when the assistant chief scrambled across the street.

"Gotta tell ya, Banks, it takes a special kind of asshole to cause a shitstorm like this in my city."

Banks grinned and was about to reply when an immense thunderclap and flash blotted out the world. The three men were thrown backward by the pressure wave caused by Dierks when he triggered the high explosive charges inside the container truck. Banks, Viejo, and Vaden flew through a plate-glass window and skidded across a marble floor, bouncing off various columns, potted plants, and furniture while they tumbled. When the world came back into focus, Banks had a high-pitched screaming in his ears. His body was numb and stiff from the beating it had taken.

"What the fuck, Lieutenant?" yelled Viejo.

"What the hell was that?" demanded Vaden.

With a momentous effort, Banks gained his feet and looked through the gaping hole where the glass windows used to be. The world outside was dust and smoke. Through the haze, he could see the gleaming white and orange blaze of what used to be the Old South delivery truck.

"It was our evidence," he grumbled.

Who the hell were these people? No matter what he did, it seemed like they were miles ahead of him.

"You guys okay?" Vaden asked.

"Yeah, I'm fine," Viejo muttered.

Banks looked at him and saw a stream of blood snaking its way down the younger man's dust covered face. Viejo must've felt it; he swiped at it with a gloved hand like it was an offending insect then winced.

Banks suddenly felt exhausted. He'd been beaten and what was, worse there were dead cops out there because of him.

"Banks!"

He snapped his head up to face his superior who was standing in front of the stairwell.

"You good," Vaden snapped.

It was more an admonishment than a question about his general well-being.

Banks straightened and checked his weapon for damage then nodded his head,

"Yes, Sir," he stated.

"Good. Move, Lieutenant," Vaden ordered.

***

Biannca didn't need to see the truck loaded with high explosive light up. She'd seen explosions before. Dierks on the other hand was entranced by the show to the point where she wondered if he was about to orgasm. He stared at the destruction with a fierce joy dancing over his features. Smoke and debris was raining down around them like tiny meteors falling from the sky before he took a moment to look her way. The expression on his face was like that of a dog that had just learned to fetch and was returning a stick to his master.

She shot him in the face, twice. He had been read in on the wildfire protocol, just not all of it.

The mercenary's body was still shivering in nerve death when she leapt from her prone position and ran for the door leading down from the roof.

***

Banks, Vaden, and Viejo cautiously made their way up the stairwell from the lobby. The dust and smoke from the hell across the street had not filled the passageway. They stopped at each door they passed to ensure it was locked or do a quick peek inside if it was open. The building was seven floors tall and in their weighty tactical vests, they were soon breathing heavy. And sweating, though they could breathe in the relatively fresh air of the stairway, the sweat they were excreting was finding all the small cuts and scrapes they had suffered when crashing and rolling around on broken glass in the lobby.

They were passing the fourth floor landing when Banks, who was on point, put his left hand in the air and clenched his fist. The three-man unit froze just outside the doorway to the floor. He had heard something, thought it was the pounding of someone running toward them. He strained to hear through his ringing ears. He was scanning the stairs above when suddenly on the landing two floors above them he saw a flash of blonde hair,

"Police! Don't move!" he ordered.

223

He could hear the sounds of someone running now.

A face appeared out of nowhere on the stairs between the fifth and six floors. For the briefest of moments and over his front sight, Banks saw the woman. Barely more than a girl, her blonde hair swung around her jaw for a moment when she stopped. Gorgeous was his first impression. Bright blue almond shaped eyes, high almost chubby cheeks, tan skin. She was smiling. Not the expression he would have expected.

"Don't move!" he ordered.

The girl disappeared once more and just as quickly as she vanished, two small items came flying down the open shaft at them. Viejo realized what those two items were. Banks was shifting position to the other side of the door to get an angle on the girl while she continued down the stairs. He heard Viejo scream.

"Grenade!"

Shit, where? His mind raced with images of a small pineapple shaped ball landing at his feet.

"Come on!" Vaden yelled and Banks saw the door to the fourth floor wrenched open by the assistant chief.

Viejo dashed through the door and then Vaden. Banks was on the far aside. As he moved to swing around the open rectangle of steel, he heard two light pings one after the other. There they were bouncing on the landing three feet away. One continued down the stairs while the other sat spinning in full view of the opening leading to the hallway. Banks went on autopilot then and slammed the door with all his weight, straining against the hydraulic piston that controlled its movement. While he struggled, he kicked his boot at the cylinder that looked like a small pipe bomb a little longer than his hand. He connected with the explosive, sending it spinning down the stairs.

Banks dove for the floor just as the grenade detonated.

Chapter Thirty-Eight

Over the radio, Wilke heard the execute signal for the raid downtown and switched frequencies.

"Go!" he yelled into the microphone attached to his shoulder.

The line of cars screamed down the winding causeway toward their target.

They approached the property and observed nothing. The raised two-story home had a covered drive and was completed in an off color brick and timber design that almost seemed Bavarian. The raid team pulled into the drive and stopped before the covered pull through.

There was no movement in the front as they bounded from the cover of their cars to the steps leading to the front door. DeGuello, holding a ram, holstered his sidearm and under the cover of the officers, approached the door. He waited to one side with the ram poised while Wilke led the others to stack opposite him. Six men behind Wilke signaled they were ready with a strong squeeze of the shoulder from the last man to Wilke. He nodded at DeGuello.

The ram met the brass locking mechanism directly and sent the expensive fitting flying ten feet into the receiving area. Wilke and the others flowed into the building, smoothly stepping through the shattered remains of heavy custom carved and stained wood door. The group fanned out covering danger areas and openings to various rooms while shouting.

"Police! Search Warrant!"

Not a sound greeted them.

They held their positions for a moment while DeGuello moved over to join Wilke. He pointed at a team of three posted at a stairway to move up and search.

Another group of two he motioned for them to move to their right. Wilke and DeGuello moved cautiously down the center of the house. Along the hallway, the regal decorations gave way to a more Spartan atmosphere. No decorations to speak of and the doors in front of them were of brushed metal. Swinging doors like those in a restaurant kitchen. When they were just outside the door, they heard the locking thud of a car door closing.

They moved in the direction of the sound. Through a professional grade stainless steel trimmed kitchen and out one more door they found themselves on a landing overlooking a massive four car garage. Two men were just entering a black Mercedes,

"Stop right there!" DeGuello and Wilke ordered simultaneously.

In response, the precision German engine fired. Wilke could see two heads moving in the front compartment and a still form with a human silhouette in the back seat. He tightened the stock of his AR-15 assault rifle to his shoulder but could not get a shot off before the car's tires screamed on the spotless garage floor and the vehicle tore out of the garage.

"Perimeter! Incoming!" he yelled and charged down the stairs with DeGuello in tow.

Wilke ran for the driveway and saw the Mercedes diving off the concrete onto the manicured lawn to avoid the perimeter vehicles. He ran for the vehicles.

That's her. She's in that car.

He felt like he was running in quicksand while he watched the black Mercedes fishtail around the cars, running away from him like he was standing still. The officers on the perimeter screamed orders when the car passed them but the driver never let off the gas. Wilke stopped at the first marked unit and slammed the butt of his gun into the hood.

"Fuck!"

Screaming tires behind him made him jump and he brought his weapon up expecting to be sandwiched between another luxury automobile and the cruiser he stood in front of. Instead, he watched as a Silver Porsche Boxster with the top down slid to a stop in front of him.

"Get in the car!" bellowed DeGuello from behind the wheel.

Wilke jumped over the door and dropped into the passenger seat while DeGuello stomped on the accelerator. The black Mercedes had a good lead on them.

"Sarge, they didn't have any cars for dudes in that garage?" Wilke asked while propping the muzzle of his assault rifle on the passenger rear view mirror and taking aim at their quarry.

"That's funny coming from a guy who drives a Volkswagen Jetta," retorted DeGuello while catching fourth gear.

The small sports car screamed down the winding road of the normally peaceful island community.

"Where are they going?" he asked.

"If they pass through the roundabout, they are staying on the island. That means marina. If they take the exit left off the roundabout, they are heading for mainland."

The Mercedes was almost a quarter mile ahead of them when it hit the roundabout. At high speed, the driver cut the corner and caught a wheel on the curb, causing the car to hop back into the roadway like a racecar careening around Watkins Glen. DeGuello saw an opportunity at the roundabout.

"Put your seat belt on," he said calmly while they approached the circle.

Wilke struggled against the belt's safety lock. He was finally able to get the belt clicked into the receiver when DeGuello dove into the traffic circle and didn't turn. The small car launched over the curb and dug through the manicured St. Augustine grass. The road tires began losing their grip almost immediately. DeGuello floored the accelerator so as not to get bogged down. The momentum of the slide pushed them narrowly past a stand of three palm trees before bouncing down the curb and into the roadway once more. The maneuver had paid off. When they hit the causeway, they were within a couple hundred yards of the Mercedes.

The causeway was dead straight for almost a half mile before a sharp curve that would join with the main road on John's Island. It became a drag race as the two German engines whined down the road.

"Call it in," DeGuello said.

Wilke grabbed the microphone on his tac vest and switched to the main channel governing John's Island.

"Control, 815, pursuit Kiawah causeway approaching Main Road, John's Island!"

"Control, all units clear channel. Go ahead, 815."

"In pursuit of a newer model Black Mercedes Benz, four door, three occupants. One of whom is possibly Detective Poppy Montague."

Before the dispatcher could repeat his statement, the Team Five shift supervisor cut her off.

"All units, converge, control patch in county, this is signal 46."

A forty-six was the signal call for an officer down. That meant every cop in earshot of the radio broadcast was dropping what they were doing and converging on the pursuit. Effectively, the supervisor had just declared war on the occupants of the black Mercedes.

The Mercedes was not as powerful as the smaller Boxer. DeGuello had made some ground on the causeway. They were within a hundred yards when the Mercedes plunged into the busy intersection where the causeway met the main road. Civilian traffic in the intersection screeched and some flew off the road into the deep marsh lined ditches trying to avoid the car as it fishtailed in a left hand turn. DeGuello didn't lift his foot from the accelerator when the Boxer hit the intersection. He dropped a gear and gunned the engine while cranking left on the wheel. The little car skipped across the roadway while the tires tried to maintain traction. Halfway through, the tires gave up and began spinning wildly against the asphalt. DeGuello drifted the sports car though the turn. Once righted, the tires caught and both men were thrown against their seats when the Porsche accelerated.

"Damn, Sarge," commented Wilke.

"I've been wheeling cars since before you were playing with Matchboxes, kid," DeGuello responded.

"Control, left on the main road heading west." Wilke gave out their location once more and the dispatcher relayed the transmission.

"Either they have a plan or they're lost," DeGuello stated.

He was weaving in and out of traffic on the narrow two-lane road that stretched across John's Island.

"What've they got this way?" asked Wilke.

DeGuello bolted out of the right hand lane to pass a Honda Civic and cranked the wheel back to the right just in time to miss an oncoming pickup truck. Ahead, the Mercedes was holding their gap at around a hundred yards. There was a major intersection a couple of miles down the road, where traffic would be thick, and a school not far past there, where kids would be all over the place.

"Don't know but we're getting close to the population up ahead. We're going to need to stop this before we get there."

"Get 'em then."

DeGuello took a brief moment to look at his younger partner sideways.

"Easier said than done."

He horsed the throttle and dove back into the left lane.

This time, he didn't dive back in after he passed a Jeep Cherokee with out of state plates. He floored the gas pedal and hoped the oncoming drivers were paying attention. Cars dove out of the way of the speeding Boxer. DeGuello gained on the Mercedes. Wilke continued to relay their position location over the radio.

Chapter Thirty-Nine

Banks couldn't hear anything. Dust stung his eyes. It took him a moment to remember where he was. When he tried to move, a vicious pain in his right hip stopped him cold.

Blinking grime from his eyes, he cringed when he squirmed to a sitting position and looked himself over. He could see a smattering of black burns along the right side of his vest beginning around his shoulder and stopping where a pool of crimson was spreading from his blue jeans. A jagged shard of blackened metal protruded from his jeans just under his belt. He went to probe the shrapnel with his right arm and heard a grinding in his shoulder,

"Ahhh." He gasped, the cutting pain in his shoulder took his breath away.

Looking over the area, he found another dark smudge highlighting a hole in his shirt. Another circle of red was spreading.

Something heavy hit the door to the hallway and he realized his rifle was gone. Looking around, he saw it perched on the edge of the landing three feet away. It might as well of been a couple of miles distant. Clenching his teeth, he reached around himself with his left hand and did a weak side draw of his pistol. He raised it just as the door kicked open,

"Lieutenant!" Viejo yelled.

Banks released his breath. "Where is she?"

The look on Viejo's face told him that he looked as bad as he felt.

"Don't move," Viejo told him. "EMS is coming."

"Where is that bitch?" Banks shouted.

"We have a perimeter set up below with what units we could scrape together," Vaden said with his back to him while he watched the direction the girl had fled. "We'll handle her in a minute."

"We don't have a minute," Banks argued.

He got a look at her face. She smiled at him before trying to kill him with a grenade. She might be it. She might be all the case had at this point.

Banks tried to move, tried to get it all out. Tried to get them to leave him there and chase her down, but they ignored him. When he tried to move, Viejo's meaty paw held him down. Somewhere along the way, things went hazy. He couldn't make out Viejo's features as he worked him over with the few medical supplies they carried in the blow out kits attached to their vests. Viejo and Vaden were still talking as well but their voices grew distant. Banks finally decided he needed a moment, just a moment to clear his head, shake it off.

Slowly he closed his eyes.

***

Burgess had just taken cover with three ATF agents beneath the engine block of one of the stricken SUV's that had taken heavy caliber fire in the driver's compartment. He got a look at the smeared blood along the dash while he dove to the ground but hadn't seen anyone inside. When he hit the pavement, the three agents closest to him jumped. For a moment, he thought they might shoot him,

"SLED!" he yelled, showing his hands.

They turned their weapons back to the building above them.

"So this is your shit show?" one of them asked.

Burgess peeked over the hood of the SUV while trying to expose as little of himself as possible toward the building where the sniper fire was coming from.

"Somewhat," he responded to the agent's question.

He heard another deafening crack and dove to the ground when the hissing sizzle of a large round passing overhead boiled the air around them.

"What the..." One of the ATF agents started to say when all four of them felt as if they were suddenly picked up off the ground by an angry giant baby and slammed into the gravel.

They were so close to the truck when the explosives were ignited that there was no sound. Their eardrums were overloaded by the violence before their brains received the information. After the weightlessness, came the heat. A rolling wave of fire washed over them. To each man, they screamed, fully believing they were burning to death. The wash of heat from the explosion seemed like it lasted forever when in reality the assault was over in less than a second. The corpses of the SUV's had protected them from the brunt of the effects. When Burgess finally opened his eyes, he noted that the tactical gear of the agents around him was smoking.

For all his worth, Burgess didn't want to move. He just wanted to lay there in the dirt until someone woke him up from the nightmare surrounding him. He wanted to hide until someone tapped him on the shoulder and told him everything would be okay. But he knew that wasn't going to happen. He groaned as he rose to his knees. He noticed the plastic frames of his Oakley sunglasses were hot and sticking to his face. As he stood, he felt his scorched shirt on his left shoulder sticking to his seared skin. He looked at his rifle and noted that it looked undamaged. He cycled a round through just to be sure and scanned the other cops he'd taken cover with. All damaged to some extent but they were moving. Slow as he was, tentatively surveying themselves for the extent of their injuries.

Burgess looked around cautiously and noted he hadn't heard any weapons fire.

He might be just waiting, Burgess told himself.

They had to find out where they stood.

"You guys cover me," he said, his eyes on the lot yard in front of him.

"Huh?" one of the agents said.

He was looking back at the condos.

"Do it," Burgess said and pushed off from cover.

He tried to sprint to the corner of a container box but his body would barely respond to him. It was more than a shuffle than a sprint. About halfway through open ground, he couldn't help but wonder if the shooter above was too busy laughing at the fool below to get a good sight picture.

Burgess made it to a set of barrels on the far side of the molting hulk that was the Old South Tractor Trailer and dove behind cover. He landed on something soft that grunted as he bounced off. Rolling and then hugging the metal he hoped would shield him from gunfire, he looked at the ground. Congressman Andrew Tulley was staring at him. His hands were up in surrender. He was covered in his own blood,

"Don't let me die," he pleaded.

Chapter Forty

Wilke could see the four-way intersection at the Maybank Highway and Main Street. The afternoon rush hour was picking up but the hub of John's Island bustled. He could see cars all over the intersection up ahead.

"Uh-oh," he said.

"We gotta stop this now," DeGuello answered.

They were now within a car length, having gained ground when the Mercedes started to hit traffic.

"All units, we're taking them out before they get to Maybank and Main. We're a quarter mile East on Main Road. Remember the white male and black male driving the Boxster are blue."

Wilke was trying to study the occupants through the tinted windows of the Mercedes. He could see vague silhouettes as the two shuffled back and forth in the driver compartment. His heart froze for just a moment when he saw a long narrow cylinder vertical between the two suspects.

"You see that?" DeGuello grunted.

"I did, Control suspects appear armed with long guns. All units use extreme caution."

"Extreme doesn't quite say it," DeGuello whispered. "Hold on."

Wilke dropped the microphone and braced himself against the dashboard and door while DeGuello sped up til the nose of the Porsche was alongside the rear quarter panel of the driver's side of Mercedes. Wilke could see much better inside the vehicle now and could swear he could see the front passenger leaning his way. Muscle memory made his movement so smooth that Wilke didn't register he'd raised his rifle and started firing until the rear driver's side window of the Mercedes shattered. At the same instant, the windshield of the Boxster was pockmarked with a ribbon of holes when the passenger of the black car opened fire. For the briefest of moments, Wilke was eye to eye with the man trying to kill him. He squeezed the trigger while at the same time fully believing he was about to die. The barrel of the rifle aimed at him seemed huge.

The cars broke away and weapons fire from both went wide. The rounds from the black Mercedes stitched another pattern across the hood of the Porsche. Steam burst from under the hood.

"Shit!" yelled DeGuello, trying to keep control of the car.

The Mercedes gained some distance while the Porsche lost power but the speeding car fishtailed wildly with a shredded left rear tire.

"Come on," Wilke urged the dying vehicle forward.

The Mercedes was fifty yards ahead when the traction of the three remaining tires finally gave out. The black suspect vehicle slid sideways into the rear of a Ford F-150 and bounced into the middle of the four-way intersection coming to a rest in the heart of John's Island.

Cars careened and slammed into each other around the intersection until the clogged roadway resembled a sick multicolored web of twisted metal. At the center of which sat the black Mercedes. People immediately started getting out of their cars, every expression from shock to rage flowing among the mangled vehicles. The arguments and bravado that accompanied road rage lasted approximately ten seconds before the suspects in the black Mercedes leapt from their car, each brandishing automatic rifles. Wilke and DeGuello fled their dying Porsche amid the first volley of rounds coming from their assailants. Two white men, one with short-cropped hair, the other bald. They wore polo shirts, the bald guy in white while the other was in dark blue. Wilke took in all this information, recording it subconsciously through the reticle of the aim point mounted to his own semi-automatic rifle.

He crouched behind the engine block of a Volkswagen Bug and could hear screaming from the driver's compartment when the hood absorbed a spray of rounds. Sliding to the driver's door, he wrenched it open to find a young blonde folded under the wheel. She was crying hysterically.

"Come on! I'm a police officer!" he yelled dragging her by the arm. "Stay low behind the engine."

As soon as she was out of the car, she was running like mad toward the gas station fifty yards away,

"Shit, No!" he yelled and turned, firing at the first subject he could get a sight picture on.

The suspect was maybe twenty yards away moving laterally between vehicles while Wilke did the same, sliding around the hood of the car. The man sprayed bullets wildly at Wilke, splintering the windshield of the bug and gouging streaks of metal out of the body. The full auto was just too powerful. Wilke knew it was just a matter of time before he got him. The man could fire on him almost continuously at double or three times the rate of the police issue rifle. He kept firing back though and moving in between the Bug and another late model sedan while a stitching of bullets chased him. Then click, his twenty round magazine went dry. He dove between two more cars.

His hands were shaking when he thumbed the magazine release with his trigger hand and scrambled with his free hand to dig a magazine out of a pouch on his vest. In his ear, over the din of automatic weapons fire, he heard the wail of police sirens. Despite his fingers feeling as though they were moving in slow motion and through setting concrete, he was able to slap a full twenty round magazine into the breach of his gun. With a *SCHNICK*, the charging mechanism slammed a round into the chamber.

He had managed to keep his eye on his subject as best he could. You always trained to reload without taking your eyes out of the fight despite your mind pleading for you to look at what you were doing. The subject continued to move, dodging around cars. When Wilke was able to bring his weapon to bear, he saw the white polo shirt dive between two more cars at the outskirt of the traffic snarl.

Wilkes back stepped, to both his relief and his horror was a white and blue county sheriff's cruiser. Smoke still billowed from the tires as he saw the gray-brown uniformed officer line up in the apex of his car door. Wilke could see the back of the gunman through the splintered rear window of the truck he hid behind. The deputy was armed with a handgun,

"Get back!" Wilke shouted but was overwhelmed by the chatter of the suspect's rifle when he popped from cover and opened up on the deputy.

The deputy got off three rounds in the suspect's direction. Then Wilke saw him spin around and drop behind his door. He was already on the move by then, charging while he fired at the gunman who had taken his eyes off him when the deputy arrived.

Wilke squeezed the trigger as fast as he could though it felt like it moved at a snail's pace. He fired a line of rounds, walking them in the suspect's direction. He saw the gunman turning his way. The rifle bore of the machine gun looked like a howitzer. Wilke saw a spark off the weapon and the suspect's support hand flinched. Three more rounds put two into the suspect's sternum and a third in his support shoulder. The gunman cringed and fell against a car. Wilke was close to emptying the magazine into the man's torso and head. His last round was spent as he was a stride from the man.

He tossed his empty weapon and transitioned to his pistol. He kicked the rifle out of the dead man's hands. The gunman stared blankly at the asphalt where he sat, blood trickling out of his slack-jawed mouth.

***

DeGuello got off a handful of rounds before diving behind the crumpled rear quarter panel of a Honda Minivan. The firepower the gunman had was earth shaking and he instantly recognized it as the same kind of weapon used against him at the ATF Lab. He moved on his knees down the side of the vehicle while bullets shattered glass, plastic, and metal all around him. At the front of the vehicle, he risked a peek when the gunman paused his assault and clicked off four rounds in the suspect's direction. The guy was moving and opened fire on him again once he gave away his position.

The gunman wearing a blue polo shirt was moving toward a stand of trees to the left of the intersection. DeGuello used the engine block of a solid old Mercury Marquis as cover and loosed three more rounds, firing wide. He leapt to his feet and bounded over the hoods of two broken down sedans while the suspect switched out an oversized magazine.

When the gunman seated and charged the weapon DeGuello was standing on the dented and pockmarked hood of a car. He fired but the suspect was ensconced between the tailgate of two pickup trucks and his bullets peppered the body of the vehicles. He dove for cover, his own magazine now dry when the gunman fired once more. Searing pain and a tugging sensation like that of a toddler pulling at his pant leg picked its way up his thigh. He landed in a pile in front on another car and heard snapping and grinding of bones. He watched helplessly with a shredded right leg as the suspect made his way toward the woods.

The man moved smoothly but cautiously, looking for him. Ignoring his injuries DeGuello reloaded and fired from prone position. The man crouched and returned fire.

Shards of asphalt stung DeGuello's face while bullets sought him like angry wasps. Still, he continued to fire. The gunman was not advancing, he shot at him as he backed toward the trees. He was getting further away and it was getting tougher for DeGuello to focus on his target.

He was tired, suddenly so tired. He stopped firing and watched, heart pounding, breath ragged, when the gunman was finally able to pinpoint him. The gunman grinned, he could tell even through his blurred vision the suspect was taking his time lining up his shot.

***

Myra Ross was staring at her tablet while she sat in her cruiser in a gas station parking lot near the bridge leading from the mainland to John's Island via River Road. Night shift was long over but she had been held over by the oncoming supervisor. Something was up both downtown and on the island but she didn't know what.

No one would tell her what was going on but the oncoming shift covering both West Ashley and John's Island had been diverted to the operation. The nearest access to John's Island from her beat was the bridge where she now sat. Whatever was going on, she knew it was big, and she wanted to be nearby if something happened. As she sat in her cruiser, staring at the bridge and watching the morning traffic pass by, her mind quickly drifted back to the document she had saved to her Microsoft Surface.

It was a business letter addressed to the Chief of Police… her resignation letter. Myra hated every word on the screen in front of her. The document thanked the police department for the opportunity and all the pleasantries one would add to a letter announcing one's departure from an organization. It made her choke as her eyes scanned the page. She'd written the letter the day before after meeting a friend of hers for breakfast. Ann, who was a nurse on night shift at St. Francis Hospital, had let her vent. The combination of greasy morning food and exhaustion had only further lubricated the wheels. At first, Myra had just complained about the men: Beach, Pluretti, and even Wayne, though now she regretted most of what she had said about them. The release through her diatribe had cleared her soul of frustration but it had also opened her up to a hard self-examination. Ann had asked, Myra thought as a half joke, if she was scared. Myra hadn't been able to get the question out of her head since.

Was she scared to be out on the street alone? Would she really have been able to fight that meth head the other morning if Beach and the squad had not shown?

Her gut answer was no! Vehemently no!

She loved being in the car, creeping through the streets at night and chasing the criminals in her city. But the squad thought she was afraid.

Why would they think that?

Myra tried to figure out why her squad mates would dislike her. The guy right before she got cut loose? She replayed that moment, those furious seconds of hand-to-hand combat. She hadn't backed down from the guy, even though he had towered over her. And she didn't panic even when he had the upper hand.

Had she?

She realized she was no longer staring at the tablet resting against the steering wheel but was looking out over the intercoastal waterway toward John's Island. She looked back at the tablet where the letter taunted her and frowned. She shut the screen off. The plan developed with Ann last night would have her in nursing school in the fall.

"Nurses make better money," Ann had told her. *"And you aren't dealing with the dregs of society."*

Myra had seen the appeal. She and Ann had drafted the damn letter together.

Now here Myra was staring at it. Could she do this job? She didn't do anything wrong. She caught that guy

241

yesterday. She initiated it, she chased him, and she would have arrested him if Beach hadn't shown up.

Right?

She replayed the incident over and over in her mind, and then played over the fight she had been in when she was still in field training. The way she remembered it she did everything right. But good cops around her didn't think she could cut it. She wasn't scared, she didn't back down.

Did she?

Her mind toyed with her and she had begun doubting herself. That doubt had culminated in the letter that was driving her mad.

The three emergency tones that started blaring out of her radio made her jump.

"Signal 46, all units clear channel for 815 (Wilke's call sign)," the dispatcher ordered.

815, a narcotics unit, Myra figured given his call sign, came over the radio reporting a vehicle pursuit on John's Island. Rushed words, interference from engine noise, and wind energized the transmission with a palpable urgency.

She looked at the bridge in front of her. She heard him say armed and dangerous. It took a second before she realized she had dropped the transmission in gear and was burning out of the parking lot.

The radio chatter was spotty and clipped. The detective was putting out his location, traveling down Main Road from Kiawah Island. They were heading her way. She wasn't completely familiar with John's Island but knew Main Road stretched across the entire island.

Morning traffic was steady as she sped, lights and siren flashing in and out of lanes, weaving through traffic. Ahead of her, she saw a white and blue deputy sheriff's cruiser heading to the scene. The deputy was not much more than flashing lights in the distance, but she noticed that the speeding cruiser had made drivers on the road skittish, which helped her in her own response.

On the radio, sudden crackling and popping followed by cursing from the detective made her heart leap in her chest. They were in trouble. At least, the detective managed to get the location out that he was coming up on the intersection of Main and Bohicket. She was a couple of minutes away and felt like her cruiser was driving through floodwaters. The engine whined but she couldn't drive fast enough. The radio was eerily silent after that final transmission from the unknown detective.

She risked a look at her speedometer and noted she was traveling the populated two-lane road at over eighty miles an hour. Traffic was peeling out of her way with regularity now while she closed on the intersection the last transmission specified. Her eyes widened as she took in the disaster area before her.

People were running everywhere. A tangle of cars blocked the major island intersection. To her left, she saw police firing into the wad of cars. Heads and shoulders bounced up and down, using the twisted metal as cover while they moved.

To her right, civilians hid behind trees and a gas station adjacent to the battlefield. Then she looked straight ahead. A man aiming a rifle toward the pile up was standing on the outskirts of the crash site, stepping toward a stand of trees next to the gas station.

She followed the direction of the rifle and saw that the man was aiming at a figure lying on the ground next to a crumpled pickup truck.

No, was her only thought.

She had seen the bright white police patch on the downed man's back when he tried to roll and find cover. Myra slammed her boot on the accelerator and took aim of her own.

She was twenty yards away when the shooter noticed her approaching. The machine gun looked like a howitzer when he turned the weapon on her. She tried to push the petal through the floorboards for more speed. He was going to shoot her.

She felt helpless strapped to her driver's seat, powerless to get away from the storm of bullets she just knew were about to shatter her windshield and tear her apart. Blood pounded in her ears. She saw the scowl on the man's face, the dark impassive features were horrifying. The man's eyes were covered by dark sunglasses.

He stutter stepped and tightened his grip on the weapon as she closed.

Myra held the wheel steady and braced herself. She swerved to catch him when he tried to get away.

The wet heavy thud against her hood when she hit him was sickening. He looked at her for an instant, mouth twisted in a rage as she drove on through the intersection, carrying him on her hood. She didn't let up and was surprised when she felt the car suddenly weightless.

An instant later, the nose of the cruiser slammed into the high wall of the deep ditch between the road and a stand of trees. Myra remembered hearing herself scream right before the world went dark.

***

DeGuello took a long slow breath and hoped Wilke and Poppy were okay. He watched the man, waiting for the hailstorm of bullets that would end his life when his killer bolted upright and shifted position. He was bringing his gun around when from out of nowhere, with the wraith of a starving killer whale, a black and white cruiser sped past, picking the man up on the hood.

The cruiser continued without braking, running off the roadway and slamming nose down into a deep runoff ditch bordering the roadway. DeGuello coughed and chuckled, and reminded himself to buy the son of a bitch driving the black and white a bottle of whiskey.

***

Ben Wilke scanned the intersection, chock full of mangled cars and bewildered, panicked civilians for threats before moving on the remains of the black Mercedes. He approached from the driver's right side and paused between two cars to conduct a tactical reload before going forward. His hands moved swiftly retrieving and switching out magazines between his tactical vest and weapon.

More cops were arriving in droves now. Black and whites from the city as well as white and blue cruisers from the county surrounded the intersection. Some officers guided civilians to safety in the parking lots of the Shell and Citgo gas stations that bordered the battle zone. Three uniformed officers made eye contact with him, and he held up four fingers indicating he was okay. He followed that with a gesture showing he had eyes on a party in the suspect vehicle. He received a nod from all three. Two flanked the left side of the car and one partnered with him silently.

"You in the black Mercedes! Show me your hands!" Wilke ordered.

He noted his ears were ringing in the eerie calm shrouding the aftermath of the shooting.

The head in the rear passenger seat of the vehicle bobbled slightly. The four officers trained their weapons on its shape. It moved again, a little more toward the center of the vehicle.

"Show your hands!" Wilke ordered again.

Chips of broken glass from the rear passenger window frame fell like clumps of snow from a tree limb to the street until finally a quaking series of fingers and a bloody hand appeared from within. Inside the car, the subject's left arm rose to the ceiling of the cabin.

"Cover," Wilke muttered to his partner then announced. "Don't move!"

He approached slowly from the right while another officer approached from the left. At the car, he grabbed the offered wrist and unceremoniously dragged a whimpering figure through the window frame. Andrew Tulley landed on the asphalt, crying and begging for them not to shoot him. Wilke manipulated the torque on Tulley's wrist until he was spread out on his stomach. Still holding the wrist and kneeling with all his weight in between Tulley's shoulder blades, Wilke waited, desperately hoping his cover officer would announce there was one more person in the car.

"Clear!" The patrolman announced.

Wilke's heart shriveled up and died.

With a growl, the detective kicked Tulley in the ribs, flipping the blathering fool onto his back. He stuck the barrel of his handgun in Tulleys eye socket,

"Where is she!" he bellowed.

The professionalism and crispness that trimmed his prior orders were now gone, replaced by a guttural rage that gave the officers around the car pause.

"No, no, no, no, please," pleaded Tulley through bleeding, swollen lips. "Please!"

"Where!" Wilke screamed grinding the front sight of his weapon into the man's head.

A feeble hand shaking and weak pointed with a crooked index finger toward the trunk.

Before he could move, a patrolman popped the trunk from the driver's compartment. Tulley shriveled into a ball and moaned when Wilke released him and dove for the opening trunk cover. Another officer beat him to it and pushed the lid up. Wilke saw his eyes widen and the man instinctively backed away a step before grabbing for what lay hidden inside.

Wilke pushed his way past the man and froze. She was there. He could make out her face though pressed and distorted in the layers of shrink-wrap she'd been covered in. Her entire body bound head to toe like a glistening mummy perfectly preserved, almost like a translucent butterfly chrysalis. Her arms were curled in toward her chest and her legs were jammed into the fetal position. Her eyes were vacant, almost sleepy while she stared past him toward the sky above.

He tore at the slick plastic wrap that clung to her. His limbs and digits shook, when he could not seem to get hold of the horrible material. She was so limp, her body and facial features slipping languidly against his movements like a bed of weeds floating on the Sargasso Sea. Tight clipped curses and stutters escaped his lips. Drips of sweat from his brow fell onto her while he tried to save her. He was fighting against his own body that could not accomplish what his soul screamed for it to do.

"No," he whimpered, "Uh-uh, come onnnn!" he howled until he was finally able to break the membrane covering her face.

Her eyes stared at him now. He recognized that cloudy emptiness that the eyes of the dead always wore. He grabbed her and heaved her out of that horrible crypt, rough carpeting on the floor of the trunk shredding his knuckles. He held her in one arm and with his free hand, ripped away the rest of the plastic from around her head. He yelped and stopped then started again when the plastic pulled at her hair too hard and he thought he might have caused her pain. When she was free, her gaunt and slack face in the open air, he held her wet and clammy forehead to his own and rocked her,

"Noooo, come on Pop," he pleaded, holding two fingers to her carotid artery.

There was nothing for his callused hands to feel. He gulped and swallowed against the worst pain he'd ever felt, tried to ignore the helplessness that slapped him in the face. All he could think about was their one night together. How they had both put themselves aside right after for the sake of the job.

What might a future for them have held? The stark truth that there would be no future for Poppy Montague was unbearable. The sensation accompanying the thought was something he could not get away from, he wanted to get away, hit the reset button, erase this horrible reality as he rocked her in his arms.

When the medics arrived, he had to be pulled away from her. He watched them slice through the plastic covering her with scissors and open up her soaked shirt to attached leads from an AED. Within only two minutes, the silent form of Poppy Montague was strapped on a gurney and she was taken away from him forever.

Chapter Forty-One

Niles Davidson cursed as he ran from the army of law enforcement that sought him. As soon as the terrible code word 'Wildfire' had passed his lips, he'd taken off at a dead sprint. He heard the cracks of high-powered weapons at his back. He hadn't even looked back when the sizzling thunderclap of the trailer exploding sent a wash of heat and force after him.

The warehouse was where he ended up. Charging through the door, he'd not let up even a stride entering the cavernous storage facility and searching for a rear exit. Running diagonally across the expanse, he'd headed for the left rear of the building knowing that the right only held a dead end road and the marsh. In the rear of the building, he found a rusting old steel door and kicked his way through. He had no weapon save for his own limbs. He knew that they would not be up to the task if confronted at any distance by law enforcement. His only chance was in using the chaos the wildfire contingency was meant to afford him.

Wildfire was a term he'd kept locked away in a deep vault in the depths of his mind. It was the end all apocalyptic trigger that was only used when there was no other chance of survival. When an operation was compromised beyond repair. Thanks to the colleagues forced on him from above, even his talent for keeping the most sensitive of assignments running smoothly through an abundance of caution and calculated action could not save the project. He cursed silently while he ran through a series of alleyways and leapt several high chain link fences dashing for his freedom. His suit was a disgrace, pants and jacket shredded as they endured the trauma of barbed wire.

If only they had listened, he told himself, knowing that there were no excuses within the organization.

He was sure he would never see the executive floor now. He wanted to scream at the idea of forever simply being a tool of management, not attaining the heights he had strived for, sacrificing every comfort in life for the opportunity that operations like the one currently melting in the warehouse parking lot afforded him.

Coming to a street, he paused for the first time since saying that awful word and peeked out from the relative safety of the alley. People were on the street. Standing here and there watching the rising cloud of black smoke the explosion left. The civilians were focused on the scene, taking videos with phones, talking excitedly about the action and the sounds, relishing in the brief exhilaration that has so suddenly provided a reprieve from their automatic suburban lives.

Trying as best as he could, he smoothed out the tears on his jacket and brushed as much of the dust and detritus from himself as he could, before stepping onto the sidewalk. He walked casually despite the screaming in his chest for him to run for all he was worth. Every cop in the city would be flooding the area within minutes yet he forced himself to remain calm. Subtlety was the engine of stealth. Strolling away, he even turned to take in the growing black cloud in an attempt to blend in further with those on the street all the while keeping an eye out.

His only hope rested on the final aspect of the wildfire protocol. No man worked in a vacuum and Davidson was dependent on others, especially in this most dire of moments. He made a block but kept as direct a line from the scene as he could, hoping she would find him.

There had not been time to work out as precise an exit strategy as he would have liked given the circumstances. There had been so many variables that they seemed to cascade over the last couple of days. He had been stretched thin in human resources. The challenges he had not anticipated and the worst had come from the one aspect he usually could count on most.

A single unit of police officers.

His organization had them out gunned and politically out maneuvered at every turn, and yet they had still managed to push on. Still digging despite his and those he employed taking everything away from them. Under more positive circumstances, he would love to have learned more about them.

Why had they been so difficult to control?

The chirping whine of a car engine made him turn when a white Mini Cooper swung around the corner of the intersection behind him. It stopped for the briefest of moments, so he could get in the passenger seat then sped away as fast as decorum would permit.

"I'm at a loss, Biannca I really am," Davidson said calmly as he secured his seat belt.

"You and me both," she responded in between smacks of gum between her teeth.

"Is the exit plan still in place?"

"It is," she said.

"Good. I need to get back to headquarters and get control of this. Was the containment successful?"

"The shipment ignited properly, the congressman, and whoever that other guy was were taken care of. Dierks was too for that matter,"

Davidson nodded as if ticking off a mental checklist. "Pity about Dierks. Brigston will be less than appreciative of that but I will explain it to him. Your plan is secure?" He knew better than to ask her for details regarding how she would remove herself from the area.

She nodded while steering the powerful little sports car onto the Ravenel Bridge, leaving the Charleston Peninsula behind them.

The drive across the bridge was spent in silence. Davidson tried to calm his mind by viewing Charleston Harbor and the wide expanse of the Atlantic Ocean in the distance.

Within hours, he would be on the deck of the organization's yacht and in international waters. He would know peace then. He could almost smell the crisp salt from the water, and the cool breeze cresting the bow. He knew the peace would be short lived, it always was. He would have to scramble to save his career when he finally was able to check in. He hoped to hear from Brigston before landing back up north so they could debrief and he could wrestle the maelstrom with a plan.

He observed quietly when Biannca exited the bridge at its base and curved around the waterfront of Mount Pleasant. She was heading for the marina. He was starting to relax. This brought about a quick self-rebuke. There was no let up until the operation was complete. He needed his faculties at this moment more than ever.

Keep focused until we're in international waters, he reminded himself.

The parking lot Biannca pulled into was quite large. It served double duty, providing vehicle parking for both the marina and the hotel that overlooked the Cooper River. Biannca had chosen their locations well. He would commend her performance despite the unfortunate outcome of the operation. It was under grave circumstances that the best or the worst always came out in people.

She pulled to a stop near the aluminum walkway that would lead him to the maze of floating docks and the waiting yacht beyond. He could see the gleaming white hull of the eight-foot vessel waiting for him at the outer edge of the collection of boats. He fought the urge to breathe a sigh of relief. It would be unprofessional to do so in front of her,

"So, I'll see..."

When he turned to face her, he felt the startling prick just under his jaw and flinched. There was nothing there when his hand rose defensively to the site of the insult. He looked at his hand and then at Biannca.

She held a skinny syringe between her fingers. Her eyes seemed just a touch sad, but there was this delicate upturn at the left corner of her lip.

"Huh?" was all he was able to say before his heart began dancing in his chest.

He wanted to scream but the pressure building in his head, chest, and eyes was so immense, he could do nothing but cringe as he started to shake. He heard gurgling in his throat and he could only breathe in gasps. His eyes clenched shut against the pain raging in his head. His last sight was of her.

That gentle face, beautiful blonde hair and piercing blue eyes, golden smooth skin. And that grin, faint as it was.

She'd been smiling at him.

Chapter Forty-Two

Biannca watched until he stopped quivering and slumped, his forehead smacking the passenger side window with a dull thud. Dropping the needle into the cup holder, she put the Mini Cooper back in gear and repositioned the little car in the far rear of the parking lot. She grabbed a small duffle and the yoga mat from the boot.

In European cars, they call it the boot, she told herself, then sighed as she slowly closed it.

She loved the lines and the agility of the little car, had really bonded with it. It wasn't fair for things to end this way for the loyal little car but such was life. She allowed her fine, perfectly manicured fingertips to trace the body of the sleek sports car from the rear window to the front headlight before letting go. She turned her back and pressed the locking button on the key fob before heading for the boat.

Twenty minutes later, she stood on the aft salon, twirling a champagne flute. A strawberry was drowning in a couple ounces of a 2003 Krug. She watched the land receding slowly behind her and waited until she saw the flash and the column of smoke rise behind the marina. It took a couple of seconds for the sound wave to reach her this far out in the harbor. She threw back her champagne and dropped the Cooper keys into the flute before tossing both overboard. Clapping her hands together, she retrieved her encrypted phone from the tight confines of her yoga pants and pressed a hot key. Exactly three seconds later, a connection was set.

"Containment complete," she reported.

She waited for further directions.

"Understood," she finally said and turned for her stateroom and a searing hot bubble bath.

Chapter Forty-Three

When Congressman Andrew Tulley first awoke in his private suite, he was surprised to be alive. The memory of the bullet striking him made him squirm, which in turn made him squeal and wheeze when his battered body flooded him with pain signals. He was groggy and weak but his faculties were present. His mind whirled while he tried to understand what had happened.

What had gone so wrong?

He recalled the first of the police vehicles crashing in on them but once the first shot was fired, everything became a blur. He did not know what his status was and he played dead when the nurse came to check on him that first time. He listened and watched. He was helpless and the realization that he was at another's mercy tortured him. He had to know more about what was happening. The second time the nurse came to check the array of equipment attached to him he could not take it. He had to talk to her, see what she knew so he opened his eyes.

The nurse's practiced expression of an open smile and encouragement didn't belay a thing. He cautiously answered her general questions as to pain and how he was feeling then he watched her as she left. He breathed a sigh of relief when the door began to slide closed. He didn't want to see his son or any other of his various hangers-on at that moment. But the door stopped mid-arc and started reversing its course. A non-descript white male in his forty's or so came in and flashed his badge before introducing himself

Shit

"I want a lawyer," Tulley croaked then shut his eyes.

A day later, Tulley was again coming awake when he noticed a familiar figure seated in one of those horrible wood framed chairs. His visitor was looking out the fourth floor window of his suite. As Tulley stirred, trying to prop himself up against the pillows without experiencing excruciating pain, the man in the chair looked away from his view of the outside.

"Adler," Tulley wheezed, "I must really have stepped in it this time if you've seen the need to come yourself."

He tried to add a chuckle for emphasis but it hurt too much. Harrison's law firm, one founded by his great-great-great grandfather before paved streets made their way to Charleston, had handled legal needs of the Tulleys for almost as long as the practice itself. In fact, the Harrisons and the Tulleys had traded the seat occupied by the congressman at various times throughout the years. Harrison and Tulley had grown up together and amassed power together.

Adler Harrison smiled slightly. "How are you feeling, Andrew? You gave us quite a scare."

"I'm sure I did. Let's get down to it, old man. How bad is it?"

"Your son survived the incident. I knew you would want to know. He has been at the residence convalescing."

"Er, right. Thank the lord for Andrew's safe return," Tulley responded. "Where do we stand?"

Adler picked a piece of lint from his tie and flicked it into the open space between the two men. As he did so, he studied his hands. He remembered when they were so strong, so strong he had felt at one time he could take on the world with only his bare hands. The bulging knuckles and green veins slithering through and between livers spots now showed something else.

"I am not entirely sure of your legal status at moment, Andrew," Adler finally answered him. "The firm and the Tulley family are no longer associated. Neither I nor any of my staff be representing you or your son from this time forward."

"Excuse me?" Tulley responded, a weak grin on his face.

He studied the old man before him for a long moment. He noted all the weight he'd lost after being diagnosed with cancer the year before. It was like his old friend was shriveling away as they spoke. He watched him for signs that he was taking a jab at him but saw no crack in the withered gray countenance before him.

"You're kidding me. Right?"

Adler did not respond.

"You've been my lawyer for over forty years," Tulley said, exasperated.

"I have," Harrison answered.

He leaned over slowly and retrieved a thick accordion file from where it had been resting out of sight next to his chair.

Tulley stared at him waiting for more. Adler watched him and said nothing.

"Why?"

"You remember my nephew. Wyatt?" asked Harrison.

Tulley shrugged. The movement caused a blast of pain to shoot down his abdomen. He cringed.

"My nephew, Wyatt, is dead, Andrew," Harrison told him.

"I'm so sorry, my friend, but I fail to see what that has to do with me." Tulley was trying to sound contrite.

"I thought you would see it that way."

Just then, the door to his suite opened. Before he could see the person entering, Tulley bellowed, "Not now!"

They came anyway. Eyes bulging and face growing red, he was gearing himself up for a tirade when he saw the face he vaguely recognized. When the man held up his credential identifying himself as SLED Special Agent Tom Burgess, Tulley remembered the face. He found himself at a loss for words.

"Glad to see you're feeling better, Congressman." Burgess crossed the room to Harrison's side.

Harrison was holding up the heavy file, which wavered in his weakened fingers until Burgess took it from him with a nod.

"Thank you, Sir," Burgess said.

Tulley looked to Harrison dumbfounded.

"Those are just some of the highlights of our time together, Andrew," Harrison said matter of factly.

"You can't do that!" Tulley raged. "You are no saint, Harrison. You will be ruined along with me!"

"You can't harm a ghost, Andrew," Harrison said quietly. "Wyatt was my heir. Your associates killed him and there is no one left to continue the firm or the family name. There is nothing left to ruin. Andrew."

Without another word, Adler Harrison rose on unsteady legs and walked slowly out the door.

Tom Burgess followed but before leaving, he smirked. "Heal up, Sir, We'll be in touch."

Chapter Forty-Four

Winston's was a popular bar in West Ashley. Today, it was closed to civilians.

Two agents from the ATF had been killed in the ambush at the storage facility and another twelve had been injured either by shrapnel or fire.

The deputy shot on John's Island lived but would be medically retired due to the damage from the bullet that had taken him down.

The ATF agents were flown home to be buried in family plots.

That left only one funeral as a result of that hellish day in Charleston.

Poppy Montague was laid to rest overlooking the marsh near Magnolia Cemetery. Her procession included over five thousand civilians and cops, and stretched five miles long as it wound through Charleston from the Lutheran Church on Broad Street to her final resting place. The governor spoke at her funeral. Her mother was presented a crisply folded flag by newly minted Charleston Police Chief, Andrew Vaden. A twenty-one gun salute and a fly over by the aerial surveillance unit preceded her end of watch as a choked up dispatcher called her unit number 842, 0-7 (out of service).

When the unit, accompanied by Tom Burgess, and Thompson's nurse, who was assigned to him as the only condition for his temporary release from the hospital at the Medical University of South Carolina. Winston, a retired cop from New York Police Department, had relocated to Charleston to open his own place and had six shots of Pappy Van Winkle waiting for them when they walked through the door. There were other officers in the gloomy brass and oak trimmed pub before the unit arrived but the drinks and the stools standing guard over them went untouched. Banks nodded and thanked Winston while they all took their seats save for Thompson who was confined to a wheel chair. His nurse tried to reprimand him proactively when she saw him reach for the shot on the bar but she didn't have the heart. Her eyes still glistened, and were red. She was overwhelmed by what she had seen. Poppy's was her first, and, she prayed, last police funeral she would have to attend. Wilke sat next to Banks and was flanked by Viejo and DeGuello who steadied himself on a pair of metal crutches. Viejo had not left Wilke's side since meeting up with him at the hospital after they had each survived their respective incidents. Wilke's swollen red eyes were rimmed by heavy bags and his jaw was set tight, as if carved from granite.

Banks raised his glass and tried to keep it steady despite a trembling hand.

"To Detective Poppy Montague," he said as strongly as he could muster.

His face bore cuts and bruises he received from the shards of concrete and shrapnel from the grenades that had gone off in the stairwell with him. His shoulder was bound in a sling and he walked with a cane.

"A finer cop we will never meet, a better person we will never know. You will be missed,"

He threw the piercing liquid down his throat with a vengeance while the entire bar repeated her name and did the same.

***

Myra Ross groaned as she used the frame of her car to lift herself out of the driver's seat. A plastic boot supported her broken left ankle. Her left arm was likewise secured to her chest by the sling keeping her from aggravating her fractured clavicle. Having two appendages on the same side of her body and the rest of her body bruised and battered made any movement an exercise in torture. When she was able to gain her feet, she took a moment to look at herself in her rear view mirror. Her eyes were still a little red and puffy after the ceremony but her make up seemed to be holding. Her brass insignia on her collar was polished and her badge had a shine. Her nameplate was obscured by the sling. Once she was satisfied that she was presentable, she gathered her cane and started toward Winston's.

She longed for her couch and her robe. She didn't want to move until her body mended itself but her need to be with the department outweighed her pain. Corporal Wayne had told the squad in no uncertain terms that he would see them at Winston's when the funeral for Montague ended. Beach had offered to driver her but she had refused stubbornly. He was the first person she'd seen after he removed her from her destroyed cruiser, and he had not given her a moment's peace since. He had stood by her from the moment he found her until the nurse had forced him out of her room at the hospital where she'd been kept in observation overnight. The big cop fretted over her like a big brother watching over his sister on prom night. When he had finally left her that night at the hospital, she'd cried. The worry on his face every moment after the wreck left her speechless. Pluretti had all but carried her to the funeral, and both of the big cops had supported her in formation during the ceremony.

She reached the door and crept inside the dark, somber establishment. She was a mouse in the bakery. She slid as clumsily as she could along a wall looking to hide in plain sight.

There was not a chance of that though. It seemed every officer in the bar had stopped when she came in. They nodded to her or gave her a smile. She didn't know most of the people in the department so she smiled and nodded back. She was three steps inside the door before Beach and Pluretti were on her. Pluretti took her by the arm and almost carried her to a chair they had set aside for her. The two big men hovered over her, asking her if she needed anything. She was only seated a second before someone came to her and shook her hand.

"Good job, kid," a grey haired cop she didn't know said.

"Thank you, Sir,"

The old cop moved on and in his wake came Corporal Wayne, carrying four sloshing shot glasses full of something that smelled to Myra like gasoline.

"I know you want to get home, Ross, but it's important that the three of you see this," he said while handing a drink to each of them, keeping one for himself. "You guys are young pups and if you stay in this job long enough, you will attend gatherings like this again. It's important for you to know that when the worst happens, we all come together. Someone will always be there for you, just like you will need to be there for them."

Myra studied the crowd around her. There were some who were talking. Some masked sniffles and watering eyes with a fake sneeze. Others just sat, quietly hovering over their drinks.

"Raise your glasses," the corporal ordered.

Myra did as she was ordered though she knew she was going to regret it. Before Wayne could start a toast, he was interrupted,

"Mind if I have a moment, Corporal?"

Myra watched as a black officer with Sargent's stripes hobbled toward them on a set of crutches. He cringed as he hung off the metal supports, but he kept his eyes on her. He stopped in front of her and nodded to her three squad mates. He held up a tumbler of his own and clinked it off her shot glass,

"Max DeGuello," he introduced himself. "Thank you."

Myra tried to keep from shaking. Though she didn't regret what she had done to that shooter, it felt strange to be thanked, and to have a drink in honor of taking someone's life.

"Yes, Sir," was all she could say and keep her voice from cracking.

The four of them downed their drinks quietly then DeGuello shook her hand.

"You ever need anything you call me," he said before hobbling off toward the bar.

Myra watched him go and saw him rejoin his own squad. She saw the empty seat at the bar in honor of Poppy Montague. A couple of them were talking quietly while others were hunched over their drinks. They were heroes, famous now after being labeled murderers by the FBI, ending up exposing a massive gun running operation.

Heroes, Myra thought. *Why do they look so sad?*

She was broken from her train of thought when Wayne said, "Myra, let me get you home so you can rest."

"No," she responded. "I think I'll stay a while."

***

If the first shot was in her honor, the following three sped Poppy on her way. Hours went by as the booze continued to flow and the family all still wearing dress blues came together like they always did at times like these. The somber quiet that had subdued the beginning of Poppy's wake shifted over time to gently rise in crescendo as here and there someone would offer a story about her. As the tone lifted, her career as well as some more entertaining personal moments were reviewed and celebrated, and even laughed at.

Night had fallen and the crowd slowly dwindled. Viejo at some point had shepherded a barely coherent Ben Wilke from the premises. Thompson's nurse had pulled his chain promptly at six. A few hangers on still mingled in corners. Banks, his heavy blue uniform blazer open over

263

his white dress shirt and tie, still hovered over a drink at the bar. Sometimes, he would stare at his glass, sometimes he would stare into the mirror behind the liquor bottles across the bar to watch the goings on around him. Burgess sat next to him in a dark grey suit. His only insignia was lapel pin that carried the SLED seal. There was small talk here and there punctuated by long reflective moments of silence between the two. As it grew later, Burgess checked his watch and ordered one more round for the two of them. Winston refilled their glasses and both drank whiskey. Burgess sighed, about to speak when Banks beat him to it.

"I feel like we lost," he said quietly.

Burgess thought about his words momentarily, "How so?"

"The girl in the stairwell, the guy at the drop point. They got away,"

"That's true," Burgess replied, "We still got Tulley, junior and senior. We got the guys who killed Poppy. A truckload of those godforsaken rifles are not going on the street. That's something."

"Maybe," responded Banks solemnly.

"You've got a hell of a team," Burgess said, "That's for sure."

Banks scoffed.

"Don't know how many folks I work with would have gone on the lam with me if the time came."

Banks didn't respond.

Burgess looked through the mirror and studied his drinking companion for a long moment, weighing whether or not to ask. Finally, he decided he had to know.

"Why?" he asked.

"Why what?" Banks asked the question, piqued by his interest.

"Why did you push? Why not just let it go?"

The girl, Allie Vandrein's face, the glimmer of hope showing through her fear, her shock, and her shame was as plain in Bank's mind as it was when he first interviewed her. He didn't know if he was vindicated now, if he could be forgiven for letting her down. It didn't matter. He was looking through the bottles of alcohol at his own face staring back at him from the mirror. His gold lieutenant's badge had a spark in it, standing out against the deep blue of his uniform coat.

"We're cops," he said quietly. "That's what we do."

End

About the Author:

John Stamp has been a Patrol Officer, Narcotics Investigator, and Hostage Negotiator serving the City of Charleston Police Department, Charleston, South Carolina. Following that he went on to serve as a Special Agent of the Federal Bureau of Investigation where he was assigned to both a violent crimes and Counterintelligence units. Following service with the FBI John went on to serve as a Special Agent of the Naval Criminal Investigative Service. He worked a wide variety of criminal investigations and served as a member of the Major Crimes Response Team and the Contingency Response Field Office where he served multiple deployments to areas in the Middle East and Africa.

John wrote his first story in the Sixth Grade because he was bored in Math class. The story, sixty-five pages all in free hand was God awful but he did manage to pass math class. He's been writing ever since and now relies on the career he's had and the travels he's made to pen novels he hopes are better than that original "work" he almost failed Sixth Grade math for. Brother's Keeper is his second novel.

Acknowledgements:

I have to acknowledge my wife for putting up with the obsession which takes up far too much of the time that should be spent with her and the kid. Thanks to the dogs, Maggie and Tiger for letting me bounce ideas off of them. Their input is always dead on. Also thank you to my select test audience for taking the time and providing the feedback I need to iron out loose ends. Also big thanks to

K.C. Sprayberry, my editor who exhibited patience and a great deal of knowledge in preparing this book for publication. Could not have made this work without any of you. Looking forward to our next adventure.

Acknowledgement also has to be made to the men and women of the various law enforcement and military components I have worked with over the years. Though you would do it anyway and more often than not feel self-conscious rather than honored when someone thanks you for your service, Thank you for your service. Stay safe and look out for the one standing next to you.
#Bluelivesmatter
#Alllivesmatter

Finally but by no means last I give thanks to God. I'm not much for formal religion but still have faith. I give thanks every day for every second I've had and those I still hope to still experience.

Social Media Links:

Facebook: https://www.facebook.com/John-Stamp-Author-Page-1512392099078916/?fref=ts

Twitter: https://twitter.com/43Stamp

Instagram: Stamp43

If you enjoyed this book by John Stamp, check out his other novel:

Brother's Keeper:

Alex and Charlie were brothers born of blood and violence during the battle of Fallujah. Then they came home and became cops. Charlie couldn't let go the adrenaline rush of the battlefield and it showed on the street. Always looking for a fight, he went dark, crossing the line one too many times until he went so far even Alex couldn't bring him back.

That's what Alex thought anyway until a terse message lead him into a gunfight and a recording Charlie left him in case the worst happened. Turns out Charlie hadn't gone dark, he'd gone deep undercover and sacrificed his entire life to do so. The worst has happened, and now Alex has to save the life of a man he's written off. As much as he doesn't want to admit it, the sad truth is brothers are brothers. Alex will run the gauntlet through anything and anyone to save the life of his brother. Then he'll kill him himself.

Brother's Keeper details to what length a man will go to save the life of a friend. This fast paced crime thriller also illustrates the dark often hidden reality that is human trafficking.

http://bookgoodies.com/a/B0182P6LWK